Micha
Fr
Writes (
to another. The first story
in particular touches on
this theme and "Ripples in the
Time of Oz" absolutely is
tied to theatre —
but in many ways it's
all the same: characters,
action, conflicts — the
whole catastrophe and
comedy.
Best,
Bob

MW00917855

Thief

Of

Hubcaps

And Other Stories

Bob McAllister

ISBN-13: 978-1482058468
ISBN-10: 1482058464

Introduction

Somewhere in all of us the people we once were remain. I'm still 10 years old pretending to be the Hunchback of Notre Dame, 12 running through the woods of Woodway Park, 16 in the throes of young love, 20 riding a motorcycle too fast on Snake Road.

Even now, my mom and dad live with me. I see my dead brother alive. I wave goodbye — perhaps for the last time. Stories endure like stones picked up on a beach in Puget Sound. We store them in a place where they can be brought out into the light of words.

We find, through time, that the stones remain but they've changed. Some have gathered together in a circle to ward off loss, others to build an altar one might discover walking another more distant beach and pause to consider why these particular stones have been placed just so and what design has placed them this way.

We imagine a story that might be true as we walk our way on the beach to find other stones to keep.

Bob McAllister

Thief of Hubcaps
and Other Stories

Table of Contents

Thief Of Hubcaps

James Dean, Deliver Me

When he was 10 years old in 1951, having seen a movie the night before about WW2 paratroopers, he imagined himself in the film so intimately that he parachuted out the back door of his family's Hudson Hornet/Flying Fortress at 30 miles an hour on Richmond Beach Road and survived, suffering a concussion and an abraded backside which took weeks to heal.

He's since realized that immersion in others to the point of losing ourselves helps us define who we are by understanding what we're not.

He remembers playing "Pearl Harbor Sneak Attack!" in Woodway Park, an enclave of expensive homes and wooded property five miles south of Edmonds, Washington. He and some of the neighbor boys would sneak onto Bill Boeing's estate—the man who started Boeing Airplane Company— by the bridge that spanned a creek where spawning salmon returned home, walk to a lawn area the size of a football field surrounded by manicured hedges and giant cedars.

Thief Of Hubcaps

The contest for the four boys, all around 12 years old, was to see who could perform the best death. One by one, with the others watching, someone would shout, "Pearl Harbor, Sneak Attack!" and the boys would run across the lawn trying to evade strafing Japanese pilots who grinned bucktoothed in the imagined sky.

On this particular day, he was last in line and determined to die with academy award flair.

When he heard "Pearl Harbor, Sneak Attack!" he catapulted into the light, zagged and zigged, got a bullet in his shoulder, lurched left, got hit in his right thigh, somersaulted over, got up, and scrambled toward safety, screaming, "O God, O God" and just before the safety of the boxwood hedges, took a fusillade of lead in his back which dropped him like a sack of cement.

He continued crawling and spasming, finally lifting his arm up toward heaven after which he breathed his last, closed his eyes and died inches from safety.

He heard hoots and applause and opening his eyes, could see through the shadows of the surrounding trees in back of his friends a silent Japanese gardener with a wheelbarrow containing the root-bole of a rhododendron awaiting transplant, staring at him with what he took as puzzlement.

He was puzzled too. His understanding of Japan and its people, circumscribed and gleaned from WW2 movies, didn't include a wizened man who nurtured plants.

At 14, he was a veteran of Lon Chaney's *The Hunchback of Notre Dame* which he'd seen at the Princess Theater in downtown Edmonds. One summer night before school started, his younger brother Tim and his friend, Doug Openshaw, who lived close by on Hummingbird Hill, led him on a rope with a cushion placed in his back to create a hump.

He crab-walked in front of them and when a car approached in the twilight, he would break loose and scuttle in front of the headlights, give them a tilted head, tongue sticking out of the side of his mouth and the weirdest eyes he could muster, gargle unintelligibly, then make for the nearest empty lot with the rope around his neck trailing after him.

He met his dream role when he saw James Dean in *Rebel Without a Cause.* He became Jim Stark as he fell in love with Natalie Wood, almost died with Buzz Gunderson in a game of "Chicken" with cars racing toward a cliff, befriended Sal Mineo's Plato, the sensitive, distraught boy who's killed at the end of the film.

The next week he bought a red Pacific Trail Jacket just like James Dean wore in the movie.

He was soon to be 16, a portentous age—one which he knew required a driver's license, a car and a girlfriend. The holy trinity. All of which was virgin territory.

The license was easy— he got it on his birthday, March 16th, and spent Friday night driving through Edmonds like a Prince fresh from Coronation in his folks' 1950 Dodge Coronet Club Coupe with Robb Gomez. He'd agreed to buy the car for $200., with four monthly payments earned from his job at a dollar an hour at Edmonds Cycle which his dad owned and where he worked serving customers, assembling new bikes and trikes and overhauling Schwinn and Phillips trade-in bicycles for resale. Shortly after he turned 16, he owned the car.

We all fall in love with our first cars especially when we've earned the money to buy them. He immediately set out to make his parents' car his own—to change it from stodgy to cool, from respectable church-going to hotrod heat-seeking.

He painted the Conquistador emblem on the hubcaps bright red to bounce against its black panther body color, removed the hood ornament and covered the holes with black electrician's tape, bought fake whitewalls, removed the glove compartment door replacing it with a curtain of white leather that displayed a grinning devil in red with a pitchfork created by Chuck Gaultier, an artistic classmate of his at Edmonds High School.

Finally, he bought white dice with red spots, placed them on the rearview mirror, sawed off the steering wheel halfway and installed what was called a knickerknob—a round swiveled fist-size knob that you could use to drive one-handed.

He had visions of a girlfriend glued to him as he drove with one arm around her, wheeling his chariot into adult ventures of sex, intimacy and love—a trinity more distant and unattainable.

He was primed for a girlfriend but other than some dismal encounters at 14 and 15 he'd had little experience with girls. One girl he dated for a football season, after they'd had a glass of champagne with Dale Oakley and Kay Brinson, allowed him to kiss her for long minutes and even dry-hump her on the couch on a Saturday night at Kay's house after Dale and Kay disappeared into the basement.

The next Monday at school he heard that she'd transferred to a Catholic high school in Seattle which wasn't called St. James Infirmary but was close to that. He never heard from her again. Rather than gaining a girlfriend he'd molested an apprentice nun.

Other encounters were equally dispiriting. He was fast starring in a novel he called "The Failures of Young Worthless", after *The Sorrows of Young Werther*, Goethe's coming-of-age novel that his English teacher, Mr. Cunningham, recommended he read because he was a hotshot English student.

There was a girl who stirred his fantasies. Her name was Pam Swenson and she was a year younger than he. He'd met her in Journalism class with Mr. Adams. She had blue, inviting eyes, russet hair, lissome legs and what caught his attention, two breasts he classified as perky that he avoided looking at whenever they spoke about leads and the who, what, where, when and how of news.

He'd found his who but couldn't figure out what to do, let alone where, when and how.

He was the star of the class. Mr. Adams had chosen him as guest editor when the class put out all the copy for a special edition of the Edmonds Tribune, the local newspaper. He sat at the editor's desk and chose Pam for Features Editor. He was willing to do anything to gain her favor.

He'd written assignments for her when she'd told him she didn't have time because of her Girl Scout and Rainbow Girls activities where she was a star in her own right. She had a Girl Scout sash that contained so many badges it must have weighed 15 pounds and was an officer in Rainbow Girls—a Masonic organization for teenage girls with offices titled Fidelity, Chastity and other maidenly virtues he couldn't remember.

Whenever he spoke to her she smiled and tilted her head which was not only the cutest thing he'd ever seen but a signal that smoked and stoked his attraction for her—that made him feel maybe he had a chance with her.

The problem was her boyfriend, Dag Lundquist, a kid who also lived on Hummingbird Hill though he was on the flat part at the bottom of the hill so he was never sure that he actually lived on Hummingbird Hill.

Dag had a gang aura he envied, wore a black leather jacket, jeans and engineer boots which he suspected contained a shiv—gang term for a knife which he liked to use because it made him feel tough which he'd learned from reading *Blackboard Jungle* by Robert Evans. Dag was best friends with Garth Woodman, already famous in teen mythos for his prowess at fighting, drinking, seducing and all around badness.

How could such a sweet girl like Pam, who looked a bit like Natalie Wood, fall for this thug? She wore Dag's ring on a silver chain around her neck which only increased his desire for her though he knew that going after a girl who was going steady was as unscrupulous as masturbating which didn't deter him from desiring both.

However, Dag outweighed and out-muscled him by 20 or more pounds. Not only in temperament but in physicality, he was a Great Dane to his anemic whippet, a Viking Warrior to his spaghetti-noodle self.

Dag, who other kids called Dag as in rhymed with "stag"— not being as familiar as he was with the

Swedish pronunciation of his name which he liked because it was a homophone for Dog and the first name of the United Nations Secretary General, Dag Hammarskjöld whom he admired—often wore sleeveless T-shirts and riding in a car, he'd place his arm on the open window to display his bulging bicep.

The last thing he wanted to do was to arouse Dag's Nordic ire. Thus, he waited, abided, looked for his chance, kept smiling at Pam to win her favor and fantasized about holding her in his arms, kissing her. Beyond that, he knew little but desired much.

As often happens, time and chance came when he expected little. 10 of the girls from his class invited 10 boys to a Saturday-night-in-spring party at a lake near Lynnwood. Knowing little to nothing about the machinations of girls (was Machiavelli a woman?), he never suspected that they were pairing them off though this realization came later when he stopped thinking of girls as a different species after he had daughters of his own.

The party was a very respectable parents-in-the front-room, kids-in-the-rec-room kind of affair. For some reason, he drove alone, rare for him because he usually went with a friend to give him confidence, to take him out of his shyness, to trade tough talk with. Maybe he was growing up. He hoped so.

He arrived a fashionable 15 minutes late along with the rest of the guys. They were met at the door by the girls and herded to the basement after meeting the standard-issue parents (she in a floral housedress, he in slacks, shirt and loose striped tie without a coat). The girls immediately served Homemade Chicken Pot Pie— a dish as popular to teenagers then as pizza is now.

Thief Of Hubcaps

Squat soldiers of coke, chilled to cold, waited on the table. The girls knew intuitively that teenage boys live and love to eat, must be fed because that's the door to romance.

After the girls cleared the dishes and the serving tables while the boys nonchalantly digested, Jolly Greenleaf turned down the lights and turned on the 45 record player which dropped vinyl wafers with one-inch holes onto the turntable. About half of the girls and guys found partners and hand in hand went to the center of the room. Barbo Green and Ramona Tuffley, the "fast" couple in the group, immediately merged into a swaying embrace and undulated almost sensuously, groping each other's hips with their hands.

He couldn't help but watch and envy though he knew the proper way for a boy to dance with a girl was with one hand on her shoulder and the other gently holding her hand as he'd been taught to do when he attended Mrs. Rosepickle's Dance lessons for boys and girls in the 7th grade as part of the Physical Education program.

He sat and yearned, trying to be cool, the outsider wanting to be in. A wind from the sliding door opening came into the room along with Dag, Pam and Garth Woodman.

They'd crashed the party or maybe they were invited though he doubted it. No one said anything. The hostess girl went over and welcomed them, then moved back to her boyfriend. The record paused between end and begin.

In the silence, Dag said, "Don't tell me what to do, Bitch!" and went out the sliding door with Garth, closing it with a thud.

The air electrified, not only at the insult but at the swear word. Boys were taught never to swear in front of girls and to do so was a slap at convention—an obscenity that defined obscenity and violated what most teenagers of that time knew as the purity of female sensibilities.

He'd first encountered Garth Woodman at the Princess Theater the year before when he was sitting with Olive Bowman in the balcony—he'd met her inside the theater because he was too embarrassed to be seen with a date.

The year before four of his envious classmates watched him making out on a first date at a movie with a Swedish exchange student named Sonia and spread the story throughout Lynnwood Junior High about how they started kissing when the lights went down and didn't stop until the lights went up which caused him never to speak to Sonia again because he thought he'd done something wrong—a cowardly act he still regrets for she had white-blond hair and lubricious lips.

On this night he was hoping for some hand-holding, maybe a kiss or two. The movie was *Scaramouche* with Stewart Granger as the poetic rake who takes up acting as a way to disguise his true identity as a heroic patriot, and two guys came in, sitting directly behind Olive and him.

He heard one say, "That Sonuvabitch..." so he turned around and said primly in his best man-voice: "Excuse me, there are ladies present." Garth Woodman leaned in toward him smelling of beer and cigarettes and said; "Yeah, what are you going to do about it, asshole?" He turned to Olive and whispered, "Maybe we should move to the back of the balcony."—which they did. Another cowardly act.

Now he looked at Pam, alone by the door, who gathered what dignity she could, forced a smile and walked to the velvet couch against the wall and sat down, shoulders slumped, eyes cast down. His heart crashed he felt so bad for her. What could he do? Dean Martin finished "That's Amore"

The next record plopped down on the turntable. It was "Earth Angel" by The Five Penguins and he knew what to do as a rock knows what to do when it falls.

He walked to Pam on the couch remembering his dance etiquette and said, "Pam, may I have this dance?" She didn't say anything, just stood up and took his hand, came into his arms and put her head against his shoulder. He smelled her lemony scent, felt the angora brush of her hair.

She put her arms all the way around him so he did the same, his hands embracing her dear shoulder blades which seemed soft as feathers. They started moving to the music.

"Earth angel, Earth angel, will you be mine?
My darling dear, love you all the time.
I'm just a fool, a fool in love with you—
Ooooh ooh ooh, oooh, oooh, oooh..."

They were one. He was one. What was two was now one. They moved together as if consecrated by the stars.

To fall in love is to lose oneself in another but also to find one's self in a rhythm you've never felt before and the first time it's so new you can't think, only feel. It's what he would later learn Buddhist monks call the eternal now. He'd offered himself to the altar of Pam's hurt in complete service and reverence but mainly because Dag wasn't there.

He knew beyond thought that this was his chance and he fell rapturously in love with this vision of everything he ever desired and now held in his trembling hands. The record stopped and the needle retracted but they kept swaying. He finally stopped, pulled back, looked her in the eyes, then lightly brushed her forehead with his lips. How cool. How romantic. How did he know how to do that?

She looked back at him and he saw as he traveled into her eyes a future he could only dimly imagine but knew contained everything he wanted to live and die for. He walked her back to the couch.

The rule was that a boy had to return the girl to where he'd asked her to dance—as if girls couldn't find their way back to where they began unless the boy took her there. He waited as she sat down, took her hand again for a brief moment, then said, as he'd been taught to do, "Thank you for the dance, Pam." and gave her his shy James Dean smile made even more attractive by the removal of his metal-mouth braces two months before.

He walked away backwards, as if going away from a princess. She smiled at him and he seemed to see his eyes reflected in hers.

This tender denouement was interrupted by the sliding door opening from which Dag and Garth entered, thankfully having missed Pam and his romantic tryst. He turned away, barely able to stand, breathing for the first time in 3 minutes it seemed, breathing hard and fast. He walked up the half stairs to the landing, out the door into the night. He muttered "my god, my god" but this was different than playing "Pearl Harbor".

This was Nirvana, Paradise, Heaven, Valhalla. He was so excited that after catching his breath, he spun in circles, opened his mouth to the moon, wanted to drink all the stars in the sky, felt himself opening like a gated lily in summer. He jumped up and down a few times, said, "wow, wow, wow", then composed himself and walked back to the party.

Who was he now? The Saint of Spurned Girls? The Savior of Loss? The Knight of Charity, The Benighted and Bespoke Lover?

When he returned, Pam was standing between Dag and Garth like an orchid surrounded by skunkweed. Too cool to dance, they seemed a cabal, a closed circuit that kept him out. He saw Dag walk toward him.

"Hey, Stud, could you give Pam and I a ride home?"— he noted the misused pronoun with disdain as well as the teenage slang for his name—"Garth's got some things to do with Tiny."

Tiny Salanga was Woodman's girl, an exotic Filipino-Native American mix, who wore white sleeveless blouses and a slash of red lipstick. It was rumored they went all the way and though he hadn't experienced what that meant, he didn't doubt it. He instantly said yes, thought of asking if he could drop Dag off first but that wouldn't work because Pam's house was on the way to where he lived.

He said yes of course—to do less was to be ungracious. Besides, he wanted Pam in his car, sitting and breathing beside him even though he knew Dag would have his arm around her on the other side. His fate was in the wind and all he could do was follow its direction. He'd heard from *Hamlet* that the readiness was all.

When they got to Pam's house with the light on above the front door, he kept the car running, listening to "Tik-Tok Party Line" on KJR which came on at midnight and played songs too risqué' for daytime radio like, "Work with me Annie (all night long)" and "One Mint Julep (was the cause of it all)".

He watched Dag walk Pam to the door, past a Mercury Cruiser parked in the driveway. "Death of an Angel" came on, a song about a guy whose girlfriend is run over by a train as she tries to reach him and as the song continues we hear the sobs and cries of the girl as the guy manfully wrestles with his grief. The perfect soundtrack for his pure teenage love.

At the door, Dag took Pam in his arms and planted his Lumpkin lips on her rosebud mouth. He turned away, hit what was left of the steering wheel. He thought, "My girl, he's violating my girl."

He knew she wasn't of course and after telling himself not to, he watched again and they were still kissing. How long could this go on?

The seven-minute record ended with trailing sobs from the dead angel who was crying tears from heaven because she couldn't be with her boyfriend. In his movie, he was both the guy and the girl who suffer tragically from a cruel loss of love.

He dropped that role when Dag came back to the car. They drove in silence until he dropped his rival off at his house with a "Stay cool, Dag." Dag didn't thank him for the ride and he drove home visiting again, like a tongue that can't stay away from an aching tooth, the scene with Dag kissing Pam.

The next day, Sunday, was "Dig out the 10x24-foot portion of the basement which used to be a crawl space with his 3 brothers and Dad" day. After two months, they were down to six foot, using pickaxes, iron bars and steel shovels on clay so hard it clanged the shovels. The family needed the room with his parents and four boys from 12 to 18 years of age living on one floor. They sang Russian work songs, slave songs, joked about being in prison, teased each other about their relative strength and it was almost enough to take his mind off Pam.

That night, precisely at five o'clock, the family sat down to dinner. His mom cooked for an adolescent army and his dad's prodigious appetite and Sunday was the most sumptuous meal—often a giant roast of beef, cooked vegetables, mashed potatoes and thick gravy, green beans in mushroom soup and onion rings and for dessert, berry pie with mountains of ice cream—all of this accompanied by pitchers of milk which was good not only for healthy teeth but growing bones as his mother frequently advised.

In the middle of the meal, the phone rang and his mom got up and answered it.

"Bobby, there's a girl on the phone who wants to talk to you who says her name is Pam. Should I tell her to call back?"

Though his heart had started beating like a trip hammer (is 16 too young to have a heart attack?), he summoned all his casual cool and said he'd take it on the basement phone. His brothers didn't say a word, they were too busy eating.

He yelled from below, "I got it" and picked up the rotary phone which, every time you dialed, displayed Elizabeth Taylor's breasts from the clavicle to the cleavage which now perched invitingly, waiting for his mom to hang up.

"Pam?"

"Hi, Bobby. I wanted to call and find out if we have any homework for Journalism."

Having read Arthur Conan Doyle and being adept at optimistic interpretation, he saw this as an excuse, a ploy, and like Wordsworth beholding daffodils, his heart leaped up. Pam was light years better at keeping track of assignments than he was. She kept an organized PeeChee with a small notebook inside reserved for THINGS TO DO in capital letters curlicued with roses and hearts, a quality he'd noted as another of her endearing virtues along with her ability to draw flowers.

Besides that, she'd said "we" which meant she saw them or could possibly see them together and she'd called him "Bobby" for the first time. Maybe she liked him. He plunged into the river.

"Pam, would you...uhh, could you... might you...uhhh...think of...well... going out with me... sometime?"

Not so smooth as he would have liked but at least his voice hadn't cracked though his nerves were blasting like cherry bombs on the fourth of July. He waited on the edge of a run down the rapids, heard her breathing which seemed to match his own in its intake, its excitement. He breathed with her. It seemed years before she replied.

"I'd like that. When?"

"Oh...okay...Friday night? Uhmmm...pick you up at seven?"

"I'll see you then. No, wait, I'll see you in Journalism tomorrow."

"Okay, Bye."

How dumb. He should have said, "Tis centuries till then" or like a French Freedom Fighter, "Adieu, Mon Amour" or even, "Tomorrow and tomorrow and tomorrow..." from *Macbeth*, which wouldn't have suited the context but was impressively Shakespearian— anything but "Okay, bye" without even saying her name which he longed to do and had done so over and over on Saturday night until he fell asleep hoping it might inspire him to dream about her wetly which he'd done before.

But he had the date, she was interested, his train puffed at the station, his ship ready for sail, his date with destiny and Pam in his pocket and he couldn't care less about mixing his metaphors.

Monday morning before school he was at his locker at Edmonds High School in the first year it moved from downtown Edmonds to the outskirts of Lynnwood though it was still called Edmonds High School. The locker room housed enough lockers for every student in the school and felt like a warehouse in a factory, which it was.

He was alone, rummaging for books, hanging up his blue suede jacket on the hook when he heard the door open and a voice saying, "Let's get out of here. Something stinks." He sniffed but couldn't smell anything offensive. He'd put Mennen's deodorant on that morning... ah, of course. That was Dag's voice. It was an insult directed at him.

Dag knew and he knew he knew. He was Raskolnikov in *Crime and Punishment,* caught out by the detective, Porfiry Petrovich. What next?

School was a blur that day. All he could think about was having to face the slubberdegullion Dag and fight him. Custom dictated that the fight be in the parking lot at the south end of school after the last bell. Such fights occurred once or twice a week over some point of honor among boys. He'd watched with interest but never came close to being one of the fighters.

With a sinking, pacifist heart, he knew if he was going to keep his date with Pam he would first have to go through Dag. He searched him out after the final bell. He found him leaned against the wall outside of Mr. Phillips' Chemistry Room. He'd prepared and practiced his gambit.

"Dag (throat clear), if you wanna' fight (throat swallow), let's go to the parking lot." He didn't say "want to", he said "wanna". He said this in his best imitation of Jack Palance in *Shane* before he shoots Stonewall Torey because he's a Southern Pig Farmer.

Dag squinted at him like a bug on a glass slide in Mrs. Hollingshead's Biology class.

"Why would I fight a dipshit turd like you, Asshole?"

Numerous responses occurred to him. "Because I've stolen your girl?" "Because Pam deserves me more than you, gangster boy?" and more clever, "Isn't dipshit turd redundant?" But he kept silent and waited.

They locked eyes for long seconds, then Dag spit on the ground, laughed dismissively and walked away.

Thief Of Hubcaps

He watched him disappear among the other kids walking toward the buses thanking, with William Earnest Henley, whatever gods there might be that not only did he have an unconquerable soul but he'd escaped imminent dismemberment or possible disembowelment from a righteously homicidal teen.

Friday night, first date at the Sno-King Drive in.

He can't remember what movie was on but does remember Pam's lips on his, the taste of her, how she snuggled into his side, how his arm accidentally by design brushed her breast, how they looked into each other's eyes more than the screen, how she patted his stomach inches above his throbbing tool, a term for what his friends called their wang, dick, throttle, middle leg, schlong, shooter, penis, in those days—how everything moved so fast he felt like he was in free fall, parachuting again as he had when he was 10 years old but this time he didn't hit the gravel.

He kept falling into Pam until they were both fitted against the passenger door, pulsing their hips rhythmically, each to each, until he had to stop. Alarms were going off and he didn't know what to do.

Is this where we take our clothes off? Do I ask permission? Should I violate her chastity to quench my carnal lust?

He disengaged, caught his breath and attempted to cool his tool.

It was too fast, too much like a dream. She'd never told him to slow down, given him a sign that he was being too forward. He knew what to do at stop signs but had never driven a car without brakes or yellow traffic lights to slow him down.

He excused himself to go to the concession stand for two cherry cokes which, after he returned, made her lips and mouth even more delicious but he kept away from anything more serious. Now he became the earnest boyfriend, the one who loved his girl so much he heroically sacrifices his needs and in so doing, preserves her honor.

He asked her out again for Saturday night and she invited him to her house for dinner to meet her folks who greeted him with open smiles and affection even though he was a potential seducer of their daughter, a renegade Romeo, a Gypsy thief. Perhaps they thought he was a more respectable boy for their daughter than the mongrel, Dag.

He hoped it was true.

That night they had shrimp cocktails, sirloin steak and giant potatoes with melted cheese and chives. Mr. Swenson was a short man with frog glasses who sold insurance, his wife a dynamo who outshone her husband in personality and charm. She flirted with her daughter's date and seemed to like him more than her husband who everyone called Sonny though being raised to respect grownups, he always called him Mr. Swenson.

After dinner, they had homemade blackberry pie with Horluck's Vanilla ice cream on the trellised patio and her dad talked about life insurance which he said was like having a spare tire in your trunk.

After dessert, Pam and he played Scrabble in the basement, knees touching under the table. When he left she walked him to his car and he kissed her long and longingly until he thought her parents might get suspicious so he left, even though their bedroom light wasn't on.

So it continued for two more weeks—he had dinner more at their house than his own. Pam and he would go for drives, park at deserted roads in the woods where he first fumbled the puzzle of a hooked bra and touched a bare breast.

The second weekend they went swimming at Silver Lake and she changed out of her wet swim suit under a towel in his car while he kept lookout but couldn't resist turning his eyes to the front seat as she stretched out of her one piece swim suit, arched her back and he caught a brief glimpse of her "down there."

Other words for female anatomy he barely knew and wouldn't use, even in his private thoughts, about Pam. She must have felt his eyes and caught him looking. He immediately turned away caught in the act but not before registering what he thought was a smile—but that couldn't be, could it?

He took a breath and resumed his moral duty to watch for perverts, feeling like one himself. She didn't know what he was thinking or feeling, did she? He hoped not. He was not one to violate the sanctum sanctorum of a Vestal Virgin. Like a Knight Templar he was determined to be honorable—a guardian of virtue, not a despoiler of innocence.

Thursday nights Pam had Rainbow Girls meeting in Alderwood Manor about 10 miles from Edmonds and he conceived a plan.

He called up Mrs. Swenson just before family dinner and asked her if he could pick up "Pammy"—which he'd begun to call her in front of her folks with some trepidation as to how intimate it sounded—after her meeting and surprise her with a ride home. Mrs. Swenson said, "Oh yes, Pammy would love that."

After dinner he washed his Dodge, Boraxed the fake whitewalls, polished the dash, cleaned the new red and white plastic upholstery, changed into Chinos, a dark blue sweater with a white shirt and polished black Buster Brown dress-up loafers. At exactly 8:39—he'd calculated the time it took to drive to Alderwood Manor so he wouldn't arrive too early and kept glancing at his watch to try to make the time run faster— he started his "rod."

It was an early summer evening with a pink-tinged sky. He was finally a boyfriend picking up his girl after a meeting.

He parked directly across the street from the entrance to the Masonic Hall. He got out of the car and leaned back against it, hoping he would look romantic and chivalrous when the girls came out.

Wind in the twilight ruffled his hair which he'd begun growing out. Girls began to exit from the double doors down the stairway. He saw Bev, Francine, Jolly, Bridget, Jane, Sandy, Sue, Kathy, Sharon, Gloria, Rosemary—everyone but Pam until the last two girls, the Byers twins, Judy and Janet, came down the steps.

He took two steps toward them and asked if Pam was still inside. They said in their contrapuntal way (first Judy, then Janet) that she'd left at intermission with Dag.

He said, "Okay, thanks." He got back in his car, bit his thumb which he tended to do when he didn't know what to do, and started driving home with a whirl of questions. *What do I do now? How can I live? What does this mean?*

Thief Of Hubcaps

Looking at his speedometer, he realized he was driving 50 in a 35 and slowed down, thinking, Who am I now? What happened to my perfect life? He knew he had to confront this betrayal, untangle this treachery. He boiled with anger and despair. How could she do this to me? What would Jim Stark, the rebel without a cause, do if he were me?

He got home, told his folks he had to go out again, changed into Levis and his best white T-shirt, put on the red James Dean jacket with the collar up, exchanged his dress shoes for beat-up black tennis shoes, stole two Lucky Strike cigarettes from his brother's Ford convertible and headed for Pam's house, considering again if he was having an early heart attack.

He didn't care if he was and maybe he was— he just needed to see this through, to follow what he felt. He knew he was headed into a tornado and wasn't sure where it would carry him off to. Certainly not the Land of Oz. He was an arrow, drawn toward disaster.

He wasn't watching a movie or reading a book. He was directing, starring, producing and writing the film. He knew it was an action flick, one that required sparse dialogue, suspense and a certain noir mood.

He drove three times around the Swenson's block before he found the right background music playing on the radio—"Rumble" by Link Wray and his Ray Men—an ominous, throbbing instrumental with insistent drums and a brooding bass guitar. Perfect chords for a teenage showdown.

He pulled into her driveway, three houses down from the street end. Link and his Ray Men thumped with menace, low and slow.

He had a half-smoked cigarette in his hand as a prop. He left the music on, the car running and walked the six steps up to her front door and knocked twice with his fist. He put the cigarette in the side of his mouth like Bogart and waited with his hands in his pockets. He'd practiced this before but it's hard to do because the smoke gets in your eyes and he wanted no blinks or tears for this scene.

The door opened and Pam appeared looking innocent and pure, dressed in a light blue terry cloth bathrobe which she demurely held at her neck. She said, "Bobby?" in a surprised wide-eyed voice as if she didn't know what he knew. He took the cigarette out of his mouth, let the silence grow while he took her in. He squinted tough like Robert Mitchum in "Thunder Road". He'd memorized his line and now he delivered it.

"Pam, it's over."

Later, he realized he'd stolen the line from a Roy Orbison tune titled "It's Over" but at the time it felt like it was his. It was his. Roy was on the radio—he was here, living his lyrics.

He put the cigarette back in his mouth and started down the steps. Reaching the car, he gave her his right profile, which he thought was his best side, took the cigarette between thumb and forefinger and flipped it in a soaring arc past the steps and Pam where it hissed out on the wet grass.

Go, man, go. He got in his car ready for the next scene.

Honor dictates that a betrayed teenager leaving his girlfriend's house must beat the shit out of his car and lay rubber as he leaves to properly trumpet his manliness.

But here, another problem presented itself.

The only way his '50 Dodge would lay rubber was to go backwards in reverse about 15 miles an hour, double clutch, slam the Zyromatic transmission into 1st gear then hit the gas. The trick was the switch from reverse to 1st which he'd tried before with varying success.

His timing was perfect. He roared backwards, double-clutched into first, rammed the gas pedal to the floor board and tires squealed, rubber burned and screeched as he accelerated toward the intersection like Lance Reventlow in *The Grand Prix.*

As the 90-degree turn approached, he realized that he was going too fast to make the hard left from asphalt onto gravel. The hotrod coupe whirled two concentric circles as he tried to control the wheel with the knickerknob then crashed against a telephone pole, scrunching the passenger side door. A cloud of dust rose and he was in it.

He breathed again, short panicked bursts, until the dust cleared and he regained what was left of his composure.

Okay, okay. I've just had my first accident after my first breakup. My car's still running, I'm alive but god, maybe it'll catch on fire.

He turned off the ignition, sat back in the seat and thought, It's not so bad if Pam didn't see. He looked toward her house and she was on the front steps staring open-mouthed in his direction.

The credits hadn't rolled yet and what he had conceived as a tale of revenge was quickly turning into a comedy starring him as a Jerry Lewis incompetent idiot.

He could save this scene.

He willed his trembling legs and hands to stop, lit his brother's last Lucky Strike and stepped out of the car. He didn't look Pam's way, just started walking down the road toward Pine Avenue—the guy who almost lost his life in a car wreck who survives, doesn't give a damn, leaves his dearest possession—his car—and walks off into the sunset and an uncertain future.

"The End" in block letters as he disappears down the road.

That's the nice thing about movies. When the end comes it's over, finished, done. You get up from your cushioned seat and go on to something else completely removed from the movie you've been watching with a hundred other people.

Living's different. The damn thing just keeps going and gets messier, nothing completes itself. It's like a novel you thought was 200 pages long but as you turn the last page, more pages appear, things won't stop multiplying and there's nothing you can do about it but keep going with the words and plot raveling incoherently on and on.

You haven't been reading the book, the book's been reading you. It doesn't need you to exist. You're a prisoner of prose, an existential inmate who watches through barred windows a life beyond comprehension or reason.

Which is what happened when he felt headlights on his back and heard the throaty purr of the Swenson's '57 Mercury Montclair hardtop with a Continental kit that made it seem 40 feet long as it pulled up beside him and he heard the power window on the passenger side glide down with a hum and click.

"Bobby. Come on. Are you okay? Get in the car and I'll give you a ride home. Come on, it'll be okay. Bobby?"

He kept walking. Pam followed him in her hearse of a car. She didn't say anything else. She kept pace with him, exactly matching his stride. It was as if she was a 40 foot elongated black greyhound and he was a wounded fox. No other cars appeared on the road. They were alone under a cloudy sky.

He had sealed off his heart, chosen to play this part in silence, perhaps forever. He didn't look at her.

Part of him knew that if he did look at her, he'd give in, be convinced he'd made a mistake, misunderstood what had happened, take her in his arms again, have a happy ending with a kiss to seal the romance and it would be more wise than stewing in remorse and hurt.

The price of that surrender was too high. He'd begun something he couldn't stop and to not go through with his act, which part of him watched as if a director on a suspended perch 10 feet above the action, would be impossible. The cruiser stopped and he kept walking. He heard the car pull into a driveway, then reverse and purr away. She'd given up.

Maybe she believed him when he said it was over. Maybe it was over.

He walked to the Edmonds Ferry dock into the darkness at the side of the pilings. He sat on a log on the stony beach, looked toward the lights across the bay at Kingston, 6 miles away. Wind came up and with it, rain. A nice touch. He looked up and felt rain hit his eyes. He didn't cry. The effect of the moisture from above created that illusion.

He was beyond tears, brave in his restraint, biting an imaginary bullet to stand the pain, watching himself.

Suddenly he realized no one else was watching.

He was alone with no audience. A couple of seagulls squawked as they flew the lowering sky but they didn't count. No one was there except him. He wasn't even sure if he was there.

He said "I'm here." out loud but felt silly and didn't know what he meant by that. The rain increased to wet and he zipped up his coat.

He could see the ferry about a mile away, heading for the dock like a lighted barge. He heard the thrum of its engines against the wind.

People out there on the dark water were headed home. He got up from the log, knowing he had things to do before he could go to sleep, first of which was to wake his brother Gary to help get his car, knowing that tomorrow would bring more unimagined scenes. He had to be at his best.

Much was afoot and his film still had to be edited and developed. It was in the can but needed work. Plus, there was more footage to shoot.

Someday, he thought, *I'll write this story with me as the hero*. He smiled at the thought and headed up Main Street toward home, walking past The Princess Theater where the year before he'd had a summer job changing the movie titles on the marquee 12 feet above Main Street by going out the window in the Men's Room. He knew there was something significant there.

Maybe he'd call the story *"Rebel With A Cause."* Nope. Too clever.

Maybe getting a title before you wrote the thing wasn't as important as living your life and seeing what happens and then later, you might write about it. How could you put a title on something you hadn't figured out yet?

That part was up to him.

Snowfall

January, 1951, two months from my birthday that will advance me from nine years to 10, I step onto the school bus on a gray morning and as if on cue, the snow begins falling in flakes that seem as large as silver dollars. I stare out the window as the trees and dirt turn white as pillow slips. Our stop is the first on the route and as more kids get on—Betty, Sharon, Buzz, Gerry, Richard, Lucy—there's an excitement, a buzz of expectation that maybe school will be closed.

By the time we get off the bus in front of Edmonds Elementary School our shoes crunch on the salted pathway to the front door and school is open but it might as well have been closed for all the school work we accomplish that day.

Mostly, my classmates and I stare out the windows hypnotized by the whirl of white as if we're trapped in a shaken snow globe.

Mrs. Myring reads us a story about an Eskimo boy and girl who get trapped on an iceberg. I remember only the subject of the story, not how they got back home or what adventures they have while they float on their island of ice. As it was the 4th grade I imagine they returned home, which is what I wanted to do.

My brothers and I had gotten American Flyer sleds for Christmas—top-of-the-line sleds which we hadn't had a chance to try out but where we lived, long lawns proliferated— perfect for sled runs. I had plans to build, with my brothers, a ramp at the bottom of such a hill and imagined myself flying off the ramp into the air.

Sometime before noon, Mrs. Myring announces that the buses will be picking us up early to take us home and we cheer and applaud.

I know now that the grade school started earlier so that when the high school buses— which were also the grade school buses—had picked up their cargo of students and arrived at the high school they were told to turn around and take the older kids home, which took some time.

By the time our buses arrive the classroom has diminished in numbers. Parents, most often mothers, of children who live close to the school have arrived at the school to walk their children home. I envy them and think that perhaps my mother might arrive but the year before she'd had an accident on the hill heading to Edmonds Park with all four of us boys in the car and this event caused her to avoid driving on icy roads.

Besides, I live five miles from school and the only way to reach my home is to negotiate several steep hills.

When Oscar, our bus driver who we used to watch secretly pick his nose in the rearview mirror to our great enjoyment, has dropped off all but three of us who sit together in the middle of the bus and starts heading south up 5th Avenue toward the hill that leads to Kulshan Road where Kris Jorgenson lives, we feel the bus veer toward the ditch. Oscar comes to a stop. He slowly backs down the hill to get straight. The tires spin, the rear end sways.

Oscar turns off the key. The bus goes silent.

We are far from home and the snow has only increased in volume. This is exciting, worthy of a Cub Scout adventure.

John Simpson, Kris Jorgenson and I are Cub Scouts with Bear badges,—next to Lion, the top rank. Kris's mom, Mrs. Jorgenson, is our Den Mother and at meetings we do Craft projects which included spelling out the Cub Scout Pledge on a lacquered board with alphabet soup letters then shellacking the whole business. We also learn to tie square knots and bowlines and learn the basic rules for survival in the woods.

The best part is that Mrs. Jorgenson makes delicious fudge and chocolate chip cookies she serves with lemonade or hot cocoa depending on the weather that's now beginning to turn from a source of adventure to a source of danger which I only dimly apprehend.

Oscar starts the engine and we can smell burning rubber whether from the tires or the clutch I don't know, but smoke rises from the hood so it must have been the clutch. We hear the tires spinning as the bus lurches side to side. Oscar shuts off the engine and we wait until Oscar speaks.

I cahn't go furder. You haff to valk home frum heah...

When you're in the 4th grade you don't question adults. They know the answers, what's best to do in times of trouble, when to go and when to stay, where danger lies and how to avoid it. We get off the bus and head toward Kulshan Road.

The snow comes close to our knees and walking is like wading through scallops of white feathers. Tree branches next to the road bend and bow toward the ground with their freight of snow.

Kris leaves us where Kulshan Road meets 5th Avenue out of Edmonds. He has about two city blocks to walk and a long driveway to climb but he isn't far from home. Fifteen years later he will die of bone cancer.

John and I trudge up the hill and when we reach the top, by the Veterinarian's Office, we say goodbye and John heads toward his house about 50 yards further on Edmonds Way. I turn down the long road that hairpins after about a half mile then continues toward a dirt road two miles from where we live.

I'd been dressed by my mom for cold weather that morning, but nothing short of bear skins and long underwear could have prepared me for the surprise of this sudden snowfall. I trudge past occasional houses set off the road, some with smoke issuing from their chimneys. I can see long tongues of icicles—which I love to break off and use as swords in play—forming at the roof eaves. Other houses are dark and unlighted.

Why didn't I stop at the houses with fires going? Because I'd been told by the Oracle of Oscar to walk home and that is the only thing I can do.

I'm wearing a lined canvas coat with a hood that pulls up over my wool cap, a wool sweater over a thick cotton shirt, jeans and galoshes over my tennis shoes. I don't have gloves so I stow my hands in the pockets of my gray coat. I keep warm by moving but the cold has begun to penetrate my skin.

Everything is silent. I hear no cars, no call of birds or dogs, only the occasional whoosh of snow grown too heavy for the branches falling to the ground.

Otherwise, a silence attends so deep and profound I've never felt its like except when our family went to Carlsbad Caverns the summer before and listened with our tour group to the dark silence 500 feet from the surface. The silence seemed enormous, to surround your ears with cotton and carried an absence made more deep by its presence.

I keep walking, never doubting I will arrive home safely.

Other than a scare the year before in the summer when I tried to swim solo to the raft at Green Lake and reached the ladder exhausted by the effort and a kid ahead of me put his foot on my head and accidentally pushed me down into the water, I've never feared for my life. That day my older brother Gary had reached down and pulled me sputtering from the water but now my brother isn't here.

However, I'm a Cub Scout. I will do my best, as the Scout Pledge says.

The snow falls so thick I can scarce see where the road ends and the woods begin. I follow the one-car road and hill that leads home. No tire tracks. Snow scrunches under my galoshes and occasionally, I have to knee my way through the drifts.

I'm getting tired when I reach the top of the hill. My breath comes in white puffs, the only sound I can hear.

Thief Of Hubcaps

Close enough to home to know I will soon be there, I have an idea: if I can just rest for a bit, I can continue on. All I need is to gather my energy. I head toward the bank by the side of the road. I don't want to stop in the middle of the road in case any cars come that might run me over. This plan makes perfect sense to me. I'm doing the right thing, what a trained Cub Scout should do.

I lie down and nestle into the blanket of snow. I snug up my feet to my chest and wrap my arms around me.

A heavenly wave of warmth comes over me. I'm happy, transfigured by a calm I've never felt before or since. My breathing slows. I drift into sleep so sound it's more quiet than snow, more beautiful than caves or cathedrals. A deep peace flows from my legs, up my spine and behind my eyes as the world turns white. And then I don't know.

This is the point in the story when the author writes "Meanwhile..." to let us know the world hasn't stopped, that other events are going on that affect or will affect the story—but I won't write that even though I already have and do so with some enjoyment to gain the benefit of both excuse for the trope and license to visit another perspective.

All three boys had arrived home when my mom called the bus shed. Dad was stuck in Seattle. The bus phone line was busy for a half hour or more she told me later, and finally she called the operator and told her it was an emergency so the operator got on the trunk line and connected my mom.

When she got through she was informed that Oscar had dropped me off an hour before on Edmonds Hill when he couldn't continue.

Now she moved fast and now as a parent, I know what she was feeling for her missing kid. It's a calm panic and driven purpose that's unrelenting until it finds an answer.

She called Mr. Allan, an outdoorsman type like the '70s Grizzly Adams, who lived in a log cabin east of us and had horses, dogs, snowshoes and a rifle. He promised he'd find me. He knew the direction I would come from and knew me by sight as he'd sometimes seen me walk home from Cub Scout meetings and wave to him as he worked in his outdoor shed with its smoking stone stove. What he did in that shed and with that stove I have no idea.

I always imagined him as a blacksmith—he had burly arms, a solid stomach and an impressive beard. His legs were short and powerful. He had a son named Mike who'd recently begun to toddle along behind him. That probably added to his urgency to find me but perhaps he wasn't doing Darwinian self-interest. More likely, he was simply a good man helping out his neighbors.

He found me at the side of the road. He said he spotted my hood, the rest of me was covered with snow. He picked me up and hurried toward our house a quarter mile away.

When I come to I'm in the bathtub in lukewarm water. My mom's sitting on the edge of the tub stroking my head. She tells me she called Dr. Torland and that's why I'm in the tub. That's all I remember—a brush with death, a day in the snow, a deep peace.

Thief Of Hubcaps

Thirty years later, teaching at the island high school on a day in May, I go to the Faculty Room during my free period. A Spanish teacher in her late 40s who I know enough to say hello to in the halls sits in the cramped room on one of the green vinyl couches. I get a cup of coffee and sit across from her. She hadn't said hello when I walked in. She seems distant, somehow lost.

She purses her lips and sighs. I ask if she's okay. The silence is like being inside a covered coffin, a sudden snowfall.

I must have tapped a spring. In a strained voice, she says that today is the 5th anniversary of her son's death on Mt. Rainier when he was 20.

The rescue team had found his body on a snow ledge near the top of the mountain. She says what she can't stop thinking about is how those final minutes must have been for him—when he knew he was going to die, when he knew he was going to freeze to death— how alone he must have felt, how terrible it was to be cold, how she wished she could have been there to comfort him.

I tell her my story about almost freezing to death in 1951.

She keeps saying "really..." not to question the truth of my story but as a way to negotiate the ice and cold and understand that what we sometimes think happens to others might be beyond our comprehension and vastly different than what we'd imagined.

I think of how time and chance happened on that particular day to bring her to a room I'd never seen her in before and how this woman, who never spoke of her life outside of school, would open up her clutch of sorrow and find a person who could offer witness as to what the approach of death might be like in the cold and snow, far from home.

Cathy Crumley at the 7th Grade Prom

My longtime friend, Rick Stafford, is a ceramic artist, which means he works with clay to create images, colors and forms that populate his imagination. Most have their origins in the natural world—butterflies, birds, shells, flowers. Daily he pulls clay from containers, kneads, dries and powders the shapeless mass, finds the dimension of both the piece and the clay, then layers in slices, dollops, circles, larger shapes, after which he places the completed pieces in the kiln to heat and cure.

This part of the process he calls "firing" but I like to call "casting" which has the additional implication of the way we cast people into roles they play in the film of our lives.

What's true about Rick's regimen is that firing fixes the piece for life.

What emerges remains as he says, "...for 10,000 years." even if in shards. It's a boat to sail into the future, malleable in the beginning then fixed in time once time and heat attend. Thus with memory, thus with people I've seen take shape and form.

It's also the way of writing. We begin with a mass of memory we knead into shapes that issue from what we've lived and recalled and place the pieces into a form that becomes, with heat and time, a written text—in most cases of vastly less permanence than ceramics because words have no substance, they're stand-ins for the furnace, for the pieces carved away and discarded to become part of something else.

My friend believes that every piece he creates should have a use. If the shape is a pitcher it should pour, if a cup it should hold liquid, a ceramic flute should play and he lives by these precepts.

He also saves odd pieces cracked by heat, broken by accident, warped by unequal expansion and contraction because the different elements that compose the piece react differently, almost whimsically, to the fire of the kiln and the potter can't always predict the outcome.

I have several of these cast-off pieces Rick's given me in my workshop. I've used parts of them as inlays in furniture and what I haven't used I've saved in odd places on shelves, in deep drawers, because what's strange or different also deserves a place.

I cannot cast these imperfect fragments away though I imagine at some future date when I'm gone, one of my children will debate whether to throw or save or perhaps wonder why I never used the piece with embossed dragonflies propelled by lilac wings framed by attendant lily pads with a border of flower stems with button blossoms that seem to float and connect the dark space that lies beneath and forms a field to contrast shape and color.

Beauty not alone lies in perfection and use—it sometimes derives its beauty from flaws and solitary disposition and now that I look at the dragonfly piece more closely I cannot see why such a piece was judged inferior. Perhaps it was intended as part of a series and didn't measure up to the others.

Perhaps the fault lies in one of the edge flowers which has a stem that's separated from the dark field at the bottom. One can see the light of what's below through the separation. Perhaps it was simply a gift from a friend.

Cathy Crumley was the smallest girl in our class at Edmonds Elementary. She wore thick glasses, had black, lank hair knotted in French braids, and in the years when girls wore knee-length pleated skirts and angora sweaters with patent leather princess pumps, Cathy wore what we could call granny dresses 10 years later—gingham affairs with white lace collars—and always, laced-up boots that looked like castoffs from a 19th century Cossack regiment.

Such difference from the uniform sameness of the rest of us invited exclusion and cruelty. Cathy played the outcast troll.

I see her alone at recess with her back against the chain link fence. She didn't play tag or other elementary games. She never sat with a group of four or five girls and made daisy chains. I can't remember her speaking in class where the top of the desk reached the bottom of her neck and the rest of us could easily rest our elbows on the top. She seemed hermetic, enclosed.

If a boy wanted to get at another boy, out of dislike or misplaced humor, he would find a time when the classroom wasn't occupied—usually before the end of lunchtime—draw a huge heart with an arrow through it on the chalkboard and write the boy's initials plus C.C. and sometimes title the whole piece "True Love." To be linked with a girl in the 5th, 6th or 7th grade was embarrassing enough but to have your name connected with Cathy Crumley was the ultimate insult and cause for a gagging throat.

I never considered how Cathy might have felt about this public humiliation until sometime in the 7th grade after I'd read some novels by Dickens, probably in the form of *Classic Comic Books*. Dickens had an eye for the orphan and a generosity toward misfits which I began to admire and hoped to emulate.

The culmination of 7th grade was the 7th grade prom, our first formal dance. To prepare for this initiation into the ways and rituals of adults, our class took dancing lessons from Mrs. Rosepickle after school on Mondays for an hour starting two months before the prom. She taught us to waltz the box step and execute a rudimentary foxtrot as we mouthed one, two, three, one, two, three, circling the gym floor.

More importantly, she taught us how to ask a girl to dance, how to end the dance and how to manage the closeness of contact with each other at an age when holding a girl's hand induced a case of the jitterjits.

She taught us how to hold the girl and where the girl should put her hand on the boy's shoulder. We practiced to songs our parents knew like "Waltzing

Matilda" or "I dream of Jeannie with the Light Brown Hair" on an ancient record player and for most of us, the steps were executed in silence and intense concentration, trying to make sure we were doing everything right.

I don't remember Cathy taking the class and I would have if she was there since Mrs. Rosepickle made sure we had a different partner for every song she played and no one was left out.

Why didn't she take the dance class?

I don't know the answer to that question but I can guess and none of the possibilities speak well of us or of the way we regard different others.

I do remember seeing Cathy with her mother after school and sometimes her mom, who looked like an expanded version of Cathy dressed in wider clothes and boots of the same style, would be waiting for her at the school door when we walked to the buses. I don't remember seeing either of them with anyone who might pass for a husband or father—another question without an answer.

At the 7th grade prom, the girls looked like lilies on their own pads—many in white flowing dresses, all of them modest with some in light blue, others pale green, most with a silver necklace at the throat, sometimes a pearl or cross and none wore makeup. The boys wore sportcoats, white shirts and mostly bow ties. I wore what my mom chose for me—maroon corduroy sport coat with gray wool pants and a church-white shirt with a maroon and blue bow tie.

We were dressed and felt like grownups. And that was the idea of the dance—to acquaint us with the doings of courtship and being adult—a dim country glimpsed obscurely, not quite imagined as real or thought of as desirable.

Masonic Temple dances and meetings were held on the top level where you entered up six stairs through massive pillars meant to resemble a Roman temple. Inside, the dance floor was polished oak and against the long walls ran a continuous line of benches that resembled church pews.

As I walked in I knew my place—boys on the east wall, girls on the west. Mrs. Rosepickle, the architect of this night and hostess, welcomed us, complimented our class as we boys, with a mix of fear and anticipation, looked at the girls seated primly on the opposing benches across 20 feet of No Man's Land.

This blur of uniformity was interrupted by Cathy Crumley who sat by herself toward the side as if she was contagious. She wore a difference from the other girls not only in her blank expression but in her salmon pink organza dress with fake begonias at the waist and shoulders. Her hair was braided on her head like a coil of ropes.

As the music started the more brave or foolhardy of the boys walked across the gleaming floor to ask a girl for a dance, always by saying the name of the girl first and then the words, "May I have this dance?" No one was refused a dance which was every boy's secret fear and prehistorically, given what happens today, no girl asked a boy to dance.

I remember after about eight dances noticing that Cathy was never asked to dance and as I looked at her I felt sorry for her. I had a notion.

Thief Of Hubcaps

I told Craig, Bob Bean and Doug that I was going to ask Cathy Crumley to dance. They looked at me like I was insane.

I walked across the floor and stood above Cathy who had her hands folded in her lap scrutinizing them as if there was a mystery she might solve by the way her fingers fit together. I said, "Cathy, may I have this dance?'

After a pause of five seconds or so—an eternity when you're waiting for an answer—she moved her head from side to side without looking up. I froze. She'd refused my offer. I couldn't speak. I waited, hoping for divine intervention or inspiration but all I could finally do was turn to see my friends with open mouths and bent smiles whispering to each other.

I couldn't go back to where they were. I headed for the stairs.

I have a clear memory of walking down the stairs to the basement which held tables of fudge, cookies, pies and pitchers of lemonade. I headed for the Men's room, locked the door and then didn't know what to do because I didn't have anything to do and everyone in the building must have known what happened but I couldn't hide forever.

When I walked out I went to one of the tables and one of the mothers helped me with a plate of dessert and a glass of real lemonade with ice cubes. She asked if I was having a good time and if I'd danced yet. I said yes to both questions but I was trying to understand why I'd been turned down by Cathy.

I was an average boy, popular and though thin as a fence-picket, I wasn't bad looking though I didn't think about it much. All of the other girls—Carol, Sue,

Lynn, Dorothy—had immediately gotten up to dance with me when I'd asked and two of them (Sue and Dorothy) had held my hand as I walked them back to their side of the room after we'd danced.

I wasn't upset with Cathy—I just wanted to know why she'd refused me.

Fifteen years later I wrote a poem about this event that I titled "Invitation to a 7th Grade Prom" and the Seattle School District used it for a number of years as part of their 7th grade curriculum. The poem describes Cathy and her refusal, "Her coat hanger nose moved east/ and west like a deranged compass" and ends with lines about my wish to ask her again, "...and we'll be alone, / no cadre of scrubbed baby boys to assist me, / no excuse but a poem to give you."

But it was never enough and I'm not sure that this story is enough and because I'm still writing about it I know it's not.

This is the second time I've put this memory into the kiln to cure and it's still warped and cracked though I believe it contains a kind of beauty.

There's beauty in Cathy's refusal, in her dignity in refusing to dance. There's a recognition that's both courageous and honorable in the decision. There's something about the act of going to the dance that's noble and speaks well of her ability to hope.

I think the reason she refused me is that she had been so beaten down she'd lost her trust in her mates, in people she'd shared a room with for years. Perhaps she thought that a fancy dress and a prom might transform her isolation into acceptance. The first half hour of the dance must have been a crushing retort.

Thief Of Hubcaps

My impulse was a generous one but I needed to have an audience so I told the three boys what I was going to do. I saw myself as virtuous and charitable toward the less fortunate and asked her not because I wanted to dance with her but because I wanted others to see what I wanted to be—a friend of the dispossessed, a boy who saw someone else's suffering and did something about it.

Now I can see a further reason why she didn't dance. She must have felt and perhaps understood that I wasn't seeing her as a person, more as a victim. There's my remorse: my self-styled hero coming to the rescue of the leper, the outcast, the weird kid and doing so not out of generosity but out of self-indulgence.

Even now as I write this story I question whether I'm not making the same mistake.

I hope not. Perhaps some stories should be shut to silence. I do know that this time with Cathy opened me in a way I hadn't been opened before. I did attempt to reach toward others and always tried from this time on to consider why I was doing what I did—whether I genuinely cared for the person or whether the root of my actions was a way of feeling better about myself. That's another question I've wrestled with.

Perhaps it's enough to ask the question and be aware that virtue isn't always selfless.

Virtue, like vice, is multifarious. It's not one thing completely or composed of one un-redeeming or redeeming quality.

Perhaps like clay that's transformed—flaked and blanged into a slurry after being taught to hold its shape by kneading, then placed in high heat—one cannot determine the final outcome of virtue or vice until the crystals of the original clay melt into each other and become glass which may be worthy of being kept.

This remains on the shelf of memory: not many years ago, driving through the streets of Edmonds I saw a diminutive woman walking on the street above Front Street and knew who it was.

I pulled the car to the curb, rolled down the window and said, "Cathy?" and then we talked for a fragment of time which I will save.

Newton, Michelangelo, Squirt Guns and Mr. Curtis

I began with Cathy Crumley but it didn't end there even though my first attempt at philanthropy was flawed.

I've come to think that nothing ever ends and Newton backs me up on this—nothing is created or destroyed, it only changes form. It's like the elder Michelangelo taking Giambologna's wax model, crushing it and then making a new model of what Giambologna had formed from the same wax—an obscure but true reference I read about in a James Fenton essay that illustrates Michelangelo's cruelty to young sculptors as well as Newton's first principle of thermodynamics.

That night, alone in his room, the insulted Giambologna reshaped the wax his master had revised into something more in keeping with his original vision, then left the next day for Rome and an artistic career that rivaled Michelangelo's. We often learn from teachers what they don't intend to teach.

This is not to say that I became a Dr. Schweitzer of giving, a Mother Theresa of sacrifice. I was also capable of cruelty and one such event occurred in Mr. Curtis' algebra class in the 8th grade but before we can go there in time I must go back further in time for a necessary digression that illustrates, for me, how stories never emerge newborn or fully formed. It's a tatterdemalion process.

Their antecedents dwell in the past and connect to the present like forget-me-not seed pods picked up from a hike in the woods.

That's why they're called forget-me-nots— they're attached to the main body and become not so much digressions as part of the ongoing story of walking in the woods of our lives, never quite knowing where we're going but having faith that we'll ultimately arrive at a destination and perhaps find something along the way even more important than the destination which we never arrive at anyway. As Frost said, "...way leads onto way."

I'd thought of myself as a hotshot math student since the time in the 5th grade when I discovered I was a math prodigy, more accurately an idiot savant as I learned later, with an interesting if ultimately worthless ability to double numbers.

On the last day of summer before the first day of 5th grade at Edmonds Elementary, my brother Timmy, Doug Openshaw and I were playing on the back lawn of our house on Dogwood Lane in Woodway Park. It was after dinner before the 1st day of school and Doug and I started boxing and flailing at each other in the manner of 10-year-olds. Doug got in a lucky blow which knocked me to the ground and I hit my head on a rock.

I was unconscious for about a minute my brother Timmy told me, and they didn't tell the folks because we weren't supposed to fight.

When I came to, the world had shifted.

I shook my head as my eyesight cleared. Dogwood trees that lined the road leading to our house assumed an order I hadn't seen before. It was as if each tree had become a part of a whole. As if a random collection of people in a parade had suddenly changed into a unified statement of what constitutes a parade. I saw the trees both new and old. Though they twined together and grew each into each other, they were also distinct and separate.

I looked at the puffy sky and the clouds distinctly placed themselves against the blue as if in a code I'd just begun to glimpse and understand. I couldn't express this puzzle nor would I because I didn't have words for its strangeness but I knew something had happened.

I didn't know what happened until the end of my first day in Mrs. Hennum's 5th grade class.

Mrs. Hennum was a formidable woman for whom I grew to have great love and admiration—I always wanted to sit by her on field trips to museums we took that year and I loved the way she knew so much about much—history, music, art, even opera— but this was the first day and I wasn't sure about Mrs. Hennum, a squat dynamo in a Nile green dress who brooked no frippery when it came to the classroom.

Several of us had been struck dumb by her glare of disapproval at our inattention or being admonished to "sit up straight and think" as she salvoed questions at our summer-idled minds.

The last class period was math. Mrs. Hennum had written the numbers 1-30 on the board and she began the class by asking which we would rather have: 10,000 dollars a year for 10 years or nothing for nine years and 11 months and then in the last month, a penny on the first day which would double every day until the end of the month.

I realized some years later that she was teaching us Malthus' concept concerning over- population and how something that seemed small in the beginning could exponentially increase in time like a snowball that begins an avalanche.

Most of us knew to add a zero to 10,000 for the first answer and $100,000 seemed like a lot of money to us. How could a penny doubled every day for 30 days be more?

Mrs. Hennum wrote "1" next to the first day, and then waited while we chorused "2" for the second. One kid said "3" for the third day but was overruled by the class. By the time we hit 16 for the 5th day, a screen opened in my mind and I said without thinking, "16, 32, 64, 128, 256..." in rapid fire. Mrs. Hennum stopped my recitation.

What are you doing?
I'm doubling the numbers.

Do you have a list? I shook my head, I wasn't a cheater.

How are you doing that?
I'm seeing the numbers in my head.

Continue....

I did, up until I reached the 21st day and 104 thousand, 8 hundred and 5 dollars and 16 cents. I'd only paused long enough to take a breath.

She looked at me and said, "What's your name?" Students in front turned around to look at me. I could feel my classmates' eyes staring as if a four and a half -foot platypus had appeared in the room. I murmured my name as my face grew hot. What had happened?

A screen opened in my head.

When I pictured a number, its double immediately appeared. I wasn't thinking, I was reading the next number and as soon as I saw that number the next appeared and on and on until I reached a million and the screen wasn't wide enough to contain all the numbers.

Later, I found out that this phenomenon isn't associated with intelligence—it's often the result of a blow to the head and MRIs disclose activity in the visual cortex, not the computational part of the brain. When I found this out I found it strangely comforting— there was a reason for my weirdness.

What I felt at the time was that I was different from the others and being a 5th grader, I didn't like the feeling.

That night I couldn't sleep. Numbers whirled and sailed through my head. I doubled and doubled and when I grew tired I told myself not to think of a number so I could go to sleep but that's like telling yourself not to think of a purple elephant.

By morning something else happened. I didn't have to think of numbers, I could call them up when I wanted but somehow I'd learned to govern them and this ability hasn't changed or diminished to the present. When I was 21 I used to win pitchers of beer on bets in the tavern where Engineering students gathered near the University by betting someone with a slide rule I could double any number they gave me past a million in less time than they could double a number past 1000 that I gave them.

They thought I had a trick—suspected fractions or a different numerical set—but I didn't and when their suspicions were assuaged I always won and was never wrong. I was filmed by the Math Institute when I was in college and when I teach, I sometimes display this odd ability, but it's a parlor trick, like finding a coin in someone's nose at a party or putting two cherries joined by a stem on your ears to look like earrings—interesting but so what?

During that year in Mrs. Hennum's class, I remember being interviewed by counselors and various men in suits in a room high above the other classrooms to determine if my ability extended to other areas of mathematics. It didn't.

I went with my mom to the U.W.'s Psychology Lab where a group of people in white coats recorded me doubling numbers and one of them told me that when I hit my head I connected a synapse in my brain that allowed me to see the numbers. I counted it as a happy accident but also realized what was easy and normal for me didn't extend to other people.

I doubled numbers without thought or effort the way we often make trouble for ourselves when we commit acts without thinking.

Thief Of Hubcaps

8th grade was a down-uppance for my self-regard not only for being voted "funniest walk" after I tried all year to imitate John Wayne's rolling gait but because algebra wasn't easy for me. I did just fine in the initial puzzle of X equals problems because I could guess and find the solution through elimination but I never learned the method so when more complicated problems arose, I couldn't find the answer to the equation.

This might have had something to do with the way I acted in Mr. Curtis's class.

Mr. Curtis was a short man with a squeaky voice who wore brown suits and white shirts with a brown regimental tie. He wore polished brown Oxfords. He looked soft from his receding hairline to his sloping shoulders to his puffy cheeks and chin. His shoulders slumped inward toward his spavined chest. He spoke in murmurs and when he asked us to be quiet in his high voice, we seldom heard him above our chatter nor did we heed him because he seemed always to hesitate in confusion when called upon to control the class.

This indecision and reticence gave us license to become even more uncontrollable and rowdy. 8th graders can spot weakness quicker than they can snap their fingers and like sharks smelling blood they attack without mercy or comprehension, driven by appetites that issue from the lower reaches of our reptilian brains.

As the year wore on, like cats that paw a mouse to make it move, we progressed from talking out of turn to throwing papers at each other to flagrant insurrection.

One day Ned Storm and I had a race around the room sitting in our desks. As we scooted and scuttled, we could hear Mr. Curtis saying, "Stop Boys. Stop doing that" which we ignored until we reached the finish line at the other side of the room.

The only way we would be quiet was when Mrs. Myring, the legendary shrike of a math teacher from the dungeon next door would step into the room and quiet us with one glare from her hatchet face. She didn't have to say a word and we'd be quiet for a spell while Mr. Curtis finished his instructions for the assignment.

Once, at the stroke of 10:20 we dropped our math books on the floor to our great delight and Mr. Curtis' consternation. We received no tirades, no punishment.

We thought of him as a thing, a beetle on the ground it was enjoyable to step on and crunch. We had no idea how old he was, what he did when he wasn't at school or whether he had an inner life. What it must have been like to realize that what you thought you might do for a living was turning into a disaster.

All teachers have visions of helping young people learn what they themselves love or at least understand and some must learn the lesson that what they dreamed can turn into a nightmare beyond their influence or control and they are helpless to stem the tide that carries away the wreckage of their dreams.

Some version of this nightmare must have visited Mr. Curtis daily as the year continued. I've seen variations on it through my decades of teaching and come home dispirited and despairing at the hard heads of my students. Fortunately I had other teachers to assist me, from whom I could get advice and counsel and quickly learned to follow my impulses when something wasn't working.

Thief Of Hubcaps

Confidence builds confidence, failure breeds failure.

I never saw Mr. Curtis talk to any other adult in the school. Perhaps he couldn't stand to, knowing and fearing what he knew, but outside of class I gave him no more thought than a slingshot target or a can on a post to shoot with a BB gun.

Once when he was out of the room I went to his teacher's platform, got his grade book and wrote in new grades for my zeros and changed others from 'C' to 'A'. When I didn't get into trouble for my perfidy, I figured it was because I was so clever in changing my grades but now I think he knew what I'd done but didn't have the will to expose me for my scurrilous and what must have been obvious forgery.

He'd given up.

Toward the end of the year he began to ignore us. We'd come in the room and find the assignment written on the board and when we'd screw around and not get to work he'd sit at his desk and stare out above our heads. This was disquieting.

I also remember the principal coming into the room and sitting in the back without saying a word. We never questioned why he was there—adults often did inexplicable things for no discernible reason—but now I know the principal was there to document Mr. Curtis's performance in the classroom which had turned from a classroom into a torture chamber.

Whether the principal ever talked to Mr. Curtis and gave advice, I never knew but nothing changed after these visits and we began to run out of ways to torment our teacher. And what good is torment if the tormented doesn't acknowledge the torment?

His indifference to us caused further eruptions of disorder.

Once, three of us boys left the room without permission and walked the halls like pirates until the vice-principal caught us and escorted us back to class. Another time one of us wrote on the board: "Mr. Curtis is a turd" which didn't rhyme but displayed our delight in bodily functions. The culprit was never punished—in fact the words were left on the chalkboard— which puzzled us. Inadvertently, he'd come upon a perfect response.

He didn't respond to our arrows. We were as invisible to him as he was to us. Quid pro quo.

The last day of 8th grade Ned Storm and I brought squirt guns to school and in the hallways had great fun shooting guys in the crotch to make it seem as if they'd peed their pants, squirting girls from behind then hiding our guns and looking innocent when they turned around. The guns were fluorescent, mine green and Ned's orange.

We'd told our moms that we'd be late coming home the last day of school. Our plan was to go to the Tastee-Freez a block away from school and gorge ourselves on French fries, ketchup and coke to celebrate the end of 8th grade. After the final bell I met Ned in the hall. He said, "Let's go visit Mr. Curtis."

We filled our squirt guns to full.

He was hunched over his gradebook at the desk when we walked in. He didn't look up when the door closed. He kept working. He ignored us.

I tipped over a desk. Ned smiled and tipped over another. No reaction though the desks banged to the floor. Adrenalized abandon told us what to do. We tipped over every desk in the room, waiting after each, checking to see if Mr. Curtis had noticed us.

After all the desks in the room were upended, Ned and I looked at each other and pulled out our squirt guns.

We walked toward Mr. Curtis who lifted his head and stood up. We weren't sure what he might do so we waited. He was staring above our heads at the back wall. I shot him in his chest but he didn't wince or change his expression. Ned joined in.

We didn't aim for his face, as if some sort of ethical boundary existed there. We kept shooting until our squirt guns were empty and Mr. Curtis's shirt, tie and coat were dark with water.

Mr. Curtis was mute—it was as if we were drenching a statue, a tree, an outhouse wall. His eyes hadn't even blinked. We looked at each other and went out the classroom door.

Ned went to the water fountain to fill his squirt gun.

Something happened inside my head—it was as if what had occurred in the last 10 minutes had just now seeped into my brain.

I said, "I think we'd better go." I felt a boulder in my chest. We walked out the school doors and headed for Tastee-Freez where we devoured three orders of fries, four cokes and a vat of ketchup and none of it did anything to remove the weight in my chest.

And what happened with Mr. Curtis after we left the room?

Did someone find him still standing damp in the room? Did he begin to choke back tears or give into them? Or was he anesthetized? I don't know. There are some things so private that to speculate is an invasion though I have just done so.

I like to imagine he smiled but I doubt that happened. I know that I've kept him in mind from that time on and I learned something more valuable than algebra. I don't even know his first name nor would I presume to use it if I did. Even after this passage of years respect must be paid for courage in the face of cruelty.

Coda: On this particular day in January of 2012, I take a break on the porch to watch the snowflakes whirl in the prelude to what is anticipated as the worst snowfall in Northwest Washington since 1951.

I watch what is gentle and soft fall to the earth and realize that our species has surmised what Newton knew from the fall of the apple.

Everything that exists on the earth obeys gravity. Adam and Eve were expelled from the Garden of Eden in what theologians call the Fall of Man. Robert Ardrey traces the fear of falling to the time when we resembled tree shrews 65 million years ago—to fall from a tree at night meant certain death from the predators lurking below—and thus we have in our catalog of fears the fear of falling, and I believe that our dreams of flying are a way to balance this fear and suggest a way to remedy what is most deep-seated within us.

When I've told the story of Mr. Curtis to my students, because I still feel shame for it but also because I hope to make them more aware of the damage we inflict on other people, I always add that two years later—a sophomore in high school and more wise—I went back to my junior high and found out that Mr. Curtis had left after that year and was now working at a math institute in North Carolina.

I would tell them that I wrote a letter to him apologizing for my stupidity and blindness but that never happened though I wish it had.

I didn't understand Mr. Curtis until I began teaching.

What's true is that he did end up working at a math institute, whatever that is. I imagine him parsing formulas, jiggling numbers, arranging equations on ancient chalkboards that leave a fine dust when you erase them which flies into the air then falls.

Rather like this day when the promised snow has arrived, shut down the schools and roads and as I stand on the porch to gauge the weather a wind comes up and blows fine particles of snow off the roof where they join with other frozen crystals so that you can't tell which are blown by wind and which fall from the sky.

First String

You have a memory of something you're not sure you witnessed or heard about and filled in the details which is close to the same thing. Memory has a life of its own and what we remember is shaped over the years as clay is shaped as it spins on a wheel.

You lived in northwest Seattle in those days and your 15 year old brother Jim lived with you. He had a basement room and had recently started Ballard High School so you must have been five or six years old. One night some older boys from Ballard High took the garden hose and turned it on Jim through the open window when he was asleep in his basement bedroom. Hearing Jim yell, your dad raced down the stairs and routed the boys.

Your next oldest brother, Gary, a couple of years later when he was nine, went to Bremerton to visit Auntie Rae and Uncle Carlos on the 4th of July.

Thief Of Hubcaps

For some reason he went by himself though we four younger brothers usually stuck together. Gary didn't know much about firecrackers and when a kid asked him to hold a cherry bomb while he lit the fuse he did so. The bomb went off in his hand and your aunt and uncle took him to the emergency room.

Gary told you the story when he came home the next day and said he felt stupid. After a week or so, Dr. Torland took the eight stitches out and Gary was left with a scar like a scarab on his hand which never faded until he died 30 years later.

At recess in the 4th grade there was a kid named Butch Morris who'd recently moved to your grade school who terrorized a select group of boys, including you, by telling you he was going to hit you in the stomach at recess and if you winced or reacted he would hit you again.

You went along with his game. He was a strong kid and his fists were hard as rocks. The blows lasted until you went numb or the bell rang. That went on for a week in a slave/master way until Mr. Hawk, the playground supervisor, caught him in the act and sent him to the principal's office.

You'd begun to realize something about the cruelty that boys inflict upon boys. You knew the term "bullies" and you would bet at times that you were one though you can't remember any specific incidents.

You were beginning to have empathy for kids who were victimized. You weren't a big kid but you were fit and played football, basketball and baseball in season. You knew it was important to learn to fight, that it was a manly thing to do, that one had to defend oneself. All the westerns and war movies taught this truth.

In the 5th grade you fought Kenny Ostensen in a "smoker" at Edmonds High School. Thinking back it amazes you such an event could happen. A smoker was organized by adults for adults and involved watching different-age kids from 10 through 16, who'd perhaps had a few boxing lessons, smash each other for three rounds in a lighted boxing ring while the men smoked cigars and cigarettes.

There was a ring with ropes, an announcer, a referee, a standard boxing bell and adults who served as seconds and laced up your oversized gloves. No headgear for the fighters. Kenny and you, since you were in the youngest division, were among the first fighters.

You don't remember much of the fight. You both hit each other solidly in the chest and face and the crowd cheered with each struck blow. You remember that by the third round, your arms felt like they weighed 50 pounds but you kept going and Kenny did too. You were both friends, both victims of an honor code that said you never gave up, you kept hitting your enemy and this was strange because you weren't enemies.

When the bell rang to end the final round you put your foreheads against each other and held on with dead arms.

The ref raised both your hands in victory and you suppose you felt pretty good at the time. You hadn't won but neither had Kenny and the crowd of adults, all men as you remember, cheered for you. After the evening ended, your dad drove Kenny and you home and you said "good fight" to each other. But something had gotten into your brain.

You realized you didn't like to fight, to hit other people. You didn't have the "killer instinct" you'd read about that great fighters like Joe Louis, Rocky Marciano, Kid Gavilan and Sugar Ray Robinson possessed.

At the age of 10 you retired from boxing. You got no thrill from intentionally hurting other people. You still fought occasionally with your brothers but it was more play and tomfoolery than violence.

You chose your friends wisely for the next four years, avoiding the nascent psychopaths and fistfights. You got into arguments and fracases during and after athletic games but you were good at talking and a fairly popular kid who didn't antagonize other boys.

Besides, you had an older brother which must have had some influence on your peers not so much because your brother was a tough guy but because he had some badass friends with names like Larry Gard, Lucky Dufresne and Dick Schwimm who looked like grown men with sideburns and drove cool cars, who carried switchblades and a tire iron under their driver's seat in case a rumble happened to happen.

You tell your writing students that most of the time when we're writing about an experience we tend to dance around the subject and often suggest cutting the first couple of paragraphs because the crux of the story doesn't need a build up. You tell them about "in media res"—the Latin phrase for "in the middle of things"—to begin with action and here you are violating the rules you profess.

You also tell them that if you know the rules you can break them.

The first year of Lynnwood Junior High, basketball season. For the first time, kids from Alderwood Manor, Lynwood, Mountlake Terrace and Edmonds are together at one school which sprawls across three acres and the competition in sports increases exponentially.

You're worried about starting which you'd done every year since the 5th grade at Edmonds Elementary. You tried out for the 9th grade basketball team and made it but when the season started you were 2nd string guard behind Jake Blount, a kid about your size (5 foot 7—you hadn't had your growth spurt yet) who outweighed you by 20 pounds. You were thin as a pencil and so immature that body hair hadn't blessed you though you were almost 14 years old.

Jake was different.

He had real chest hair, not exactly simian but manly strands at his sternum and a thatch at his gonads which you'd enviously glimpsed in the shower room. He had articulated muscles. His biceps were balls of muscle where yours were straight as uncooked linguini.

Two years before, you'd played baseball with him on a Little League All Star Team and you were vaguely aware of each other. That fall at Lynwood Junior High, he'd run for Boys Club president against you but you'd won, probably because you'd also won the contest for naming the school mascot (the Lynwood Lancers because you were reading about King Arthur, Knighthood and Lancelot and you understood the allure of alliteration) and because you had the inspired idea to link up with Jim Miller and Gary Minugh on a candidate slate with posters that extolled the virtues of the three "Ms": "Vote Me, Minugh and Miller." You became a DJ at the Noon Sockhops and a popular kid.

You didn't think about how this might have affected Jake's feelings toward you.

The basketball season began with mixed success. You won two out of four games. After a dispiriting loss against Everett Junior High, Coach Doyle on the bus home, who was also your History teacher, sat down with you and told you that you were going to be starting guard at the next practice which was Monday. He told you not to tell anyone.

You're not sure why he did this but you went along with it because you'd been to taught to respect your elders and Coach Doyle was one of your heroes because he was your basketball coach and a man who fired your fuse for American History. Plus, he had more confidence in your abilities than you had in yourself and you hoped he was right.

For the whole weekend you were elated, ecstatic and felt your dreams had been answered. You were going to be starting guard for the Lynnwood Lancers!

You planned your outfit for Monday over the weekend. You chose a pink wide-collared Mr. B shirt in a piquant hue of pink which would have branded you as a "queer" if you'd worn it on Friday,—white peg pants, blue suede shoes and a blue suede jacket—all of which your mother had bought you from her earnings working at the Bon Marche at Northgate in the Foundations Department—an archaic term which meant she fitted and sold bras, girdles and corsets.

You liked clothes and chose carefully what to wear, unlike most of your peers, perhaps because you liked colors and saw how you could change depending on what you wore. It was a way to wear a costume, don a personality.

The year before, your model was the cowboy walk of John Wayne but the new popularity of Elvis Presley in 1955 and all the screaming girls who surrounded him soon made you change your outer skin. On the coolest day of your life you wanted to look the coolest you could. You wanted to glitter when you walked, as the poet wrote.

You remember nothing of that Monday except basketball practice after school. Coach Doyle performed a ceremony before every practice.

He would tell everyone to sit in the bleachers, place a ball at one end of the court at the top of the key and stand at the center line with five scarlet and white Lynnwood Lancers silk tops. He'd look at the fifteen of us then announce in a stentorian voice: "Starting at center (guard, forward)..." and then announce the name of the player. After he'd named Cal Southworth, the tallest kid in the 9th grade at center and others whose names you don't remember, he came to your position.

"Starting at right guard…"—then, by god, he said your name.

You ran out, grabbed the precious jersey and took your place with the other four starters. You picked up the ball, threw it to Cal who began a series of layups while the others watched and put on their white practice jerseys over their white T-shirts to play against the first string.

You practiced well. You were almost flawless, fluid on the floor. You faked, juked, made some hook shots, layups, jump shots from the key, one long swisher from the end line and got several rebounds. You hustled, ran to defend, you lost yourself in the game. You didn't give a thought to Jake Blount.

After practice you did your usual dawdling in the locker room so you wouldn't have to parade naked into the tiled communal showers.

You always grabbed your towel to cover your privates and waited until most people were out before you went in. You'd never liked communal nudity ever since your dad took you to a YMCA naked father/son swim when you were eight years old. Or perhaps it wasn't the YMCA.

It might have been an activity your dad signed you up for that took place on 1st avenue near your dad's Sporting Goods and Bicycle Store on 1st and Stewart in Seattle.

You knew something was wrong from the moment you stepped out into the pool area. You remember feeling embarrassed and uncomfortable at the sight of all the grown men and their sons without clothes on. The sheer palpability of grown men with exposed body hair and imposing penises frightened you.

After you'd showered and left the building, your dad, who was a good man, put his arm around you and said, "Bobby, we don't have to do that again if you don't want to."

You never did.

On this Monday you were the last to leave. You got dressed, grabbed your fake-leather zippered notebook that contained your PeeChee and school books and headed out the door to catch the activity bus home. The walk to the bus went past three buildings with a space between each about 15 feet wide. You were tired, hungry, and happily reflecting on your prowess as a basketball player.

Rain had begun while you were practicing and small puddles shone on the asphalt avenue where you walked. Halfway to the bus area you saw Cal and Jake step out between two of the buildings, walk to the center of the asphalt and wait while you walked the 20 feet or so toward them.

You didn't think to wonder why they were there. You've always had optimism and a slow sense of impending danger. You were in a haze of dream fulfillment, of achieving what you'd wanted for so long—a kind of happiness that included the whole world and couldn't imagine anyone else, especially your teammates, wanting to hurt you. Perhaps you even thought they were there to congratulate you on being first string because each had a smile on his face.

You walked to where they stood and stopped. You said: "Cal, Jake."

Jake took two steps toward you and punched you in the stomach so hard you lost your breath and levered down.

He caught you on the nose with his next punch which made you see stars. He shoved you back and used both fists to pound on your back as you fell to the ground. It was like being caught in a cyclone that came from nowhere you could tell. You put your hands over your face, tried to catch your breath which now came in racking sobs.

The last detail you remember was a pause after which Jake kicked you twice in your stomach. You were lying on the asphalt in the wet and you heard Cal laugh and then the sound of their footsteps scuffing slowly away.

They hadn't said a word, only that final derisive laugh. You must have moaned.

You began checking to see if anything was broken but other than a bloody nose you were okay. You sat up.

Bits of gravel and dirt clung to your suede coat. Your suede shoes were wet with dark splotches and your white pants were dirty. You brushed yourself off, tenderly checked your nose and stood up.

What had happened? You'd been massacred, beaten, humiliated. You hurt all over. You stopped crying, wiped your face and picked up your notebook which had flown out of your hands when you first got hit.

You knew you couldn't get on the activity bus. It would announce your defeat, your shame. You walked slowly toward the bus area and waited out of sight until you heard the bus leave, then walked to the road from Lynnwood to Edmonds and stuck out your thumb, hoping for a ride which came after about 10 minutes.

Was it raining? Probably, but you didn't notice.

You got home and entered by the basement door. You yelled upstairs to your mom that you'd missed the activity bus and walked home and needed to start your homework. You shucked your clothes, put them in the washer and set your shoes and jacket by the heater. You took a shower and looked at your nose which you could see was a bit swollen but you were presentable enough not to draw suspicion when you ate dinner an hour later.

The next day you avoided Jake Blount. You made sure you were with Robb or Ernie or Doug in the halls or at lunch. You didn't go in the Boy's Room by yourself.

At practice you avoided eye contact with Jake and Cal and were able to forget the beating for a while. You took a shower first for a change, sacrificing modesty for safety and walked to the activity bus with a third string guard named Ernie and Cliff, a doofus second string forward. You knew you were under a curse but you didn't know how to lift it. You hadn't told anyone about what happened—not out of honor but out of fear that once you'd told, your humiliation would become real.

If you didn't tell it would be as if it hadn't happened. You'd done that trick before and it took you about four years to realize lying to yourself was as dishonorable as lying to others.

The next game was away. You started but played terribly—where you used to be able to fake out whoever was guarding you and drive for the basket, your feet got tangled up and you double-dribbled or lost the ball. Your passes were intercepted and normally an accurate shot, you missed the backboard several times until you stopped shooting because you were locked up.

Mercifully, Coach Doyle substituted Jake for you halfway through the opening quarter. You walked to the bench and hung your head.

You realized that you weren't the basketball player you thought you were. Just because you had an 'A' in History didn't mean you could play ball. Mr. Doyle thought because you knew facts and could understand ideas and concepts about the Declaration of

Independence and Western Expansion that those skills would transfer to the basketball court.

You were a loser, maybe even third string, certainly not first string.

You kept going though. You didn't quit basketball and continued avoiding Jake Blount who, now that he was first string, didn't look at you as if you were an insect. He just looked at you as if you weren't there. You didn't mind being invisible though now you realize it's the worst insult you can give someone else.

Mostly during that time you were numb. You knew something about physical shock after an injury but it would be years later before you realized you were in psychic shock, a precocious version of PTS.

A week later, you took a cap and ball pistol your mom had given you for Christmas the year before to school.

It was a beautiful Derringer made in the early 1800's with a walnut fob handle and Mr. Doyle had told the class you could get extra credit if you brought an item made before 1900 to class. Your mom knew you liked old guns and you did—not because they could fire bullets but because they represented the past and were marvels of engineering. Whenever you held the Derringer, you imagined other men or boys who'd held the gun.

It was a way to visit and touch the past—much in the way writing does.

Today, carrying a gun to school would land you in the principal's office for suspension and intervention by the authorities but these were different times before school shootings. You'd looked up information about the Derringer in your family's set of *World Book Encyclopedias.*

When it came your turn to speak, you talked about how the Derringer was a gambler's favorite because you could hide it in a pocket or boot without a holster. Mr. Doyle gave you twenty extra credit points, the highest possible score, though you already had a runaway 'A' in the class.

At lunch, Jake Blount came to your table, said hello for the first time in weeks and said he'd heard about the gun you brought to school and asked if he could see it. You handed it to him and he admired the gun, turning it over in his hands.

He smiled at you and asked if he could take it home and show it to his dad. He said he'd return it the next day. You said yes. You figured that this was his way of apologizing for beating you up, that now he was ready to bury the hatchet, to make peace. You breathed easier the rest of the day.

The next day after basketball practice, you asked Jake for the gun.

You'd seen him at lunch but you didn't want to embarrass him by asking for it. He said that he'd forgotten it. He hit himself on the forehead and apologized, said he was sorry. Well, you'd forgotten things too but you began to feel a buzz at the back of your head which buzzed even more the next day when he made the same excuse.

He said he'd for sure bring the gun on Monday.

The first thing you did on Monday after 1st period was ask him for the gun. You said— some part of you knowing that you'd been beaten again, another part thinking maybe you were wrong to be so distrustful—"Jake, I want my gun back."

He considered this for a long moment and you wondered if you'd offended him by being so straightforward. He looked away as if he couldn't see you and told you he'd lost the gun. He didn't apologize or make any excuses. He didn't say anything else, just looked at you and waited. You couldn't say anything because you didn't know what to say. Jake turned and walked away.

The sound of voices in the hallway and doors opening and closing disappeared down a sinkhole. You were alone, all your thoughts bunched up like dead leaves in a drain. You didn't have any words. You felt sick. You said you were sick to Mr. Doyle and wouldn't be at basketball practice.

You took the bus home and went to your room. You didn't read anything as you usually did. You just laid on your bunkbed and looked at the pine ceiling. You counted the boards.

When your brother Tim came home from school you went upstairs and he talked about Pam Eastman, his latest girlfriend. He made you a peanut butter and jelly sandwich—your price for throwing the football around with him on the front lawn—and you ate and then went out and passed long spirals to each other. That helped.

After, you went inside and sat on the living room couch.

Sometime later—it was getting darker—your mom came in from the kitchen, sat down beside you on the couch and with the radar of all good mothers, asked you what was wrong.

No one else was there or perhaps they were but at that age, the whole universe is in your head and whatever your problems are assumes an immensity beyond the universe that stops us from seeing anything else but ourselves.

You started crying. You could barely get the words out and said something like: "Jake Blount stole my Derringer and he won't give it back." Your mom knew you'd taken the gun to school—you'd asked her permission to do so the week before— and she asked for more details. You told her what had happened but didn't tell her about the fight you'd had or more truthfully, though you couldn't tell the truth, the beating you'd received. She said, "We'll see about that." and went back to the kitchen.

Within an hour the gun was back, you're not sure how, but it must have involved a call to Mrs. Blount who lived twenty minutes away.

What happened next? Many things and some that need writing about, some that you've forgotten, some contained like fossils in limestone that bear inspection but nothing that connects with Jake Blount.

The year continued and you finally got your growth—everything that your genes and older brothers by their height had promised. Between the 9th and 10th grade you grew six inches and though you were still "too skinny" as your mom noted, you weren't completely uncoordinated.

Your voice deepened, reassuring hair sprouted. You needed deodorant. Your dad got you an electric razor for Christmas.

Jake Blount disappeared by the time you got into high school, maybe even before. You still avoided fights and luckily didn't have another, though you came close several times. You began to see that not fighting was more brave than fighting. At least you saw it in one of your best friends, Robb Gomez, who refused to fight David Denby, a guy who resembled a feral rat, even after David called Robb every obscene name in the book of taunts outside the bowling alley in Lynnwood.

Robb had braces on his teeth and didn't want to chance damaging them and said so in language to David that you're pretty sure Denby could barely understand because the words contained more than one syllable. Other kids called Robb "Chicken" but that didn't bother Robb. He was a smart guy who you believe agreed with you that words were stronger than blows, that better fights could be waged with language and ideas than with fists and blood.

Final chapter, if there is a final chapter in any story. You've learned that most of the time when we think something's over, it pops up again somewhere else, given time and place.

You're 21, working construction half the year, going to the University of Washington the other half. You've grown into your body, stronger at this time than possibly ever again because framing houses is like doing an eight hour exercise regimen five days a week which, if you survived, left you with corded muscles and the strength to not only carry a 200-pound beam on your shoulder but run with it.

You were 6 foot one and 175 pounds and won money arm wrestling lumberjacks in Anacortes who thought they could whip you because they had 30 pounds and three inches of height or more on you. You hadn't lost a match in two years nor were you beaten until 20 years later by Neal White, football coach and former high school quarterback, at a Faculty Retreat in Port Townsend. You say this perhaps with pride which you don't like to admit but also part of you wants to say, so much for the stick boy you were when you were 14.

Now you could hold your own.

On payday Fridays in the summer your crew wouldn't take the 10 minute afternoon break or drink any water so that you could leave 15 minutes early, drive to Edmonds Tavern after work where Chubb, the bartender, would have frosted schooner glasses in the fridge into which he poured tap beer so you could toast the end of the week. That first drink after a parched afternoon was so exquisite it shivered all the way down to your scrotum.

After you'd ordered your second beer, sitting at the bar in your sleeveless T-shirt and cutoffs, you looked toward the back of the tavern and saw a guy sitting in a booth by himself. Jake Blount.

You rolled that in your head for a minute, then walked to the table and stood in front of it. He looked up with a blank stare. You said: "Jake Blount." No inflection. Each word of his name was a boulder. 9th grade had returned but now it was different. You felt your eyes narrow, go gimlet.

He screwed his face up toward you, squinted a bit as if you'd taken him away from a train of thought and said your name. You nodded yes and smiled but it wasn't the kind of smile that was open. It was closer to the kind of smile Jake and Cal must have had when they saw you step toward them on the asphalt path. It was a smile a guillotine might make.

Thief Of Hubcaps

Jake stood up. He barely came to your shoulders. He was same size he'd been in the 9th grade, a bit thicker perhaps. You had a thought that if you wanted to, you could pick him up and throw him 10 feet into the bar mirrors, shattering the glass.

This was followed immediately by another realization as Jake stuck out his hand and said "How ya doin'?"

The anger drained out of you. The injuries you'd received had long since scarred over, even healed. You barely recognized the person you were when you were 14.

He was still inside you but you knew more of the ways and way people are out of control when they're young— they respond to their parents' upbringing, the twist of their lives, the multiple desires not met the way the brain and body yield to hormones and urges beyond reason— swamp-borne and unswerving in their command.

You knew enough to know you didn't know everything about Jake.

You shook his hand. You smiled in a genuine way—not so much because now you understood Jake and believed in ultimate goodness and the human spirit and all that feel-good crap but because you'd gotten rid of something you'd carried around for awhile and hadn't known it were there until it was gone. You felt lighter.

You sat across from him and spoke of the past.

He'd joined the Navy when he turned 17 and gotten married because his girlfriend was pregnant. He'd recently divorced but still saw his kids and spoke of them by name. You asked him if he remembered beating you up in the 9th grade. He got a puzzled look in his squinty eyes and said, "Nope... I don't remember that but I could have. I was an asshole in those days." You both laughed.

What was scary and frightening had now become a source of laughter—an alchemy that helped you get through some tough times in the past and would do so in the future.

He said he was working at Northwest Fur Breeders doing maintenance work which you knew meant cleaning out the chinchilla and nutria pens. You toasted Friday Payday, your future lives and tamped down the wedge of satisfaction you got from knowing he'd arrived at cleaning shit out of cages while you were building houses and preparing to be a teacher.

At this point in your life, you still thought in terms of winning and losing, something you're still working on and getting better at, thanks to Jake Blount.

Even Now In A Gas Station Head

Always an omnivore of Lit where he widely roamed and fed, at 14 he began to realize that living in words separated him from the world. He hadn't read Hamlet yet but when he did four years later, he recognized the failing in the Dane as his own.

He'd read of men being in war but hadn't dipped his toe in battle, He'd read of romance and passion but had barely kissed a girl and knew as much about them as he knew of Einstein's theory of relativity—which is to say that he recognized both by their designation but knew nothing of their substance. He was also of the age when strange urgings took hold of him at odd times and dreams were no longer only of monsters but contained females and friction that ended with evidence requiring a washing machine.

Movies also spurred this urge. Romance was everywhere to remind him of his ignorance—in war films as GIs got letters from sweethearts back home, epics of Rome and Egypt with sinuous dancing girls an obligatory feature, musicals that always had at their heart a boy-gets-girl conclusion. He remembered the song lyric from *Casablanca*, "You must remember this, a kiss is just a kiss..."

Even the Hunchback of Notre Dame, who he admired and impersonated, loved Esmeralda and died for her. He didn't want to die but he sure wanted to live and love a girl. How to get the taste of experience?

He hadn't had a real kiss yet. He'd played Spin the Bottle at Nina Harris' birthday party when he was 13 but other than a peck lasting as long as a giggle he was a yearning acolyte. Once he met a girl in the balcony of the Princess Theater when he was 14. He knew the film was going to be romantic so he suggested that every time the couple in the movie kissed they should do so too. She looked at him with arched eyes and said no.

Throughout the rest of the film, he kept his distance though every time a kiss happened on the screen he looked sideways at the girl but she kept her eyes screwed to the movie and being brought up to respect females in an all-male household except for his mom, he honored the girl's refusal to play what he thought was a clever game but also knew that he'd violated her virtue and felt a measure of guilt for doing so.

Maybe the key was to find a girl with experience in these matters.

Thief Of Hubcaps

On a summer day in late August he found a message above the urinal in the Richfield Gas Station across the street from Edmonds Motors. From his standing position he stared at the words gouged in red: "For A Good Screw, Call Tess Daley, Prospect 4152."

He admired the rhyme of screw and two and received this as a timely message from god—a revelation like discovering that Rock Hudson was "an honest-to-god homosexual." He knew Tess Daley from Lynnwood Junior High. She was a bouncy girl with blonde hair, blue eyes and a sweater that displayed two promising mounds which deserved capital letters—Breasts, Bosoms, Tits, Dugs, Boobs, Boner Meat, Bra Stuffers—he knew the words but hadn't played the game.

Tess, though food for lust, always seemed an innocent girl who teachers called Teresa. She didn't dance close at the Noon Sock Hops, didn't squeal and giggle, didn't hold your eyes and look mysterious. She seemed a modest girl you might see in church. She couldn't be a fast girl, could she? He certainly would have heard about it but not a whisper.

At 14 he came upon two momentous concepts that we all discover and think they're uniquely our insights whereas they're as old as trilobites and ancient as the wheel: things change and appearances often lie.

Tess may have evolved over the summer—sometimes three months can be like three years, especially for a girl. Most guys remained the same but maybe that's because he was paying more attention to girls in that time—and he'd read enough to know that outer appearances often disguise inner truth. Milady

DeWinter from *The Three Musketeers* was a mud shark skank.

Though sometimes, like the hunchback, an ugly face and deformed body hides a beautiful spirit. However sometimes, like a vampire, a handsome face, tuxedo and cape conceals a blood-sucking bat. What we see and believe is often deceiving. Angels may disguise devils, devils angels.

He walked out the door and saw a phone booth. He went inside and got Information. He called Tess and she remembered him. He asked how her summer was and other inane questions which were tossed back and forth like beach balls. He finally asked her for a date and she said, "Sure." He hadn't anticipated this instant success. Next he had to tell her where and when. Events were going so fast, he was dizzy but he trusted his teeming brain.

He told her next Friday he'd call for her (he actually said "call for her" a phrase he must have learned from British movies set in the 19th century) about seven and they'd go to the Carnival at High School field. He'd seen the roustabouts setting up the rides and booths on the football field that morning on his way to Edmonds from Hummingbird Hill where he lived.

It was a perfect place for a date. They could ride the rides, eat cotton candy, maybe see some sideshows and he wouldn't need to fill the silence. They said goodbye.

He had a romantic date with Tess Daley in two days— Matahari, Scheherazade, Delilah and Bathsheba awaited his carnal quest.

Thief Of Hubcaps

Friday arrived and with it two showers, Old Spice aftershave from his brother's bottle, Wrigley's Spearmint gum for breath and dressed in chinos with a light blue sweater over his best white shirt, he walked to Tess's house which was two blocks toward the water from the Richfield Gas Station where he'd discovered her true nature.

She greeted him at the door in a blue and white-checked gingham dress with a white sweater around her shoulders and a silver cross that hung from her neck towards the scooped bodice—a word he liked because it resonated with body. Her eyes were open and he saw no temptress in them, no smoldering lust or flirtatious filly. She looked innocent as a primrose, as untouched as an orchid.

He smiled at how easily deception deceives, how canny he was to be privy to the network of knowledge available in Men's' Rooms.

The carnival was a whirl of organ music and motion. Acrobats worked their way through the crowd, clowns in costume mimed and played the children. Barkers invited them to throw darts, shoot guns, throw balls in baskets, toss hoops on spindles, ride the Octopus, see The Bearded Lady. He had two dollars to spend so he chose judiciously.

He tossed footballs through holes and won a cheap charm bracelet for Tess. They played a lever machine with metal balls that rang bells but won no prizes. They drank what's now called a Slushy but then was called a Snow cone, a ball of ice with grape or orange sprayed on top which you sucked for pure sugar lust.

He saw some friends of his brothers walking hand in hand with their dates who sometimes held large Teddy Bears they'd won at the game booths. They walked past the rides, most of them designed to make the riders dizzy or scare the bejabbers out of them. A roller coaster occupied 30 yards of the football field but cost 50 cents to ride and looked rickety.

He saw the Ferris wheel at the far corner of the field turning like a giant Mandala, lighted against the deepening night with spokes of lightbulbs.

He could see young couples sitting close together in the coach-like seats, the guy's arm around the girl, the girl snuggled close to the guy, their heads together in meditation upon a kiss.

In the sky the full moon beamed with saffron bliss.

It was a place to be alone, to wait for the time when the wheel would stop and you'd be suspended and alone at the top while riders got on or off and you could take the chance to smooch, to taste another's lips. He asked Tess if she'd like to take a ride. She smiled at him and he surmised she was looking forward to the chance to be alone and lock lips as much as he was.

It couldn't have been more perfect. They sat close together with the lever pinning them in the cracked leather seat. The wheel started up as organ music played "Shine on Harvest Moon." The first time they got to the top, the wheel stopped.

They were alone, rocking back and forth in a gentle sway. Now was his chance, now was his instant of possibility.

He must have grabbed her shoulders roughly, perhaps even surprised her with his abruptness because

he heard her exclaim "Oh" as he leaned toward her
mouth like an arrow toward a bull's-eye. She pulled
back and slapped him and as in Kepler's law that every
action has an equal and opposite reaction, he jerked
back into his original position and compressed against
the cushion.

He instantly knew three things: Tess was not a
hothouse whore, he'd made an unforgivable error that
would result in eternal shame if not eternal hellfire, and
writings on bathroom walls were not to be believed.
He'd never been slapped by a girl before and until this
moment thought that his inability to be aggressive with
girls was part of his lack of success. He'd never been
slapped by anyone except some boys he'd fought with
on the playground who did it to humiliate. He was
humiliated, his cheek stung and a heated furnace burned
in his stomach.

The rest of the ride lasted forever, falling to
earth again and again. He'd seen the painting by
Brueghel that shows Icarus falling from the sky while
his father, Daedalus, watches and he relived that feeling
of falling again and again.

He couldn't speak, the words were trapped in
his throat. He'd done something that he couldn't excuse
or explain. Out of lust and ignorance, he'd harmed a
girl. Out of his careening desire for closeness he'd
separated himself from decency.

His mother would always tell accusers, when he
and his brothers were charged with minor crimes like
stealing fruit from the next door neighbor's orchard or
being seen throwing apples at cars traveling on the road
beneath their pasture or ringing door bells (for which

they were often guilty): "Oh no, my boys would never do anything like that."

Years later, he realized that she probably knew that they did such things but by believing in her children's goodness she held up a standard of conduct that her boys could aspire to though sometimes fail to reach. Or maybe she was deluded— all mothers are a bit blind when it comes to their children—and now he'd not only let himself down, he'd let his mother down.

He was beneath contempt, beneath speech. He avoided Tess's eyes after they got off the Ferris wheel and asked her if he should take her home now.

He kept a careful distance as they walked the five blocks toward the duplex where she lived. He was silent as a shut door as was Teresa. He kept biting his lip as if to injure that part of him that got him in trouble. Her silence and brisk walk were further injury but he knew he deserved more. How could he possibly make this up?

He left her at the door of 625 Pine Street. He said, "Thanks for the date" but she didn't respond. He was 14 and already a convict of the heart, a prisoner of sex and desire, a boy doomed to live in vile infamy.

He was also a kid with a short memory. Soon enough, he sailed into other dangerous waters, committed other acts he winces at now. Soon enough he learned to rationalize his faults, to excuse his actions but also to tamp down the worser part of him, to forgive himself for his blunders and see them as a part of, even necessary, to his becoming something he could live with and even respect but that would be a long time coming with events he couldn't anticipate or imagine.

Thief Of Hubcaps

Even now—a phrase he picked up from *The Chauraspanchasika*, a poem written in the 11th century that begins every stanza with "Even now" about a Brahmin lover who's sentenced to death for his illicit love with a promised princess and writes a poem the night of his capture, the night before his execution—a poem whose final lines are recited by Doc in *Cannery Row* at the end of the novel which contains an insight far beyond words gouged on bathroom walls—he remembers that innocent and tawdry time.

Even now, in his septuagenarian stage, he knows he's still capable of such lapses, though the optimistic part of him hopes that such failures are over.

He knows the final stanza of the poem by heart:

> *"Even now*
> *I know that I have savored the hot taste of life*
> *Lifting green cups and gold at the great feast.*
> *Just for a small and forgotten time*
> *I have had full in my eyes from off my girl*
> *The whitest pouring of eternal light.*
> *The heavy knife. As to a gala day."*

The Sexual Barrier Reef and King Tut's Tomb

I see her between two giggling girls in our 5th grade class picture at Edmonds Elementary. In the spring of that year I thought less of girls than important things like baseball, football and basketball and what we'd have for dinner that night.

Sally Ann's lissome in the back row, a bit gawky with long black hair, a giggle in her smile and a scarf around her neck. She's thin as a dowel. She wasn't afraid to get her hands dirty in crafts class and seemed less of a mystery than other girls.

At the start of the 8th grade in Mr. Warnecke's History class, I saw she'd pupated over the summer. Her hair was shorter, slicked back on the sides and she wore lipstick, mascara, a white shirt with the collar up and the sleeves cut off to display her pale arms.

Thief Of Hubcaps

She'd also sprouted breasts, or so it seemed from the gentle rise underneath the silky fabric which I could glimpse from my third row desk as she leaned into the boy beside her in the front row and whispered in his ear.

This was an intimate act between a boy and girl on the first day of school. She put her hand on his shoulder and seemed to be speaking inside of him. After an interval, the boy jerked back as if stung by a wasp, his face turned red and he turned wide-eyed away from her.

Word quickly spread of what Sally Ann said to the blushing boy: "Cool your tool, fool, I'm wise to the rise in your Levi's."

I admired the rhyme and was surprised by the revelation that some girls knew what a boner was, perhaps were wise in the ways of what happened not only at night after heated dreams but in school at the oddest times when we prayed we wouldn't be called to the office or have to stand up and recite because we had a bulge in our pants or worse a flagpole sticking out at a horizontal angle and for anyone, especially girls, to see that would be social catastrophe.

It was a secret all boys knew and sometimes kidded about with terms like "hard on" (as if an electrical switch had suddenly been thrown), "boner" (as if one carried an extra femur in one's pants) or "Hey Buddy, gotta rocket in your pocket?" and the ultimate, elephantine secret that everyone knew but no one talked about, being accused of "playing pocket pool" which implied the sin of self-flagellation, another cool term I'd learned from my Methodist Church upbringing.

No girl I'd ever known had any knowledge of such mysterious matters. I was intrigued and a bit frightened though I'd had my first kiss with Cassie Devlin the year before when we walked down three consecutive dark alleys in Edmonds after a football game before I worked up the courage to kiss her. My older brother had coached me on how to kiss, telling me, "It's easy, just shut your eyes, tilt your head and head for her mouth." I followed instructions but she tilted her head in the same direction as I and we bumped noses. She giggled, I blushed.

The following summer I went to Sherry Ravelle's house. She'd recently moved to Edmonds from Ballard where it was rumored the girls were "fast" and knew their way around boys.

I'd seen her at the Princess Theater the night before and she'd asked me if I wanted to come over to her house the next day. I told her I had a Babe Ruth Baseball game but I could stop by before the game.

I showed up at her house in my Edmonds Lions baseball uniform. I was a catcher, which I liked as much or more than pitching since I was involved in every play and I was pretty good at outfoxing the hitters by calling for curves and changeups at surprising times.

But that was baseball, a game I'd played for years. I knew the rules. This game with girls was different though there was some cross-fertilization of terminology. Boys used the metaphor of baseball with girls perhaps to make understandable something they didn't know much about by comparing it to something they knew something about. I'd heard older boys talk about "scoring" with girls, which seemed to mean a degree of sexual intimacy I only had the vaguest notions about.

They also talked about "striking out" on a date which for me, meant you didn't get a kiss but I suspected, at 15, there was more to it than I knew. I was a rookie, unsure of myself as a 10-year-old in his first year of Little League baseball.

She met me at the front door with a smile and a blouse with three buttons unbuttoned which created an interesting V which pointed to a place that interested me. Luckily, I was already wearing my jockstrap and cup which kept things in place. She told me her parents weren't home and we'd be alone. I tried to read her signals.

Sultry? Inviting? Seductive? I was certainly aware she had curves. I could see them in her swaying backside as she led me down the hall to show me her room. I'd never been in a bedroom of a girl my age but I did have an interest in archeological discoveries—I'd thrilled to Howard Carter's description of entering King Tut's tomb—so I followed her.

Growing up with three brothers I knew what guys rooms were like: messy, with clothes strewn on the floor, pictures on the wall of Willie Mays, Mickey Mantle, the Associated Press All American football teams, Bob Houbregs (who I admired for his hook shot) and copies of National Geographic which sometimes showed pictures of African woman with bare breasts.

Sherry's room was different.

Her bed seemed fit for a princess with a white bedspread with pink flowers, two silver cushions at the headboard and on the walls, pictures of fairies and water sprites. She had a makeup table with a mirror and various concoctions whose secrets I couldn't surmise on the glass top. Everything seemed double when you looked at them. I saw a bottle with a bulb at the end which I recognized as a perfume puffer like my mom had.

The room smelled of sweet citrus and was a newly painted mint green that complemented Sherry's natural red hair which bounced with highlights and electricity as she talked to me.

She asked if I wanted to kiss her. This was a clear signal I caught. I kissed her and then again. And again. Soon we were fumbling in each other's clothes. The clothes began falling like leaves, like secret passageways revealing Tut's tomb. I was out of breath and she was too. We panted like racehorses.

She said, "Let's go in my parent's bedroom."

I didn't think that strange at the time but now I think it was. Perhaps it seemed okay to me because we were going to do "grown-up things" and what better place to do so than in a grownups' bedroom?

We were down to our underthings—me in my jockeys and jockstrap, she in her panties and bra when we heard a car driving into the carport. The en flagrante delicto of teenage nightmares.

Sherry grabbed her blouse and skirt and ran from her parents' bedroom to her own. I grabbed my baseball pants and T-shirt from the room, raced to her room (barely missing colliding with her on her way out the door), got my cleats- stockings-jersey-baseball cap and headed for the bathroom where I began assembling myself to look like a ballplayer and innocent youth.

Within seconds (Sherry was indeed fast) I heard her say to her parents— loudly so I could hear: "I have a friend over. He has a baseball game but I wanted to introduce you to him before he had to leave. He's in the bathroom but he'll be out shortly."

My fingers were shaking so bad I had trouble buttoning my jersey and pants, tying my shoelaces. But I was quick and took a final look at my flushed face and bright eyes in the mirror and I seemed okay. Later I would realize the comic aspects of this situation but for now I knew the next seconds were crucial.

I was sweating more than in the final inning of a seven-inning game in summer heat.

Girding my loins, a phrase I'd learned to love taking Bible Camp in the 4th grade which seemed especially pertinent here, I walked into the front room to meet her parents who, in retrospect, probably knew what was going on—they smiled at me and seemed to share a secret mirth as I spoke of my baseball prowess and bloviatingly told them how beautiful the day was and welcomed them to Edmonds. I asked for the time, the father glanced at his Bulova watch and told me and I said I'd better hustle or I'd be late.

I said "Bye, Sherry", grabbed my Schwinn bicycle which had my catcher's mitt and a warm-up ball on the rear carrier and pedaled off toward another game.

When she called that night and said that maybe I could ride over some night and she could sneak out her bedroom window and we could go to the woods by her house because she wouldn't feel right " doing it" at her house, I knew there was something brewing beyond my ken, as the poet Keats might say.

I told her my family was going to leave for Yellowstone Park for a week vacation, which was true and I'd call her when I returned which wasn't.

I never called.

What she'd said and the idea of "having relations"—a term I'd heard that I knew told little and disguised much— frightened me more than my recurring dreams about being blown up by a Russian atomic bomb.

A month later, my best friend, Robb Gomez, was dating her and had begun to smile more in a week than I'd seen him smile in the previous year. He took me aside at the Princess Theater and showed me a condom he had in his wallet which he displayed like a Medal of Honor.

Sherry had actually given him a rubber! I'd seen condoms floating down the creek in Carkeek Park when I was 10 and thought they were deflated white balloons until my older brother, Gary, laughed and told me different.

And what of Sally Ann? When I began this story I imagined it would be completely about her but one must consider the prelude before the main melody. Sally Ann deserves another story with a concluding coda.

Girl in the Class Picture

I kept Sally Ann in my fantasies but did nothing to make them real until a year later in the 9th grade when Sam Gamble asked me if I'd like to go on a triple date to the Seattle Kustom Kar Show at the Memorial Coliseum. Barbo Green and Ramona Tuffley, the fastest couple in our grade were going, Sam had his driver's license (he'd flunked the 8th grade) and a hot girlfriend named Candy, and I loved hotrods, Chuck Barris' flame-painted cars and I'd never gone on a triple date in a car with other teenagers.

The only thing I needed was a girl to go with me and I knew it couldn't be a respectable girl like Sarah Woodley, my date to the 9th grade winter prom, who was precociously breasted in a backless prom dress which scared me every time we danced as I put my damp hand on her bare shoulder but who was also a future valedictorian who was referred to by teachers and parents as a "nice girl with strong morals."

At my age I wanted less morals and more contact than a bare shoulder. I was ready for a girl who was fast, who could show me more than I knew, put into practice what I'd read about in racy books like *Peyton Place*.

Reading and school were easy for me. Teachers asked questions, gave tests and I answered. I could analyze plots, talk about characters in a novel, short story or poem. I could solve story problems in math and history was a way to live in the past and learn about heroes and villains.

I was a regular at the Edmonds Library which perched above the police station just off Main Street by the Safeway store. I'd won the *Summer Book Worm Award* twice for having checked out and read the most books in a summer and I hadn't cheated. Books were a way for me to not only escape my present by knowing the past but a way to live and adventure in words and ideas. Girls were a different story.

I thought Sally Ann might show me a different story, teach me something that might help me uncover the mystery. I called her and she agreed to go.

On Friday night, Sam picked up Barbo Green and me and we drove to the girls' houses where we acquired our harem. Sam and Candy were in the front seat, Barbo and Ramona, Sally Ann and I in the back of Sam's '54 Olds Sedan, close as ball bearings in a Bendix brake. Sally Ann held onto my arm, giggled and whispered with Ramona, winked at me twice and snuggled next to me.

My arm cramped, wanting to put it around her. I had learned the trick of stretching my arm up as an excuse to put my arm around a girl at a movie but had begun to realize that ruse was a cliché and an obvious subterfuge. I wanted honesty and unbridled passion. How to do that? I waited to see what would happen.

At 15, most people believe that everyone's like them, that they share the same interests. Later we realize how wrong we were but at the time, I suspect along with Sam and Barbo Green that everyone would love to attend a Kustom Kar Show.

We cruised the hotrods, ogled the '50 Mercs, low-slung Studebaker Hawks, Model T roadsters with chrome engines whose hoods couldn't contain the chrome carburetors, '55 Buick hardtops with Dagmars (a term for the front fender chrome bullet guards taken from a television show featuring Dagmar, a plutonium blonde with prodigious breasts) and supercharged cars so shiny and exciting with their louvers and leather, fender skirts and Continental kits that they were another kind of wet dream for boys who loved both cars and girls with equal desire.

The girls followed us around, oohed and ahhed with us, taking our lead and what were they thinking?

Were they bored and comatose with all this machinery and shine? Probably. but that thought never entered my head at the time. I was just happy to be with Sally Ann who held my hand, which this night wasn't damp. It was good to not have to think about what might happen in the car on the way home.

We spent a couple of hours touring the inside of the building, imagining being the owner of such powerful and lovely cars and left shortly before the show closed at 10.

On the way home, Ramona and Barbo immediately started making out in a double liplock.

Barbo had Ramona pinned against the traffic side of the car. I realized the time had come. Girding my loins, I put my arm around Sally Ann which triggered an amazing reaction. She moaned, scooched into my side and thrust her tongue in my ear.

I'd never imagined such a thing was possible—this wet, warm tongue thrust into my open ear.

I'd never imagined meeting God before but this must be close to what it might be like: the sudden power, the discovery of another existence, a kind of glory unimagined in its epiphany. I shuddered and gasped. I'd heard about French kissing but never conceived that French tongue thrusting, which had now become a rhythmic pulse inside my ear canal, could be so cataclysmic. With every thrust Sally Ann gasped in heat.

I was heated too when she pulled back to gauge my reaction. My eyes opened wide. I stared into the river of her blue irises, placed my mouth on hers and tentatively, my tongue into her mouth which she began sucking as if it was a banana Popsicle and our tongues began undulating and I was moving like a runaway train.

She moaned and I answered in moan. We were like two peacocks calling in a language I was just beginning to learn. I rolled my hips and she rolled hers. I felt like I was in a pornographic novel. Time stopped.

I later learned that there are 10,000 sense receptors around the mouth and the tongue and all of my receptors were firing and I was beyond myself, inside a breaking wave, until I felt the car stop outside Sally Ann's house.

Thief Of Hubcaps

I swam up to the surface, pulled back from Sally Ann's mouth, took a deep breath and got out of the car so I could walk her to the door in the darkness. When I stepped out of the car, I fell to my knees and almost fainted. Sally Ann put her hand on my head and asked if I was okay. I said I was but I wasn't. She had to hold me by the arm so we could navigate the 20 feet to her door where I tasted her tongue again and wrapped my mouth in her mouth until Sam honked. I said "Thanks for the date." Sally Ann laughed and said, "Anytime" and I turned toward the car and took a last look at my siren of sex in white pedal pushers and a red silk blouse framed in the doorway. She waved and I waved back.

These cataclysms happen in our lives and we remember the main thing that happened in exquisite detail like a favorite film we've watched 20 times. As we relive these memories, which is for me is what constitutes most writing, we strain to remember more—what happened the rest of the night, what we said to the others, what we thought about in bed that night but most of the footage is gone. Somehow we've sorted out the essential story from the mundane surroundings and something else happens in relationship to truth.

Even now I wonder if what happened 55 years ago happened as I think it happened. Probably not, but the main truth remains as well as some of what happened later as well as another coda which occurred six years later when I'd turned 21.

After that "Night of the Tongue Thrust", I didn't ask Sally Ann for another date, probably because I'd heard through the rumor mill that older guys had sensed something going on with her (hard to miss for randy upperclassmen with acute hormonal sensors) and she could be seen on Friday and Saturday nights, cruising Edmonds' Main Street strapped to the side of senior hoods in hot rods. That was out of my league.

She dropped out of high school when she was a junior. Word was she'd gotten pregnant and married a Navy guy from Bremerton. She'd moved on to places I could scarce imagine and after awhile I stopped remembering her.

After high school, I took a year off to make some money and then starting attending the University of Washington and took every class I was interested in—Philosophy, Psychology, Eastern Religions, Astronomy, Physical Therapy— until finally settling in as an English major.

Shortly after my 21st birthday I decided to go to the Owl Tavern now that I was of legal age. I wanted to go inside a place I'd heard stories about and seen on my way to the Sno-King Drive in. It was reputed to be a den of vice, a place where fights occurred, women could be scoped out and workers often stayed with their weekly paychecks draining out on the weekends.

I had a sociological interest in the Owl Tavern as well as a scatological curiosity. I'd taken both Anthropology and Sociology, had graduated from off-campus Sexology 101 assisted by three young women—singularly, not "ménage a qua"— and besides, there was a neon sign outside the tavern on Highway 99 that blinked: "Live Dancing Girls Fri. and Sat. with Rusty and Gladys"

As an English major I wondered if they ever advertised dead dancing girls and what that would be like but I'd never seen a stripper and this was before the age of zombies. At my age and disposition I was eager for the experience.

I went by myself. By now I was in my Raskolnikov phase, having graduated from my James Dean phase and being just before my Actor phase, though all of it was Personae Pro Dramatis.

I'd read *Crime and Punishment*, devoured Dostoyevsky's novel about a brooding intellectual who kills two women in a botched theft because he has a theory that exceptional people are above the law. He was also intelligent and a would-be writer like me and besides he'd finally found love at the end of the novel with the beautiful Sonia, the former prostitute who saved him from a life of barren lovelessness and self-absorption. I became so involved with the novel that I would sometimes miss a class because I lost track of time in the Art Building coffee house devouring this life of late 19th century Russia.

I'd taken to wearing dark Goodwill jackets, checked gabardine pants, and colored short sleeve silk shirts when I could afford them. Sometimes I'd add a scarf, all of which I thought made me mysterious and alluring. I still wore black Converse tennis shoes from my days of playing basketball.

The past meets the present—often in surprising juxtapositions.

I loved the idea of juxtapositions, a word I'd learned from Professor Angelo Pellegrini in his Shakespeare class which I instantly realized made sense when applied to living in this world with its odd combinations of opposites and opposing forces of truth and hypocrisy, love and hate, past and present, on and off, light and dark, and yin and yang which I'd learned in Professor Smullion's Philosophy class where I had trouble understanding Leibnitz's concept of "monads" which I still don't understand.

I think of monads as something like those dust motes in summer air which you can barely make out or the brief lights you see against your lids when you close your eyes. They're there but they're not—the way events happen and we don't understand them until later, if at all.

I arrived at the tavern in my beat-up '51 Chev coffee-colored coupe a half hour before the show which started at 10. Inside was a room about half the size of a basketball court with a bar on one end and a small stage on the other. Green felt tables and booths surrounded the room where mostly guys sat, drinking beer and smoking cigarettes— Pall malls, Lucky Strikes and Camels.

As I was walking in I passed a guy who gave me a push with his shoulder. He looked drunk. I turned around.

You wanna fight? Let's go outside, boy.

He looked about my size and weight but older and he swayed as he eyed me with his tough-guy eyes. I didn't want this. I was interested in girls, not guys who had tar roofing on their pants, wore dirty T-shirts and construction paints splattered with white paint.

After all, like Raskolnikov, I was a college student. I had a brain and I didn't like being called a boy.

If you want to fight, I'm game. But I have to warn you, my hands are registered weapons.

I'd learned that ploy from Mark Lecount, a friend who was now in the Coast Guard in San Diego.

Besides, I hadn't had a fight since I was massacred in the 9[h] grade by another kid after a basketball practice. I waited to see what would happen.

I was strong from framing houses and hammering nails. I could sink a 16-penny nail into a Doug fir stud with one blow of my 28-ounce hammer. Plus, he was drunk. I flexed my shoulders and went into my best imitation of a Kung Fu stance.

After what seemed a minute, while he registered what I'd said, he blinked his eyes, shrugged and kept walking.

I was surprised he was fooled by my tactic but pleased at my success in avoiding the fight. I sat down at a table and ordered a Rainier beer from a comely waitress whose nametag said Violet, took out my copy of Dostoyevsky's *The Idiot* and assumed a scholarly air which was soon interrupted by Rusty and Gladys and the lights coming on over the stage.

Rusty pounded a Wurlitzer organ, Gladys beat the drums and sometimes sang. They played a couple of numbers then Rusty said, "And now what everyone's been waiting for: Stripper girls you won't believe and dancing you've only dreamed about in your dreams!" He began a low thumping bass, the standard strip music. Gladys played a counterpoint drum roll with a sultry rhythm. A spotlight hit the center of the varnished floor. My first live strip show!

Out of the darkness from the side of the stage came a young woman dressed in feathers and a diaphanous negligee.

She began to bump and grind. Her smile was not so much a smile as a pouty sneer that might invite a spanking. She removed her negligee, then threw off her headdress.

Now she was in a spangled bra and panties which caught the light and threw brilliant flashes when she moved. Her shoulders and feet were bare in the bright light. She began the meat of her act, pumping her hips forward and back in time to the music, caressed the cones over her breasts and the crotch of her panties, kept dancing.

What we could all see now was how thin she was. She had shoulders and a ribcage like a starved sparrow. Her breasts didn't bulge. A couple of guys began chanting "Keep it on! Keep it on" instead of the usual encouragement of "Take it off! Take it off!"

I began to feel sorry for the girl. She was the opening act and it wasn't working for a roomful of guys used to Playboy boobs and big time cans. She was thin as a dowel.

I realized that it was Sally Ann up on the stage who was now gamely unhooking her bra, then twirling it three times before throwing it stage right.

This move brought derisive chants from the audience but she kept going. She had a routine that had to last the whole song which she'd obviously rehearsed. She wasn't a bad dancer and she was different. I admired that.

She started pulling down her panties, slowly, as if peeling a banana with a tough skin.

She turned around, pulled her panties to her thighs and stuck out her rear, rotating it back and forth as if saying hello then turned back and winked at the audience who were now faking their enthusiasm, yelling, "Whoow Whee"s and "Oh, Momma"s.

Thief Of Hubcaps

There must have been some rule about total nudity because she never took off her panties. The song ended and she ran offstage covering her breasts to scattered applause. I stood up and applauded. I knew Sally Ann and liked her. She deserved applause.

I expected sybaritic but got sad. I wanted salacious and forbidden but received what I'd learned from Flaubert and Chekhov—any attempt that involves courage and dignity that fails is ultimately tragic and noble—not in Aristotle's sense of the term but in what I knew of the human spirit and the dignity we all search for and desire which often involves pathos—the blunt edge of expectation crushed by the brute force of the world— more to be pitied than censured.

I took some solace in that but I also knew I had a debt to pay.

I spotted her at a solitary table at the side, covered up in a bathrobe. She sat in the chair with slumped shoulders, eyes on the green felt of the table. I walked over and sat down.

I said "Sally Ann" and this time I wasn't acting. I took her hand in mine. I didn't say anything else. She looked at me, took another look and said my name. She opened her mouth in what might have been a wince.

She told me she had two kids, that she'd divorced her husband, that this was the best paying job she could get. She lived alone in Everett, 10 miles up the road. She could be with her kids all day, work for 4 hours a night and make enough money to pay for food, rent and a babysitter for the kids at night when she worked.

She'd been doing this for the past year. It was the best of all possible worlds as Voltaire wrote ironically in *Candide.*

We talked for awhile as another stripper, more buxom, began gyrating to Rusty and Gladys' organ and drums but I was lost in Sally Ann. I stood up, put my hand on her shoulder and said goodbye.

I wish I would have said more but I knew she had her way to go and I had mine. I walked out the exit without a glance at the voluptuous Ginger, arrayed in a Catholic school outfit open down to her belly button which revealed a transparent bra with tassels covering the nipples.

On the way out the exit door I wondered how she used the tassels in her act.

Coda: at my 50th high school reunion I told this story in abbreviated form after four hours of talk, food and drinks when our class president asked for memories of our time together. I waited until the popular ones of our school—the kids we called "Soshes" for social-suckups—had finished their recollections and stories and raised my hand. Something in me wanted the others to know that high school life and what happened after wasn't some a sentimental fairy tale with a happy ending. I thought I should be a voice other than a Hallmark card.

I still owed Sally Ann. By that time, I knew from teaching high school for thirty five years that for most of us, high school is not the best time of our lives as parents often say. God help us if it is.

The story received about as much welcome as Sally Ann's dancing at the Owl Tavern when she and I were 21. The class president said after I finished: "Okaaaaay Bob, that was an uplifting story." He understood irony.

One of my classmates, who didn't understand irony or much about why people do what they do, grabbed my arm as I walked away from the light and said, "You don't know much about Sally Ann. I heard she screwed three guys in the same room at the same time through three different holes when she was a sophomore. She was a real whore."

I said, "Really?" and walked out the door. I didn't expect to see Raskolnikov's Sonia that night nor did I but the idea and the feeling of what could be lost and found remained with me for a long time and still does.

Thief of Hubcaps

On a Sunday morning after church in early September I call Danny Irwin, a neighbor boy on Hummingbird Hill, who, like me, is 15 and playing junior varsity for the Edmonds Tigers football team.

I'm an aspiring quarterback, Danny a fast, hard-hitting, defensive back. We've been friends through grade school and often play in each others' backyards.

I ask him what he'd done on Saturday night. He says that he and Sam Gamble went to Everett and stole hubcaps and it was really cool. This interests me. My brother, Gary has a '47 Ford baby blue convertible with white top, tan leather upholstery and tear-drop spotlights. My dream, when I turn 16, is to borrow the car so I can cruise the streets of Edmonds but why would he loan me his car?

Hubcaps are the flashpoints of teenage cars in the fifties. Some are Olds' spinners that resemble a dead starfish splayed on a convex cone, others have blades of chrome that resemble the chariot wheels in *Ben Hur* and some few have full moons—an expanse of chrome that shimmers and shines as the car moves through dark and light.

All are advertisements for cool...the black of the tire to denote the lure of night and secrecy, the pervasive wide whitewalls for contrast and at the center, the rotating Gods of Chromos that flash and hook the eye of every kid who wants to ride Friday and Saturday nights through main street in our town, scouting the girls, looking for action, blaring rock'n'roll on the radio, watching and being watched.

The wheels flash and pulse like extensions of the driver and the kid who has to drive his parents' car with routine hubs registers zero as an outcast square.

You could have a '48 Nash Rambler with primer spots all over it like leprosy but if you had a set of chrome hubs with wire spokes from Shuck's Auto Supply for 25 dollars, the car had a cachet of cool, like putting fluorescent shoelaces on scuffed suede shoes. The wheels said, "I'm moving, I'm rotating, I roll, I flash my shine."

Hubs are the ticket to Paradise, entry to the Teenage Hall of Fame. They're as necessary to being a teenage boy as having a rubber in your wallet even if you never have the opportunity to use it.

My brother's car had baby moons—acceptable but a bit understated for my taste—and I knew immediately if I could get him some gaudy hubcaps it would be like money in the bank when I turn 16 and ask to borrow his convertible. Midnight Auto Supply was the answer. It solved the problem of having to pony up the money and offered an adrenaline adventure if one had the moxie and smarts. I believed I had both in abundance.

Danny, the veteran of hubcap theft, tells me I'll need dark clothing, fast shoes and a long screwdriver to pop the hubcap. We arrange to meet at twilight in the gully south of Daley Street, four blocks above Edmonds.

After dinner I tell my mom I'm going to the Methodist Youth Group meeting, always a good excuse to get out of the house. I leave by the basement door after I've changed into my dark blue Levi's, black T-shirt, black tennis shoes and a reversible black jacket which is bright orange on the inside.

Though I'm an apprentice thief, I know the advantage of having two disguises in one. I can do the crime wearing the dark side then to evade detection, turn the jacket inside out. I will defy description—the thief of many colors, many disguises.

I'd grabbed the longest Stanley screwdriver I could find from my Dad's workshop in the basement and have it hidden at my hip under my jacket like a gun. When I get into the darkness of the gully, I whistle and Danny, after whistling back, appears from the woods to the side. We grin at each other and I listen as he tells me about the plan of attack.

We'll approach the car on the side away from the house, insert our screwdrivers into the space between the hub and the rim, look at each other, nod, then count 3 and with one fluid move, pop the hubcap. We'll run to a pre-arranged place and wait to see if anyone comes out. If we get separated we'll meet at the Edmonds High Football Field and whistle in two-minute intervals until the other shows up.

Thief Of Hubcaps

We grin again and walk toward town.

Just before we reach the end of the gully we spot a bulky '47 Ford Sedan parked 15 feet from its owner's one-room house. The hubs aren't much—dingy chrome circles that cover only the lug nuts—but we figure we need a practice run. We agree to meet directly across from the house in the woods across the dirt road. We walk to the car as if on a night stroll, keeping an eye on the house, squat suddenly down, look at each other, nod, count three and then with one sound and motion, pop the hubcaps, race to the woods and wait.

All we can hear is our own breathing. Side by side, we watch the house. No one comes out. We grin at each other. Our first prize but what do we do with these clunky hubcaps?

We decide to put them back on. After all we both attend church, Danny's on his way to being an Eagle Scout and it's like only eating what you kill. This is when I first realize what honor among thieves means.

Noisily we replace the rims—it's harder to be quiet putting them on than taking them off— but nothing stirs from the house. We leave for Edmonds, for better bounty, having met our first theft with honor and expertise. My confidence soars.

This is far better than sitting in a closed room listening to our youth leader, Chet Bennet, talk about the problems of growing up and becoming adults though I'd found that walking Penny Kingdon home from the meeting holding her hand and anticipating a kiss almost made up for what I didn't want to listen to or understand.

On a long waterfront street just off the Edmonds ferry dock we spot our first victim: a '55 Buick with full chrome rims that look like sideways birthday cakes with a red Conquistador emblem in the center. No need to speak. We walk side by side looking for any sign of activity from the houses or street, step out to the street side and pop the hubs.

We run across the street into a vacant lot punctuated by Scotch broom and wait. Perfect. We leave the hubs in the middle of the barren lot underneath a pile of slash. In the next hour we get two Olds Spinners and two Dodge Lancers. We're slick as the Butch Wax we rub into our crew cuts to make them stand up straight.

After the Lancers it's close to 10 o'clock, our curfew on a school night, so we collect the other hubcaps, put them in a burlap sack Danny's brought along for the occasion and walk toward Dr. Magnuson's office about two blocks away, hiding when we see headlights turn onto the street from one car. Not much traffic at ten on a Sunday night.

We hide our booty in the alley in back of the dental office behind the trash cans. It's getting late and we have six hubcaps, all of them beautiful. A good start. I can see that stealing something is a lot easier than paying for it and it's much more fun. We're blooded in crime, bonded in theft and have successfully begun our criminal careers.

On the way home we decide to walk past the Safeway store next to Edmonds Library perched above the Edmonds Police Station. Why not walk past it we decide; the evidence of our crime is secure in the alley. We have nothing to hide. Just two guys walking home late from a youth group meeting.

Thief Of Hubcaps

That's when we spot in the alley next to the police station a '52 maroon and white Studebaker Hawk with full moons. Though the door to the station is open—it's a warm summer night—there's no one in or near the car.

We come to a halt. We've chanced upon the mother lode, the Eldorado of hubcaps, the ultimate challenge for two brilliant thieves. The door's open, the police sure to be inside the station but the challenge is too inviting to walk away from.

There will never be danger and opportunity so twinned in our lives. We turn our heads to each other, look into each other's eyes, and smile. Brothers in crime.

We step back into the darkness and conceive a plan. We'll approach from the sidewalk next to Safeway, turn up the alley, take the rims and meet at the football field after 15 minutes. I add another wrinkle. I'll be on the alley side of the car, Danny toward the street.

When we have the hubs we'll split our forces. Danny will run past the library up the long street toward the football field (I'm pretty fast but Danny's a rocket).and I'll head up the alley. I have a vision of the police coming out of the door and seeing two dark figures running in different directions, crashing into each other like the Keystone Cops while we escape.

We take a breath, walk to the end of the block, cross the street in the crosswalk to obey the law and head toward Treasure Island. It feels like just before the kickoff at the start of a football game when the whistle blows and the ball soars into the air toward you from the kicker's toe and you wait, gather all your energy so you can ignite into action.

Past the Safeway, turn up the alley, me first against the brick wall parallel to the front tire, two steps, crouch down with screwdriver in hand, find the place between hub and rim, insert the lever, catch the other's eye, count three and catch the moon. Fast and flawless.

Out of the corner of my eye as I explode up the alley, I catch sight of two figures emerging from the open door. My stride lengthens. I'm a Panther of Night; I've never run so fast before. Twenty yards and I see a three-foot garden fence and high-jump over it.

I throw myself to the ground, spot what I take as large cabbages and burrow underneath the long leaves. I make myself as small as possible, listen for pursuing footsteps. I pray for my panting to stop. I wait, catch my breath, listen to my trip-hammer heartbeat.

I'm not sure what I expected but this isn't it. The cops know our crime. Best evidence from the lack of footsteps is that they've run after Danny. Maybe they caught him.

There'll be a manhunt for me, maybe sirens, guns, searchlights. Keep calm, I tell myself. I'm a smart kid. I've read about criminals, how they outfox the authorities. All is not lost. I have to hatch a new plan. Think, I tell myself.

Forgetting about our agreement to meet at the football field I think about how most criminals get caught. They blow it by revealing their guilt. They return to the scene of the crime. But...what if I do what they expect?

Thief Of Hubcaps

It would be a double bluff. Head up the alley, get to the end, then take a left and approach the police station from the other way as if I'm taking a night stroll.

They'll never suspect anyone of normal intelligence would be stupid enough to go directly back to where he'd just committed a crime minutes before. Who would have such moxie, such nerve? It was brazen, audacious and bold but dangerous times call for dangerous actions. On the edge of a stiletto, I know this is what I must do and it's brilliant.

The plan has an added attraction: I can see what what's happening at the crime scene, if they've caught Danny, if the TV reporters from Channel Five have shown up yet.

I leave the moon under the cabbage leaves. Before I go over the fence I take off my jacket and reverse it. The bright orange glows like a fluorescent popsicle. I've donned a new identity—no longer a Panther of Night, I've become a bright orange harvest moon from the waist up. I'd read about *Be On the Lookout* Bulletins, standard police procedure that always described the clothing the criminal was wearing. I'd altered that. I would appear as if I had nothing to hide. I could probably be seen from a block away.

That's what I want. Why hide when you have nothing to hide? I prepare to enter the Lion's den, the Gangway to Dracula's castle by nearly rupturing myself as I try to go quietly over the fence without jumping.

Halfway down the long block toward the police station I see headlights come up the road. I spot the red bubble on top. I force my breathing to slow. I'm a typical teenager who can't sleep, taking a walk on a Sunday night to catch the air. I start humming "Meet

Me Tonight in Dreamland", a song my mom used to sing to me before sleep, to calm down.

I look up at the stars so I won't be staring at the approaching car. The trick, I know, is to act natural but not too natural.

The headlights catch me full on as the car pulls over to the curb and the window rolls down. A voice says,

"Hey, buddy, what's going on?"

Oh, hi Officer. I'm just out on a little walk. (I know not to offer too much information. My voice is cool, collected. I force it not to crack.)

You got school tomorrow, don't ya? A little late to be out walking the streets.

What time is it?

Almost past 10:30.

Wow....I must have lost track of time. I finished my homework and went to bed (excellent line here to establish myself as a good student) *but I couldn't get to sleep. My dad told me if that happened to try taking a walk.*

He'd never said that but that was a good line to put in—it established that I respected my father's advice like all good sons and established the reason why, unlike any other teenager with a brain, I was out walking on a Sunday night. So far, so good.

Did you see anyone about your age running in this area in the last 10 minutes or so? Hear anything?

"...your age" catches my attention. Is this a real question or does he suspect I'm the criminal? My brain whirls. As Ambrose Bierce wrote in "Occurrence at Owl Creek Bridge", I thought "...with the rapidity of lightning." To say too much is as bad as to say too little. Best of all is to deny any knowledge of anything.

Now the fuse is lit. The battle of wits has begun.

Hmmm...(a nice touch that implies I'm thinking about the question. I scratch my head and look around to see if the culprit might be in sight. The cop doesn't say anything. I can feel his eyes boring into me.)

Nope. Haven't seen a thing... (and now an idea enters my head which I immediately recognize as genius) *Wait a minute...I think I saw a guy dressed in black running toward the A&P down the street when I crossed the crosswalk. I work there on Saturdays so I always look toward the store.*

Was the working at A&P a good thing to add? It said that I was a responsible kid but maybe it was too much. The cop doesn't seem to notice. I begin to wonder if he's noticed my fluorescent orange jacket.

Okay. I'll check it out. Have a good evening.

He drives off up the road. I start breathing again. I glance over my shoulder and see the cop car at the end of the block start to take a right and it's too much to contain. I begin running, not in fear but in exaltation and as I pound down the sidewalk I look back and see that the cop car I thought had turned right has done a U-turn and now is heading down the street toward me.

I run harder, not thinking, until I look ahead at the end of the block and see lights in the corner law offices of Chet Bennet, my Methodist Youth Fellowship advisor. If there's anything I need now it's a lawyer and advice from a guy I know and like. I think in exclamation points! I live in exclamation points! Fate's on my side! My luck holds!!!!!

I feel the lights on the back of my neck, hear the engine near as I run into the office. Chet rises from his chair. I see by his wide eyes I've startled him. I blurt my story.

Chet! The cops are after me. I stole some hubcaps. They're right outside. I don't know what to do.

Wait here. Calm down. I'll talk to them.

After a few minutes, Chet returns. He sits down at his desk across from me. He looks into my eyes and asks if I know that he's the prosecuting attorney for the city of Edmonds. I swallow. I didn't know that. He smiles. Chet has a great smile, he's a man in his 30's with black hair and a rumpled look. He makes a tent of his fingers.

Tell me everything.

I spill my guts—I include Danny, who Chet knows from MYF, the six hubcaps we've stolen at the waterfront and ditched behind the theater, the moons taken from the Studebaker and my ignorance about what's happened to Danny.

Chet leans back in his chair.

Well, you certainly did it this time. You stole those moons from Officer Yomans' personal car. I have to charge you for that. Here's the deal. The first thing we need to do is return the hubcaps you stole from the cars on the waterfront. If we can do that, I won't have to charge you and Danny for them. We'll get those back and then find Danny if he's still waiting at the field.

What about the cops?

They left you in my custody. Let's see what we can do.

Thief Of Hubcaps

Chet waits in his beat-up '50 Ford 4 door Sedan while I retrieve the ditched hubcaps then drives me down to the waterfront where I put the hubs back on the cars as quietly as I can. I cough loudly every time I replace the hubcap so I won't wake anyone on the dark street.

At the time I think this is a smart thing to do. We drive to the football field. I seem to be in some sort of nightmare that won't end.

I get out of Chet's car under the streetlight and whistle, then realize I'm being stupid and yell Danny's name toward the football stands. I see a figure emerge from the darkness running low, one hand cupping a chrome moon like a discus. When Danny gets near, I get in the back seat.

Danny jumps into the passenger seat, flashes me his bright eyes and turns to Chet as if seeing him for the first time.

Chet! Glad you're with us!

If I wasn't so close to crying I might have laughed. Danny thinks Chet's our getaway man, our accomplice in crime. As Chet tells Danny what's happened Danny falls silent. Chet tells us he'll drive us home and talk to our parents.

I wait in the car while Chet and Danny go inside the Irwin's two-story house at the top of Hummingbird Hill.

At my house, my mom and dad listen to Chet and barely glance at me. He tells them the police will be talking to me at school tomorrow sometime in the morning. My parents tell me to go to bed. I've done enough for one night.

From the time I get to school the next day I keep glancing out the windows to see if a cop car has shown up. It's a fear I still have to this day. I'll be at school and even though I'm teaching if I see a police car I'll get a hole in the pit of my stomach even though most of me knows I'm not in trouble and don't have much to feel guilty about.

Experiences don't die, they echo.

2nd period in Biology class an office aide arrives with a note and gives it to Mrs. Hollingshead. I'm ushered into Principal Bromley's office, a man who looks more cadaverous than a corpse, who sits behind his desk with kerosene eyes. He orders me to sit on the chair in front of him. I look back and to my right and see Chief Rube Grimstad, an imposing six-foot-six in blue uniform who matches the ominous look of Mr. Bromley. I don't know whose eyes to avoid so I keep mine down.

What they say is a blur. I respond with few words other than "No, sir" and "Yes, sir". The full extent of the trouble I'm in has seeped into me. Chief Grimstad tells me my court date will be Wednesday night at 7 o'clock and I should bring one or both of my parents.

My dad and I enter the police station door at 6:50 and sit in the third row facing the judge's raised bench. I don't remember anyone else being there but there must have been others. I see Chet at a table at the front wearing a dark blue suit with a red tie and white shirt. He looks legal and patriotic and I fear him. I sit close to my dad in his best brown suit and white shirt which he wears to church. And this is almost like being in church. It's serious.

Thief Of Hubcaps

I've never seen my dad so serious. Danny's there along with his stepfather, Mr. Sundstrom, who's a fisheries professor at the University of Washington and reminds me of Rube Grimstad with his face like a cold mountain peak. The night before his parents told Danny that we couldn't play together anymore outside of football practice. No more Bingo ball with plastic bats and balls.

That's not what I'm thinking about as I wait for our names to be called. The fear of every teenager who lived in the Northwest was that he'd be sentenced to "Juvie", the prison for juvenile boys in Everett with cells and guards. All of this for stealing two (really eight) hubcaps?

I was being initiated into a precipitous world which didn't seem to offer second chances or a way to wriggle out of mistakes.

The court clerk calls our names. We stand and walk to the front and are sworn in, something I take seriously because I have to swear to tell the truth while putting my hand on a Bible. We say "guilty" to the charges Chet had described and noted in legalese.

The judge tells us to step toward the bench. He impales us on his eyes and intones our names as if he's reciting the Ten Commandments.

Robert Charles McAllister and Daniel Lester Irwin: I sentence you to one year at the Everett Juvenile Detention Facility...."

He pauses. My stomach lurches, My knees quake. I seem to suck in every particle of air in the room. I feel my head expanding and see bars, a cell, a prison sentence. After an hour of seconds, he finishes his sentence.

...suspended... on condition that the defendants have no further misdemeanors or felonies until they reach the age of 18. Defendants will be on parole for a year during which time they will be required to go to a church of their choice every Sunday and are further required to have a curfew of 9 o'clock each night, at which time they must be home with their parents. If these conditions are met, this case will be removed from the defendants' criminal record when they reach the age of 18. If not, they will be remanded to the Everett Juvenile Detention Facility.

I understand now that this was a small town's way of dealing with small town crime for juvenile boys. It was a way to scare them into compliance with the law, a way to warn them that if they didn't obey the law they'd wind up behind bars.

I also believe that Chet had a hand in the decision and though I saw him at various times until I moved from Edmonds five years later, we never spoke of it and I never thanked him—an omission I regret to this day.

And what of that year of Sundays spent walking alone down the hill from our house, past streets of snug houses, past the police station and library towards Edmonds Methodist church and the inevitable hour of sitting with adults on mahogany pews, hearing Reverend Proudfoot speaking his faith in Jesus and God, standing to sing the hymns, putting the quarter my mom had given me into the collection plate?

I believe it gave me the gift of isolation which in a way is a prelude to enlightenment, for lack of a better word. It taught me to be alone.

Thief Of Hubcaps

The adults, I think, saw me as a pious youth but they didn't know me and the guilt I concealed. As the months passed and I maintained perfect attendance (though at times I pleaded with my mom to no avail that I was too tired or sick to go) I realized that a forced term at a specific place could not imprison me as long as I had my own thoughts to think.

I saw that the world was endlessly captivating— all the way from the well-kept yards of the houses with flowers in season to the glimpses of families sitting at breakfast through the misted windows, to the robins and wrens I watched flying and waving on branches and in the air, to the short German couple who dressed for church as if they were going to a funeral and sat with their three children who wore always colors of the rainbow. Even the mole on Reverend Proudfoot's cheek and his subtle lisp when he pronounced "Sabbath."

I began to realize, through that year, that I rather liked being with myself.

On the last day of my confinement I go to church as usual and sit in the very back of the church as is my custom. Then I have an idea and though I'd learned that not all my ideas turn out well I can't help myself embracing this one.

I wait until the moment the collection starts and ease out the back door. It's a sunny day and I want to end my sentence with something other than routine. Perhaps it was a way to say I wasn't completely reformed, at least not in the way that the judge may have thought I would be. I was still a bit of a rebel and besides, I deserved a reward for enduring all that churchgoing.

I walk past Crow Hardware, Millie's Clothing and head toward Benz's Fountain, hoping it will be open. When I walk in, the ship's bell on the door rings softly and I see Mrs. Benz in a plastic apron doing dishes in her light green dress and plastic hairnet behind the marble counter top. I wait, not sure if she's open or has accidentally left the door unlocked.

She's humming "Beautiful Dreamer", a song my mom used to sing along with "Meet Me Tonight in Dreamland" to help me go to sleep. Soap suds bloom on her arms and rose- colored rubber gloves. She must have felt me near and turns with a smile. I see two of her and two of me reflected in the sectioned mirrors that run the length of the counter.

"Bobby, how nice to see you. What can I get you?"

I'd always liked Mrs. Benz—she was an adult who always looked you in the eyes and seemed to regard everyone as if they were her grandchildren no matter how young or old they were. She made me my first Green River when I was 10 years old served in a fluted vase-like glass which I liked as much for its emerald color as for its sweet taste.

She made milkshakes thick with ice cream and fruit and always left the frosted silver container it was made in by the glass so you could have every last luscious drop. I'm not sure how old she was but she always seemed the same age and ageless in her age.

I ask for a Strawberry Sundae and she smiles as if I've made a perfect choice. We're alone in the morning and I watch as she makes a mountain of vanilla ice cream topped with fresh strawberries in an extra-large dish. I watch her blue-veined hands in the mirror and listen to her humming. Was "Beautiful Dreamer" her favorite?

Beautiful Dreamer, wake unto me....hmmm, hmmmm, huhm huhmm humm hu humm humm hu humm...

It's the only song I remember her humming and it's accompanied by the thunk of ice cream scooped from the containers inside the gleaming kitchen counter like another kind of music that I like better than church music.

She places the dish in front of me on the swirled granite countertop. As I eat, she watches me and this is when I begin to understand how two people of different ages can have a communion without words, engage in a ritual as old as human time when an older one serves and the younger takes the service and knows it means more than food and becomes a different kind of nourishment to feed a hunger beyond food.

It reminds me of how my mother used to watch us boys finish our dinners after she was done and the light from the dining room chandelier reflected in her auburn eyes.

When I finish I put the quarter my mom had given me for church collection money on the counter and say, "Thank you, Mrs. Benz." She smiles out of her blue eyes and says, "You know, Bobby, if I'd had a son, I'd want him just like you."

Of all the words I heard in church and school that year of my parole, those were the words I remember most.

As I close the door, I hear the ship's bell ring again, followed, as if on cue, by the sound of bells coming from the church down the street announcing the end of Sunday Service.

Indian-Bent Pine

When you and Ned Storm were 12 years old you played in the woods every chance you got. Ned was your best friend whose house was a wooded 10-acre path away. You lived in Woodway Park, an enclave for the well-to-do where Bill Boeing had a mansion, Morris Graves had recently built an artist's compound and the head of Pacific Northwest Bell lived in a gabled castle next to the only bridge in that area.

The woods were dark and deep and more than lovely, they were places for adventure consisting of old-growth firs, cedars that blocked out the sun, kingdoms of ferns, convocations of mushrooms, hills to run down as if in battle and one stream that ran under the bridge where spawning and Sound-bound trout swam.

Most of all, the woods harbor memories of you and Ned.

Once you found an abandoned well covered by rotting wood and removing chunks of termite-infested planks to peer below, you saw a gray shape at the bottom that rippled like a scarf then slithered out of sight. Both of you saw it and wondered what you'd seen.

The thing looked wet, perhaps a wolverine but its flesh was pale, almost like what you imagined a skinned corpse might resemble. You covered the hole and never looked again. Perhaps it was a trick of the light, the way something appears at the moment looked at from a distance of 50 feet or 50 years and you can't be sure if it was real, imagined or misunderstood.

You walked the soggy banks of the stream under the bridge that led from a larger pool to the beach where it emptied into Puget Sound. You fished the stream and caught trout 6 inches long. You were caught doing so by Mr. Whitcomb, the guardian of law in Woodway Park who your dad called Whistlebritches for reasons appealing to 12-year-old boys—not quite a flatulent Sherriff of Nottingham but close.

He reproved you for poaching the stream and took you home. Whenever the two of you fished the stream from that time on you'd listen for the rumble of Mr. Whitcomb's Army Duck, a war surplus vehicle he drove as if he was General Patton advancing on Anzio.

You found a steel safe thrown from the bridge that landed in the stream some years before and was covered by long shoots of vegetation. The door was open, the water runneled through in silver and foam and you wondered but never found out the story of what the safe contained or who stole it. The outside door slanted askew, there was a hole where the tumblers opened the safe but now it was vacant and emptied of what it had once held.

Thief Of Hubcaps

Almost like memory, almost like trying to recall events once lived with clarity but now so far in the past they're obscured in mist, elided by the stream of time.

Other events seem to increase in meaning as distance increases and perhaps writing is a way to attempt to discover whatever meaning the events contained, even if they contain questions that will never be answered which offer another kind of meaning. All one can do is attempt the untangling, to trust whatever direction and destination the mind leads you to.

Outside the bathroom window on the spacious back lawn of Ned's house was a tree that you both called the Indian-Bent Pine.

The base of the tree grew straight from the ground about two feet then curved in an elbow about four feet long and continued upwards to a height above the peak of the roof. Ned's father told you and Ned that the tree was bent by Native Indians, most likely Clallam, to point in the direction of a destination— perhaps a camp, perhaps another trail—to find your way through the woods.

That explanation and sense of history appealed to you especially as you'd read and revered stories about Indians since you were in the 4th grade and your heroes were Crazy Horse, Cochise, Tecumseh, Sitting Bull and the fictional Uncas and Chinguchgook in *Deerslayer.*

You had a Boy Scout compass that told you the tree pointed southeast and once Ned suggested you both take that direction and walk to see where the vector led even if the journey took days but you never did that and you're not sure now exactly what you might have found or where the elbow pointed, let alone why.

Memory isn't a stream or a path. It's a place you travel that's marked by events that lodge in our minds, followed by long stretches lost in time.

Sometimes those events are like finding an empty safe or hooking a silver trout or being caught by a game warden or looking down a shaft and seeing something you can't tell you've seen and still aren't sure of its provenance.

For you, the events proliferate and grow still.

You were introduced to sex and masturbation when you were 13. Ned showed you his father's playing cards that displayed nude women in sultry poses and the rubbers in his parents' bedside table and one day, he told your older brother and you to watch from outside the bathroom window and you'd see something interesting.

From your hiding place behind the crook of the pine, you saw Ned enter the bathroom, go to the shower curtain, grab his 15-year-old sister Wendy and wrestle her naked body out so it faced your direction.

You saw breasts, a dark space at the junction of legs and waist and heard the high screams of Wendy who also seemed to be laughing and giggling. That event produced inspiration for many nights of the hand friction that prompted coming, as you called it.

Once he peed on you from a cedar tree he'd climbed next to your outdoor basketball court. You're not sure why he did it but you were so angry you told him to go home—to "Get off my property."

The next day he called and invited you over, told you to meet at the camp you'd both built—a hole you'd dug in the woods next to his house covered with long branches and dirt for concealment. When you got there he'd planted a forked stick in the ground that held a smoking Camel cigarette. It was a peace offering you took and soon forgot being pissed upon.

The first time you went all the way with a girl you did so after you'd double-dated to the Sno-King Drive-In in your '50 Dodge and this seminal event happened with Ned's counsel. He told you that she was ready—as if she was ripe fruit or a Bundt cake in the oven—and said you could park in the field outside his parents' house, that no one would bother you.

The event was notable for its clumsiness, for its darkness, for the way that after it was over, you weren't sure if it had happened. After it was over you weren't sure if either she or you remained a virgin but that question was soon resolved by repetition.

Some months before you'd gone to the Greenwood Roller Rink, where you planned to skate and perhaps pick up some girls. When the Lady's Choice part of the night came Ned was asked to skate every time by cute girls who smiled at him, even winked at him.

You watched from the side as he swept around the circle, holding the girl by the waist, leaning into her, pressing her into his side.

When there was a break you asked him why he was so successful with girls.

You were outside, having a smoke. He told you your problem—you'd known each other for three years but this was the first time he told you his theory—whenever a girl looked at you or indicated she might like you, you fell all over yourself to please her. The trick with girls, he told you, was to never let them know you liked them, to keep them continually insecure, to be mysterious.

You received this judgment as a revelation not unlike reading Kerouac's *On the Road* for the first time. You didn't realize that much of the reason Ned was so popular with girls was that he was good looking.

He looked like a more masculine Sal Mineo, a younger James Dean with black hair and Cherokee cheekbones he might have inherited from his dad who owned Crow Roofing, which name later suggested to you that the company might have been named to honor his Indian ancestors. Storm Roofing seemed a more fitting choice.

You knew one thing for sure.

Since he was 13 and Peggy Ashworth, the rich girl down the road, had invited both of you for a Saturday swim in her parents' swimming pool and wrestled with him
(you saw this and envied it) and thrust her hand down his bathing suit and grabbed his wonker and he had slipped his hand into the top of her bathing suit and from below the water had worked his other hand under her suit and into her...what did you call it in those days?—her pussy, her snatch?—you knew he knew about things about which you were blind-ass ignorant.

He was playing in the major leagues while you were still playing Little League ball.

You vowed to take his advice, to be the man of mystery, the one who was aloof, who held his emotions in check but at the first sign of affection you couldn't help yourself. You sent notes, bad poems, gifts of candy bars and flowers left after class on the girl's PeeChee.

Thief Of Hubcaps

Maybe you weren't cut out to be a Don Juan. Ned sure was.

When you graduated high school Ned went to Washington State College in Pullman, joined a fraternity and when he came back at Christmas, filled you in on college life. You visited him once in Pullman and you were appalled at the life he was living. The first night you attended a jockstrap dinner where all the guys wore only jockstraps and threw food at each other.

The next night you went to what they called a Pre-Function at The Paradise Motel in Pullman—an event where guys and girls drank rum and cokes before the main event of a dance—and Ned disappeared for a 20 minute tryst with a comely Sigma Chi in another room. He was a popular guy at the frat but when summer came he said he liked the social life but not going to school.

You and Ned rented a trailer near Lake Serene and live the bachelor life. Ned was working at his dad's roofing company and you were working at Edmonds Lumber getting ready to attend the University of Washington in the fall.

It was the summer of the World's Fair in 1962 when the Space Needle was newly completed and Elvis Presley came to Seattle in a pink Cadillac. Ned got a job as an Escort for the Seafair Princesses—rather like hiring a mongoose to guard an egg factory.

Girls were still a problem for you. You'd decided you couldn't heed Ned's advice about being detached. You realized you were what you were. You did date Carrie Olson once. She was a beautiful girl you'd admired from a distance for her looks and curves.

You'd heard a story that she was in the crowd when Elvis showed up at the Space Needle and from the back of his pink Cadillac, Elvis pointed at her and said in his Elvis voice, "Hey, darlin, want a ride?" and Carrie replied, "Nope, I've got better things to do.'

You admired that. You've never been a celebrity hound and also, you were envious of Elvis and saw in Carrie's refusal a strength of character that was at least as attractive as the way she walked with a rolling sway and smiled with wet, glowing-red lips.

On impulse you called her and miraculously she agreed to go out with you. You made your plans. After you picked her up at her apartment near Green Lake, you drove her to an isolated road above Lake Washington to watch the sun go down.

You'd written a poem, mercifully lost to memory and time, which probably rhymed atrociously and contained allusions to future happiness and images of flowers and moons and sunrises.

Claptrap—but you believed in it and wrote it at the time. After you finished reading what you now know doesn't deserve the title of poem, she was silent and you thought she was so impressed by the passion and beauty of your words, she was speechless.

She finally said, "You wrote that?" You said yes and she didn't say anything else. You still don't know what she meant by that but at the time you interpreted it as a compliment, that she thought you might have plagiarized your words and in a way you had—you didn't have a voice then, you had a chorus of junkyard scrap to steal from.

The sun went down in silence and you drove to Seattle on Highway 99. On the way four guys in a

Buick Century hardtop with the windows rolled down whistled and waved at Carrie sitting beside you. She smiled and waved back at them and they hooted and hollered even more until they turned off toward Seattle Center.

You asked Carrie if she knew them and she said no. This wasn't a good sign. These guys had horned in on your date and she'd liked it.

After the movie she asked you to take her back to her apartment. You still had hopes. You'd put your arm around her during the movie and she'd snuggled right in. You'd held her hand until you got back to the car and as you opened the door for her, she looked you full in the eyes and smiled. She scooted over to you as you drove and put her head on your shoulder and her hand on your hip.

You could taste possibility.

When you got to her apartment, a third story perch above a courtyard and swimming pool, Carrie introduced to her roommate, Lucy Lushus—a name you found worthy of a porno star but you weren't sure if that was her real name or if they were yanking your chain.

Carrie disappeared down the hallway leaving you in the front room with a bearded guy about your age who had his stocking feet on a case of Rainier beer. He had sweat stains under his undershirt, wore jeans. You were dressed up in a dark blue sweater with a white shirt and gray slacks. He asked you if you wanted a beer. You said "yeah" but he didn't move to give you one.

Loud music, people jawing in the kitchen, multiple couples nuzzling. You didn't know anyone. You sat on the couch like a carbuncle.

After 20 minutes or so Lucy came back into the room and you asked her where Carrie was. She said she was in the bathroom with her ex whom she'd broken up with the week before but it sounded like they were getting back together. You gathered yourself and walked out the door.

You stepped to the railing and looked down three stories. You could throw yourself off the balcony, commit suicide. Another thought: the way you screwed up things, you'd probably end up in an emergency room with shattered legs.

You kept thinking. You thought of Holden Caulfield in *Catcher in the Rye* and his troubles. The Joads from *Grapes of Wrath* came into your head. You figured that what you were going through didn't have half the dimension they had or the reasons to be depressed. You laughed at yourself, your high drama, your theatricality. You got to your car and drove home.

You talked to Ned when you got home to forget yourself and this night. He told you about Sarah Inglebrittson, one of the Seafair Princesses.

He told you he had a plan to snag this most lovely of princesses who he was positive was a virgin. He would ignore her. She was always the center of attention, the girl that guys lingered over, that guys told stories to, that guys asked out but she always refused.

She was polite, even sweet, but seemed to be an apprentice nun. He told you it would take 4 weeks tops to top her. In retrospect, you realize this quest wasn't about romance or sex; it was about conquest and victory.

Over the next three weeks he gave you updates in clumps. After the formal events they were scheduled for—country clubs, Kiwanis meetings, Seafair Pirates events—there was always some sort of get-together. He didn't acknowledge Sarah, unlike the other guys who gathered around her as they would attend a shrine to Aphrodite.

After the second night of this treatment she introduced herself and asked his name. He gave it, then excused himself and went outside.

The next week, she tried to have another conversation and he thanked her for talking to him and looked her in the eyes. He told her he liked poetry and did she? She said she did and he recited the first four lines of "Shall I Compare Thee to a Summer's Day" then got a catch in his throat and said he couldn't remember the rest—which was probably true.

He left soon after without saying goodbye but knowing she'd hear the sound of him disappearing on his motorcycle.

You both had motorcycles which you'd financed because Ned had zero credit. You bought them for $4000 each from Dewey's Cycle Shop on Broadway on Capitol Hill. You chose a 750 cc maroon Triumph Thunderbird and Ned picked a black 750 cc BSA.

Neither of you had driven a motorcycle before when you picked them up so the mechanic gave you a crash course in the alley behind the shop explaining the shifting, brakes, choke, reserve gas supply and how to start the engine.

You left as halting amateurs but soon wheeled the machines with increasing confidence and over the next 3 hours, after taking breaks to swig from a pint of Jack Daniels and rest from the exhilaration of having all that power at the squeeze of your right hand, you ran into a sleet storm on the way up Stevens Pass and Ned ran out of gas.

Ned hopped on your bike and you got to the summit where you stole a can of gas from the Ranger's truck, hitched a ride with a trucker to Ned's bike in the driving snow, got it started and returned to the top of the pass.

Since you hadn't driven motorcycles before you didn't know how to dress for the weather. You were both drenched clear through from wearing jeans, sweatshirt and Levi jackets which looked cool but didn't do a damn for warmth or rain protection. You didn't know about the benefits of leather or insulation.

About midnight, you wheeled your bikes into the public restroom, stripped off your clothes and hung them like drapes over the stalls to dry, had another swig of whiskey and lay on the heavenly-heated floor to grab some sleep.

In the morning you were awakened by a wide-eyed father and his 2 sons who came in to use the facilities and found two near-naked boys, a forest of clothing suspended in the air and two gleaming motorcycles instead of a public restroom. You got dressed and ripped down the freefall road to Leavenworth to have breakfast and buy some warmer clothes.

That day you rode for four hours straight past Wenatchee, on the road to Spokane, over mountain passes, on high mesas, on straight roads where you kicked the accelerator and reached speeds over 100 mph. You took a break for lunch and kept riding.

You didn't know where you were going, you only knew the speed, the flash of new scenery, the pulse of power between your legs, the way folks stared after the two of you when you drove by. You were free, powerful and 20 years old—in love with freedom, yourself and your motorcycle.

This was in the days before mandatory helmet laws. The wind blew your hair as you rode, the air sirened past your ears. You developed muscled right calves from the kickstarter which you'd stand on and power down to roar the engine.

Once, without Ned, you pulled up between two Corvettes at a red light in North Seattle. The drivers looked around you at each other and nodded, the signal to have a drag. When the light changed you poured it on and were half a block ahead when you hit the next light and you looked over at both of them, cool as ice, romantic as Brando in *The Wild Ones*.

On the third week, Ned came home to the trailer and said tonight was the night.

Sarah had given him her phone number after he'd told her he'd had a recent breakup he didn't want to talk about. She told him if he ever wanted to talk, to call her. He called her and you heard him say that he needed to talk to her, could he come down to her apartment?

He took a shower, changed from his Seafair Princess Chaperone navy blue blazer and khakis into black leather jacket, faded jeans, white T-shirt and a purple scarf and took off into the night. It must have been close to Midnight.

Later he told you what happened. He got to her apartment, she buzzed him in and he didn't speak at first, only looked at her. He finally said he wanted to thank her for letting him believe it might be possible to love a girl again and since Seafair was almost over, he wouldn't be seeing her again but wanted her to know why he'd been so silent for so long and how she'd given him a reason to live.

He said he had to go, needed to go, got up and went out the door.

When he got to his motorcycle he stood there posed, shook his head then looked up at Sarah's window on the third floor. She was watching him— which he counted on—and when he looked up she first waved at him then turned her hand the other way gesturing for him to come back.

He hung his head, looked away, then looked again at Sarah in her bathrobe, nodded and started for the entrance. He was a master at Romance, a Leonardo of Lust, an Adonis of attraction, a demimonde of drama and Sarah didn't long keep her innocence.

He mentioned the floor of the living room, up against the wall in the hallway, in the shower and in the bed, on top, underneath, forward and behind, though you have no way of verifying this description of Kama Sutra conquest. Your response was admiration and envy. You'd seen pictures of Sarah in the *Post-Intelligencer*'s Sunday supplement.

She was Scandinavianly beautiful with a bright smile, eyes like stars and a body that invited at the least a licking of lips. You could tell this even from the black and white shots.

When he brought her over to the trailer at various times during the next weeks she was even more beautiful in the flesh and she was intelligent and seemed to have just awakened after sleeping in a field of lilies.

She seemed fresh as morning dew.

Ned wasn't home much for the next three weeks. You used this time to have dates with a few girls and invite them after to the trailer where you read them excerpts from Rostand's *Cyrano de Bergerac* in hopes that the stunning, romantic words of Cyrano would help you earn some intimacy.

You read them parts of the balcony scene where Cyrano defines a kiss—"And what is a kiss? A promise given under seal....a rosy dot over the "I" of loving, a secret whispered to listening lips, together, apart, a promise given under seal..." hoping they might pick up your cue. You also read them the "I carry my adornments on my soul" speech because you wanted the girl or anyone else, including you, to realize you were more than you appeared to be.

You didn't have a large nose but you had a tender soul.

The girls must have thought you strange and when you tell your college students about this folderol, they think you even more strange.

You've realized we're never strange to ourselves. Everyone makes sense of what they do. You remind yourself to remember this when you're quick to judge others' actions—you also remember the line that helps to excuse strange behavior, that it is often "more to be pitied than censured."

Regardless, your literary invitation didn't yield results and maybe it doesn't matter that it didn't. You excuse yourself for this deception on the grounds that you didn't know it was a deception. You loved saying Cyrano's words. You thought because you loved something that others might love it too. This too could be a deception but it's one that's allowed you to have a career in teaching, maintain some self-respect and enjoy your living, for the most part.

But there's a catch with age and it's not so much wisdom as it is perspective that comes from living a long life.

You now believe you admired Cyrano because he had qualities you wished you possessed. He was patient and faithful in his unprofessed love—he never told Roxanne he loved her until he died and only after she realized it was he who had been her lover all that time, always waiting in the shadows, letting others take the applause and she tricked him into admitting it. Then he died.

You couldn't stop yourself from saying your love. And you must admit that you've had trouble being faithful. Three marriages and a brace of affairs attest to this failing.

Once you hurt someone badly and still grieve over that act but that's one of the few things you don't talk about because it's so close, so searing. You also worry that at this point in your story you've treated yourself as a hero, not an accomplice, not one without blame.

Thief Of Hubcaps

Perhaps you've skewed your memory to reflect your virtue more than your vices, of which there are many.

To the point: once in your early 30s, five women, including your separated wife at that time, got together for a hot tub soiree with champagne and discovered that they had all had flings with you in the past year and none of them were aware of the others' involvement. They vowed to confront you but it never happened.

When they got to your house you weren't there. You only heard about this event 5 years after it occurred. You shake your head at such wantonness on your part and hope by writing this you've put some dents in your armor, if not your idealistic portrait of your actions. God knows you had examples of betrayal in your experience but it's far easier to censure someone else than to admit to your own failings.

Ned grew tired of Sarah after about three weeks. On a Friday you were at a party at Steve Johnson's house in North Edmonds. Cases of beer, shots of tequila, dancing, hot girls, Little Richard and Chuck Berry on the phonograph. About 10 o'clock the phone rang and it was Sarah telling Ned your trailer was on fire.

You ran to your motorcycles and sped up Snake Road toward Lake Serene. You remember going 80 or so on the dark twisting road, following Ned's motorcycle ahead of you shooting sparks from his footrest as you both leaned into the curves and your headlights scanned the darkness against the dark woods that lined Snake Road.

When you got to the trailer there was no fire or fire trucks, only Sarah sitting on the front steps wearing Ned's flannel shirt and nothing else. Ned went to her while you waited and shut off your engine. You could see she was sobbing, out of control, hysterical. She went into his arms.

You looked away—she was so raw, shattered in spirit, naked. You started up your motorcycle and spent the night at Steve Johnson's house. You were relieved there was no fire at the trailer but pierced by what you saw of Sarah's grief and what you knew was probably the cause of it.

A year later when you had a coffee date with Sarah she told you she'd been in a mental hospital for six months. She was doing fine or so she said but she did ask what had happened to Ned and you told her honestly you didn't know, though if you had you might not have told her. She seemed breakable. You'd seen *Splendor in the Grass* with Natalie Wood and Warren Beatty and seen what damage love could inflict.

You never spoke to her again nor do you know if she became happy in love. You hope so. There are many things you will never know.

In late August, after Ned had been absent for 3 or more days—which didn't worry you because you both felt free enough not to have to explain why you were gone or check in with the other—two Lynnwood cops knocked on the trailer door on a Tuesday night with a search warrant for the premises.

They also had an arrest warrant for Ned Merrill Storm, wanted for passing $2000. worth of bad checks in the area.

Thief Of Hubcaps

You showed them in and watched as they searched Ned's bedroom which was missing some clothes and boots you were familiar with. You told them you didn't know where he'd gone, which was the truth.

The next week you discovered he hadn't been making payments on the motorcycle loan to the bank and you were responsible for the debt which you ultimately paid off. Without someone else to help with the rent you moved back home and began your life as a student at the University of Washington.

After five years you'd married an Art major, graduated from the university and started teaching high school in Eastern Washington. At some point toward the end of that time you heard that Ned was in San Francisco working at Fillmore West, the rock mecca that featured artists like Jimi Hendrix, Janice Joplin, The Doors and other luminaries.

You got a San Francisco phone book from the library, found a listing for Ned M. Storm, and dialed the number.

It was a late night, you were lonely for some reason—and he came into your head. You no longer cared about the money he'd walked out on. You remembered more the times you had together. Maybe a part of you wanted to brag about what you'd accomplished since you last saw him but most of all, you'd lived through much with him and much you remembered with fondness for its adventure, danger and exhilaration.

You knew he had flaws but knew enough by now to know you did too. You were alike. You'd both traveled dark roads.

He answered your call and you were talking to a stranger. You knew his voice but didn't recognize what he was saying or the slurs and jumps in his conversation. He was probably high on mescaline, peyote, LSD—who knows—it was a strange time in the '60s.

You realized when you said goodbye that he'd taken one direction, you'd taken another. He was lost to you and after you hung up you felt sad for days though you didn't tell anyone about it for months. You nursed it like a wound.

20 years later you're divorced from your second wife, raising two girls on your own in a cheap rental across the street from the waters of Port Blakely Bay. You'd checked on Ned in the '70s and found out through your friend, Pete Mair, who was a U.S. district attorney, that Ned was in the Oregon State Penitentiary serving eight to ten for cocaine distribution.

You wrote to him but he never wrote back.

In 1984, a year you remember because it finalized your divorce from your 2nd wife and was the title of Orwell's novel that featured a cage of rats put on Winston Smith's head to make him see that what he thought was true wasn't, you heard Ned was out of prison and planned to come up in the summer to the Seattle area.

Summer came and on a Saturday night in August when the girls were with their grandparents for the weekend and the blues had hit— maybe because the girls weren't around to keep you safe— it struck you that the summer was almost over and you hadn't heard anything of Ned.

Thief Of Hubcaps

It was after 11 and you remembered you'd heard that Ned's sister, Wendy, who you hadn't talked to for 20 years, worked at a VIPS cocktail lounge near Renton. You got the number from Information and called.

After you said hello and longtime/no hear, you asked about Ned. She said, "My god, you haven't heard? Let me get to another phone and we'll talk."

She told you, as you sat on the rummage sale couch in the dark of the living room, that when Ned got out of prison he'd started up The Northern California Marijuana Growers Association, lived with an Indian woman named Bett Lafitte and had a concealed field in the foothills of the Diablo range. He was dead.

She said it that way: "Ned's dead."

The police report said that he'd picked up a pint of tequila on the way to his hidden marijuana field and killed it on the way. The field was about 20 minutes from the liquor store and they found the empty bottle in his 4 wheel with the door open.

Wendy told you they figured he was so blasted by the tequila that he parked on the wrong side of the road and when he got out of the vehicle, he fell 150 feet and landed on the rocks below.

During that first night, he'd built a shelter over himself—he was proficient at both camping and drinking as well as seduction—and dehydrated, bones broken and body contused from the fall, the next day had crawled to a stream where they found him 3 days later, dead in the water.

There wasn't much for you to say other than you were sorry.

Later that night the description of events didn't make much sense. It seemed to you that Ned had died not from an alcoholic mishap but from a Mafia hit or some rival's vendetta. From the time he was 15 he could hold his liquor, was legendary for chugging—"slamming" in today's vernacular—consecutive beers without swallowing—a trick you'd tried but couldn't accomplish.

How could he have been so drunk he didn't see the edge of the cliff?

That night you looked out at the dark waters of Port Blakely Bay and couldn't make out where the land ended and the water began. The woods were a humped cloak that scaled down to the ink of water flecked with foam.

You caught a reflection from the glass through which you looked and it seemed to contain not only you but behind you, Ned. You looked again but the reflection was gone. You shook it off as imagination and ghosts that sometimes appear from the past.

Other ghosts obtain whose provenance you know. Phil died this year of suicide, a great friend gone. Your brother's been dead from the same cause for 32 years and you dream of him and are glad to see him alive again. You dream of your parents and they're alive in the past—sometimes your mom's in the kitchen, your dad's on vacation at Yellowstone Park with all of you boys on a fishing bridge with a string of trout.

You never dream of Ned, perhaps because like the safe in that stream in Woodway Park when you were 12, you never knew what was inside him, his provenance, which is probably true for all people but for some few it's even more cryptic and disturbing.

You think too of the Indian-bent pine and the direction it pointed to which you now think wasn't a place you could go to and find but more a place in the distance you don't realize you've come to until you've already arrived.

You don't think you're there yet but you're getting closer —though the markers grow further apart, the woods more dark and deep.

Psycho Shower

On a Sunday night in February, when I was 18 and newly graduated from Edmonds High School, working at Edmonds Lumber without a thought of going to college, being more concerned with turning my Titian Red '50 Olds coupe into a hot rod with louvered hood and Lake pipes, I watched Alfred Hitchcock's *Psycho* with my younger brother Tim who was 16 at the time and a ferocious linebacker on the football team.

We'd both seen the ads which stated that no one could get in after the movie started—which I found intriguing. I liked the title and I'd lusted for Janet Leigh after I'd seen her in *The Vikings* with Tony Curtis and Ernest Borgnine. I admired her bosoms, a term I wasn't sure was singular or plural. I didn't know much else about the plot.

After the movie's setup where Leigh's character steals money from her employer and drives a long distance in the pouring rain to finally find shelter at the Bates Motel and meet the sweet Tony Perkins, the motel manager, the indelible scene happens.

Like Spielberg's *Jaws* 25 years later it traumatized a generation who believed taking a shower or swimming in the ocean was safe.

At first, we see Janet Leigh luxuriating in the Bates Motel shower, water streaming down her face and hair then against the opaque shower curtain we see a shape that suddenly lifts a butcher knife and rips open the curtain. Then we see a psycho grandma with an eight-inch knife raised over her head.

The music begins a cat-yowl screech as the knife plunges into Janet's milky flesh.

We watch the arm of grandma as it pulls back and plunges in. The camera follows the stabs in time to the music. We see water swirling down the drain as it turns dark with blood. In the final scene of the sequence the camera pans into Janet's dead eyes.

I think Tim and I grabbed hands across the armrest and after Janet's dead eyes, we finally breathed and watched Tony Perkins as Norman Bates, the son of the grandma, clean up the carnage, finally depositing Janet and her car into a convenient bog hole swamp. But there was more.

We watched grandma strike again; this time coming down the stairs to the insane pulse of the music to slash the private detective and leave him dead at the bottom the stairs. How could a grandma move so fast and strike so quick? We soon found out.

Grandma's disguise is taken off after another attempt at butcher knife murder and we find out that the shy, kind Tony Perkins, the motel manager and resident taxidermist, had dressed in his mother's clothes and a wig and out of guilt, had killed what he feared. In an echo of Faulkner's "A Rose for Emily" he's preserved his mama's corpse and put it into the bed he'd killed her in.

At the end of the movie we see Tony dressed in his mother's clothes in the police station and we hear what he's thinking inside his head and he's become his mother and a certified psycho who says she won't hurt a fly.

My brother and I usually laughed at what frightened us. This time was different. We drove home in the dark and didn't say much. We went to bed because Tim had school the next day and I had to be at work at Edmonds Lumber by 7:45.

In the morning, from my top bunkbed in the basement, I heard Tim make his way to the bathroom. I had an idea.

After he turned on the shower, I took off the mop head—a long cotton string affair which I placed on my head—grabbed the toilet scrubber, wrapped a sheet around me and stole into the bathroom. I knew the moves.

Our shower stall was a cheap tin contraption not attached to the wall. I placed the toilet scrubber in one hand, jerked open the curtain, screeched in psycho sound and stabbed toward my naked, wet brother who turned with his eyes open wider than I'd ever seen them, screamed and threw himself against the shower stall as I kept stabbing.

The stall almost fell over, then righted when he shrank down to the floor as water poured over him. I stopped the screeching and he said, "Goddamit, Bob".

After that, when we showered, we each locked the bathroom door until I moved out that summer to a trailer near Lynnwood that fronted a lake, rooming with Ned Storm. Other horrors, not of the shower stall variety, happened there, and I sometimes remembered the look of terror on my brother's face when I tore open the shower curtain. It was a good memory for me.

However, some people are patient with revenge and as elephants are reputed to do, they never forget.

Thirty years later, happily married to Merry, living on the Island, I arrived home after a Saturday working construction, itching with fiberglass insulation picked up from working in a crawl space the whole day. I kissed my wife hello and told her I was going to take a shower, get the itch out of my skin.

The pleasure of a hot shower when you turn 40 is close to the pleasure of a cold beer after a day of framing houses in the hot summer when you're 20. I turned the shower on and sighed as the water cleansed my body.

The shower curtain ripped open with a metallic rush. I turned and there was a large woman with platinum hair wielding a 12-inch knife, screeching in psycho and stabbing toward my defenseless body.

I screamed, slammed against the wall, put out my hands to guard my face and slid down the tiled wall. Looking up I recognized the maniac eyes of my brother Tim as he screeched and I realized that what I took for a knife was a giant carrot from our garden.

After I could breathe again, I said, "Goddamit, Tim" And then we both laughed like loons.

Roistering with Brother Gary in a Room of Jars

How to get inside a story when the story's inside you?

How to uncap so many jars so long ago secured to see if what's inside still has the tang of jam, to discover if it's turned bitter, if it's still good to spread like blackberry jam picked from dusty late summer bushes, to fight through thorns and find lush berries plumped by the sun and carefully choose them, then use them to create something new, something preserved, which retains some of the sweetness with which it grew?

Gary's gone now but I still see him live. He visits me in my dreams at times and it's mostly a good thing. I remember introducing my friend Charlie Hamilton to my oldest brother Jim after he'd met my younger brothers Tim and Lee. Charlie said,

"Wow...how many brothers do you have, Bob?" I said I had four.

Jim said, "Three Bob, Gary's dead." I said I have four brothers and Jim and I looked at each other. Jim raised his eyebrows.

Jim's the older brother, the one who's a millionaire, who has two houses, one on Hood Canal, the other in Palm City, California. When he was 19, he won the Volunteer Park Art Show Exhibit for best painting by a newcomer.

He went to Northern California Art Institute and painted his last painting when he was 21, when he began working at Aurora Cycle near Green Lake which he ultimately bought from our father. We're separated by 12 years and a continent of experience.

Jim was born in the Depression and the Depression has colored him like a painting by Rembrandt. As Steinbeck said, "He pinched the eagle so hard it screamed." This year Jim's been diagnosed with cancer and "metastasized" has become another word like Auschwitz which scalds my tongue. I grieve for him and know that one day soon I'll miss him.

I miss Gary. Though he was my older brother by two years, from the time I was 15, I thought of him as a younger brother, someone I needed to watch out for. Not that he couldn't handle himself, he had a way of retreating from that which was dangerous or unpleasant.

He was what we call today mellow—relaxed in his good looks, something of an athlete though he didn't have the competitiveness that marks high school athletes and possessed a weird sense of humor as engaging as a jackanapes.

Gary's a cool guy in 1956.

He wears Levi's low on his hips with suede belts of colors from dark pink to lime green. He wears Pichuco suede boots with dice shoelaces, black leather jackets and thick gabardine shirts that drape his 6-foot frame. He has friends like Dick Schwimm, Larry Gard, Lucky Dufresne, Royal Roles, Steve Johnson—all of whom are my hoodlum heroes.

Gary has a sultry, seductive look like a sleek Rory Calhoun. At 17, he dates a girl with black hair like a waterfall of dark and bluebell-bedroom eyes named Heather Fields. Her tight sweaters over Botticelli breasts make me tingle. She has lush legs and a smile that sirens sex from her lubricious lips.

She also has Lance Matson, a Marine Corps boyfriend who was stationed at Camp Quantico in California and had recently won the Camp Welterweight Boxing title.

When Lance Matson returns home on leave, word gets out that Lance wants to kill Gary for fooling around with his girl while he was gone. Gary leaves for Arlington on a Friday night with Steve Johnson in Gary's '49 Ford Convertible. He must have made some excuse to our parents to explain his absence but I don't know what he said.

All I know is that he's in trouble.

Saturday morning I call Lance at his home, tell him I'm Gary's younger brother and ask him to meet me at noon in front of Engels Record store in Edmonds. He says he will.

I'd recently seen *High Noon* with Gary Cooper as the cowboy hero and the time seems appropriate though I never consider wearing a gun to our meeting. I have a plan. I know if I say the right words to Lance I can save Gary from a beating. I believe in the saving power of words.

I wait in front of Engels Record Shop until Lance arrives precisely at noon. Lance wears his Marine fatigues with spit-shined black shoes like mirrors. I introduce myself and we shake hands. I try not to wince when he squeezes my hand.

He looks sculpted, his muscles have muscles. His arms and chest bulge underneath his olive green jacket. He has a buzz cut and a mean look in his eyes. I'm 15 and though I've grown about five inches in the past year, I'm immature and breakable as an egg.

Lance, you know and my brother knows that he's made a mistake. He likes Heather as a friend. He told me she was so lonely and sad when you left he thought he could cheer her up so he asked her on dates. Kind of like a brother would watch out for a sister. He's not really a fighter and to tell you the truth, he took off when he heard you were back in town.

I know you're mad at him but if you need to fight someone, I'll fight you. We could go to the High School Field right now if you want.

I'm ready to do it, to be the sacrificial lamb. I wait. Lance looks hard at me, then he smiles—it's like the sun appearing through a thundercloud—and says "No, we don't need to do that." He lets out a low laugh and I can see he isn't a monster.

Maybe he also laughs because he can see how easy it would be to whip me and maybe he thinks it wouldn't be honorable to fight me. He's a warrior; I'm a clown on stilts. I say, "Thanks, Lance" and watch him walk, as if on parade, down toward Main Street. I hear in my head the Marine Corps Hymn. Somehow the fight's stopped and my brother is safe.

I don't tell Gary or anyone what I've done until six years later when I turn 21 after Gary and I have three schooners at the Richmond Beach Tavern where he'd go on payday Fridays and sometimes blow his whole check playing punch cards. Until then, it was a secret with me and I think I didn't tell Gary because I didn't want to embarrass him.

He was a sensitive guy.

He went off and on to the University of Washington where he majored in Accounting—exactly the worst choice for a wacky, non-conformist guy who told jokes about crows with submachine guns, whose favorite singer at the time was Bob Dylan, who liked to write crazy accounts of drunk zucchinis, who did a dead-on imitation of Elvis singing "Blue Suede Shoes" right down to the hip thrust wiggle-waggle, who never took too much seriously, it seemed.

It seems to me telling that he thought he had tumors in his chest when he was 18. He didn't tell anyone. He thought it was cancer and didn't find out it wasn't cancer until he was examined by an army doctor for the draft two years later and was told that he had a blocked mammary gland that could easily be fixed by minor surgery.

Until then, he thought he was going to die but he kept it in a secret jar inside himself.

What must that have been like, to bear the weight of certain death while you were laughing, drinking beer and roistering?

As it turned out he was declared '4F' because he had a busted eardrum. That was good because the army would have suited him as well as Accounting. He began working at Aurora Cycle for my older brother Jim whose business was thriving so much that he could take afternoons off with Gary managing the business.

He had a kind heart.

For my 21st birthday he throws a party for me and four of my friends at El Gaucho, an upscale restaurant in Seattle's Belltown district, which features waiters in tuxedos and high priced food and drink. He rents a private room for us—a room which I will enter 49 years later into a surprise party thrown by my daughters and sons-in-law. One of them, Mike Strassburger, plays the guitar and sings Pink Floyd's "Shine On, You Crazy Diamond" to me. All of the girls give lovely speeches. The past returns.

This night Gary's like a Pasha, an Epicurean priest initiating us into the world of booze and decadence. He pays for everything from the beginning rounds of rum and coke to the shrimp cocktails to the slabs of prime rib and exquisite potato concoctions on silver plate.

We gorge ourselves, gossip about girls, tell risqué jokes, increasingly laugh as the drunk- meter rises. It's a grand party.

After two hours of sybaritics, Gary taps his sterling silver knife on his crystal glass. He announces it's time for wine and rings a bell for the waiter. The sommelier comes into our room with slicked-back, black hair and the demeanor of an English Lord. Gary changes his voice to French Ponce.

I would like a room-temperature bottle of Chateau Lafite, preferably 1947. Do you have such an item?

The waiter nods and after an interval returns with a shiny cart that displays a silver bowl containing a dark wine bottle wrapped in a silk towel. The wine master takes us all in, then gestures toward the bottle as if we're in the presence of a sacred odalisque. Gary nods. We're silent, immersed in mystery and booze.

The waiter stands at attention, then with a downward tilt of his head, glances inquisitively at Gary who slowly raises his index finger.

Reginald, you may uncover the wine for my inspection.

How did he know the waiter's name? I accept it but know now it was Gary's way of adding even more divertissement to the ritual.

The waiter gently unwraps the towel and with two hands lifts the bottle of Chateau Lafite from its cradle. He steps to Gary's chair at the head of the table and displays the bottle. Gary nods then looks at us as if we're underlings, which we are.

Reginald, in full sommelier, with the exquisite timing of a magician, smoothly moves his hand to the inside of his white swallowtail jacket and presents a stainless steel corkscrew topped by a pearl handle. The act invites applause but none of us is sure of the protocol so we hold back. This is as serious as a baptism, as weighted as a funeral.

After a pause, he sets the bottle on the linen tablecloth and inserts the corkscrew. He inclines to his work like a master diamond cutter, turning the handle with three compressed twists of his wrist, fluid and powerful. He removes the cork which pops and echoes in the silent room. After removing the corkscrew and putting it back in his side pocket, he presents the cork to

Gary as if it's a doubloon from a sunken Spanish frigate.

Gary matches his noblesse. He seems almost bored as he takes the cork, and holds it to his nose like a golden truffle. He closes his eyes, takes one sniff and holds it. Another pause—we can almost hear the discretion and exquisite taste oozing from him. He passes the cork back to Reginald and nods.

He looks up and away—he's in a different country, some region of northern Bombay where people dine for hours after dressing in candled rooms assisted by deliquescent servants as Chopin's Etudes play on the Victrola in the fading twilight of a Rangoon plantation suffused with civility and the plangent decorum of the aristocracy.

Reginald drapes another towel over his arm, places the open bottle onto it, then steps toward the table. He pours a thimble of wine into the clear crystal glass and steps back.

Gary picks up the glass. Again he sniffs with closed eyes. He swirls the wine in his glass and observes it as if it might reveal the 7th Sacred Secret of Aesculapius. Finally, he takes a sip, rolls it in his mouth without swallowing, his tongue barely appearing, then swallows.

He puts down the glass, closes his eyes, sits back in his chair and looks upwards. He returns his eyes to the glass then slowly looks toward the bottle that sits 6 inches away on the table. Again the glass, then the bottle. It's like a ping pong match played in taffy.

A long pause which ends as Gary grabs the Lafite tips it up and chugs it in gurgling Adams Apple-bobbing-swallows which pour onto his pale blue shirt and spangled tie. He slams the bottle back down on the table, wipes his mouth like a longshoreman, looks at our wide eyes which are beginning to grin and says:

Enough of this claptrap! Reginald, bring us five double shots of Tequila and your most sinful chocolate cake.

We hoot and holler as the waiter leaves the room with a barely suppressed smile. It's a performance unlike anything I've ever witnessed. It's another reason I love my brother and bring him back now in all his whimsical wonder.

Gary got married in his late 20s to a woman named Esther who took care of him after he crashed my Triumph motorcycle (too many beers, too sharp a curve) on a mad weekend on Orcas Island in the San Juans.

She had a boy named Tommy who Gary loved and I still have a picture of him watching the first moon landing with the eight-year old Tommy. They were both dressed up as astronauts and it was hard to tell who was more enchanted—Tommy or Gary. In some ways he was like a little kid—he had the same enthusiasm, the same adventurous eyes.

He and Esther had a girl they named Laurie. I have a grainy, jumpy Super 8 film of Gary holding Laurie when she was a baby. He's looking down at her like a proud dad, then he unbuttons his shirt and offers his breast. You had to smile at him.

The marriage broke up after Gary took a trip to Japan to a Suzuki motorcycle convention and got involved with a Japanese woman. Esther found out and they split the sheets as we used to say back then. Gary seemed okay.

Thief Of Hubcaps

At his 20th high school reunion he took his current flame, a black woman named Portia—an exquisite Nubian gal he'd picked up with who was as smart as she was beautiful. The majority of his classmates were against inter-racial relationships and many ignored him for his racial blindness. I admired him for the same reason.

He loved the blues.

He told me one time when we were at a nightspot in Lake City, listening to Sonny Rollins play his blues guitar, that when he died he wanted to be reincarnated as a black Blues singer. He had vinyl records of Blind Lemon Jefferson, Bessie Smith, Bobby Blue Bland, Slim Harpo, John Lee Hooker, Big Bill Bronzy, Mama Thornton and Lightning Hopkins among others.

I think he saw in the blues the way pain and suffering can be transmuted by music into a kind of agonized bargain with living a life. The way you can sing about how life's a goddamn road of suffering but you're still singing, still trying to get through the day even when the day squeezes you so hard it makes you pop.

Something about finding courage in misery. Maybe he knew that's what he needed.

His life started to go south in the early '80s. He moved to Oregon with Portia, couldn't find a job and was reduced to selling magazines on the road. I talked to Portia during this time and she said Gary needed help, was depressed all the time, had trouble getting out of bed, they didn't have much money.

I talk to him during this time, tell him he should come back up where his family lives, get a job. I try to get at what he's feeling, what's wrong but I never feel like he tells me what's going on deep inside him. He tells jokes, deflects concern by laughing at himself.

He tells me at the end of my life I'll have something I can be proud of, I've taught kids. He says he doesn't have a damn thing—no woman, no job, no prospects. The blues have gotten into him.

He comes back to Seattle and we brothers try to help him out. My older brother Jim gives him some money for clothes and to get by on, gets him a job with Don Ribelke at Lynnwood Honda Motorcycles.

He lives in Olympia for awhile with Tim and his wife, Sharon, who try to get him out of his funk but he mainly sits around the house, watches TV and stays in bed.

After a month of this, Tim decides to do something about Gary's lethargy. He thought exercise might be good for Gary so he asks Gary help him work on a fence he's putting up around his house. Fresh air, hard work, something to do are three good things to pursue when you're bummed out.

Everyone knows that but when you're depressed trying to do anything except breathe seems impossible. What's the use? But Gary says he'll help.

After about an hour of working solo, Timmy comes back in the house and Gary's watching basketball on TV. He tells Tim he'll come out after the game's over. Tim goes back to work but Gary doesn't come out.

Finally, Tim goes down to the basement, gets out his chainsaw, goes upstairs into the hallway by the TV room, starts the chainsaw and comes running into the room toward Gary who screams and heads for the back wall.

It was funny. It gets Gary's attention and he comes outside for awhile but his spirit is on the long road to despair. He didn't give up though. I see that as a kind of courage.

He moves back to Seattle, gets another job doing paperwork at a motorcycle shop. He moves in with an older woman I briefly met who seems good for him though I don't think she's good enough. Maybe he's getting better. I talk to him on the phone once or twice a week and he puts up a good front.

It's summer—things always get better in the summer, don't they?

He drove a '60 Olds maroon two-door hardtop— a classy car, low and sleek with rumbling tail pipes, whitewalls and a hot sound system. It was 20 years old but it was in great shape, a car I would have lusted for when I was in my 20s, and I realized then that Gary was living in the past, the best time of his life and he was having trouble finding a future.

He wasn't looking forward, he was looking back, maybe trying to figure out what went wrong, how he'd come to this pass.

When Gary was a sophomore in high school, he, as I, was a quarterback, a passer. He was also a punter for the varsity and executed the fake punt and pass move a couple of times for notable gains. We both quit football after our sophomore seasons probably for the same reasons: girls, parties and a native aversion to the petty cruelties of jockdom.

In cards, when you don't have a winner and a bet is placed, you pass, which is a way of giving up, not taking the bet. With a girl, a pass is an invitation to possibility which sometimes works, sometimes doesn't.

Coming to a pass is the realization that you've arrived at a place you barely knew was a destination but when you got there you knew you'd arrived somewhere that wouldn't let you go elsewhere. You were fixed in position like a broken compass or a stopped watch.

Somewhere in late June of 1985, Gary's fired from his job but he doesn't tell anyone, even the woman he's living with. For a week, he leaves in the morning at eight and comes back at five.

What did he do during that camouflage time? I have no idea but at some point he knew what to do next. Perhaps he had to work up to it, like an animal who knows he has to jump a chasm but circles and circles to get the courage to make the leap.

I have the medical examiner's record from King County dated July 8, 1985, the day he was found. Date of death is listed as July 1st with a question mark. Both days are Mondays but the first Monday is the one that intrigues me. There's something about a Monday which marks a new week that we sometimes resent after a weekend of relative freedom. Then we must go again through our routine and sometimes that's disheartening.

Gary seems to have used up his heart by July 1st.

He drives to the outskirts of Duvall, Washington and finds a dirt road obscured by overhanging branches and trees. He drives 232 feet, almost the length of a football field, on the road into the deep woods. He takes the vacuum cleaner hose he'd taken from his girlfriend's house, attaches it to the exhaust pipe then puts the open end in the driver's side window.

He packs the hose with towels to eliminate the draft. He puts a note on the black leather dashboard.

He restarts the car. Robert Johnson's Mississippi Delta Blues plays on the tape deck. His mind goes heavy, he lies down on the seat as if going to sleep. He breathes in carbon monoxide until he doesn't have breath to breathe. The heater's on, doors locked.

Two guys looking for property in the area find him a week later and notify police.

I like to think that Gary had some small measure of something after he'd parked the car and hooked up the hose. He listened to "Robert Johnson's Mississippi Delta Blues". I know because the Coroner's Office gave me the tape. I hope he turned him up loud. Franz Liszt said that great music should be played loud enough to hurt the ears, to reflect the suffering that created the music.

He lay down on the seat and slept.

I still have the Robert Johnson tape but tape players have been replaced by CDs and none of my current cars have a tape player so I haven't listened to it for awhile. I don't have to play it to know the sound.

Blues derive from suffering and the songs sing their trouble. Gary listened until he was silent, the car ran out of gas and the battery went dead.

The note said, "I can't go on anymore. Hopelessness has eaten me up. People and family have tried to give me love but it's no use. Forgive me for this."

Three years before Gary died I drove to one of our family reunions at Jim's house near Ballard, Wa. I was going with a woman too young for me and she had an MG convertible with wire wheels which I loved to drive. The car stopped running 4 blocks from my brother Jim's house.

I put the hood up and looked inside but all I could tell was that it had an engine and it wasn't running. I've never been much of a mechanic. Internal combustion engines mystify me. I called for help.

Gary and Jim show up with beers in hand. They don't say a word, hand the beers to me and my girl. Gary walks over to the car and begins a seriously Sioux war dance, whooping and chanting as he circles the car. Jim joins in and they circle the car twice.

Hay, yai, yayah,, Hai, yai, yayah....

They stop and consider. They know the value of pause. Gary takes the beers from us, hands one to Jim. They walk over to the car and begin chanting again while they pour beer onto the engine. Gary says, "Okay, you can start it now."

I get in, start the car and it runs fine. It's magic or at least as close to it as I've witnessed.

At the Coroner's office after I pick up the certificate and note, I ask where Gary is right now. I say it that way: "Where is Gary, right now?" The man behind the counter says he's in the storage room and gestures toward a dark steel door at the end of the room. I ask if I can see him.

The guy, for the first time, looks directly into my eyes and says, "I don't think you want to do that."

I think about that. 80 degree days for a week. No fingerprints of the deceased on the death certificate, the space underneath the category filled by the word "Decomposed" in capital letters. Gary alone in the car through 6 days and nights. No one there as he fell apart.

Thief Of Hubcaps

I look at the dark door again and say, "Yeah." and nod my head. I walk back to the ferry and go home.

It's 27 years later now. Jim's coming up to Seattle for chemo at Fred Hutch. I'm writing this story about my brother Gary as a way to make him live again through the magic of words, to bring him back from the dead and it almost works.

We bargain with time which takes and gives in equal measure. It takes away those we love but gives them back again through dream and memory.

It's an odd-even game we learn to play until the paragraphs run out but the story keeps going until the telling ends and we come to the place where space begins and Gary remains in a room of jars I open and taste again for the sweetness and tart.

Rendezvous in Ritzville with Camus

In his first week teaching English at Wenatchee High School in 1965, in a three story brick building built in the Depression, he had his first taste of having to wield authority, which he'd never really liked directed against him, but now he was on the other side.

He was a guy who'd marched the Seattle Freeway to protest the Vietnam War, who listened to Angela Davis and chanted "Fuck Reagan" along with 10,000 other students in the U-Dub stadium, a guy who'd flunked mandatory ROTC classes by refusing to attend and endangered his graduation until the State Supreme Court ruled that a state college couldn't require Reserve Officers Training Corps.

Albert Camus became one of his heroes after he'd read "What is a Rebel" where Camus writes, "A rebel is someone who says both yes and no."

He'd cut his long hippy hair and doffed his tie-dyed shirts. wore sport coats and ties, carried a briefcase, had gotten married the year before, and signed a contract that paid him $4800, a year to teach high school kids.

He was part of the establishment. That year he'd even joined the Elks Club in Wenatchee mainly because they had the best, cheapest food in town and inexpensive well drinks.

He was an adult now. At least he was good at pretending he was in order to escape the Vietnam draft because public school teachers were thought to be "vital to the country's interests." But he also loved teaching and had begun to see that he was pretty good at it.

The end of that first week after the final bell he headed down to the office to check his mail. Reaching the stairs above the second floor landing he saw a crowd of people and heard voices yelling. Two guys who'd removed their shirts were slugging it out, punching each other in the face and body. He pushed his way through the crowd saying, "Stop! Stop!"

He stepped between them.

Both guys were taller than him and outweighed him by at least 30 pounds—this was Wenatchee farm country with a feared football team coached by Bo Boffo whose name fit him perfectly and these guys looked like interior linemen—but that didn't stop him from doing what he was supposed to do.

Surprisingly, when he stepped between them, they both stepped back. This heartened him. He took the next step, "All right. Come with me to the office." Everyone was silent. Then one of the fighters put his hands on his hips and said, "Who's gonna make me?"

He looked around at the faces of the kids. He knew none of them. He was the only adult in sight. He had a vision of being assaulted in his first week on the job, perhaps having to be taken to the hospital. He remembered Shakespeare's line from *Henry IV* that, "Discretion is the better part of valor."

He looked both boys hard in the face as if memorizing them and said, "Okay but you'll be hearing about this." and gathering what dignity he could, he left them to their own devices.

He didn't report the incident to the office, perhaps thinking his actions wouldn't be taken in the best light and even more than that, he didn't want to begin teaching in a school with his reputation among students tarnished by violating an honor code he was familiar with and lived by in the recent past but part of him knew he'd violated an ethical imperative.

At home on the back deck of his rental he had a beer and thought about what happened and didn't feel good about it. He was responsible after all. But what else could he have done? He called Lyle Schwarz, a fellow English teacher and English Department chairman about his age and told him what had happened.

Lyle told him he'd done what he could and in his place he'd have done the same thing. That was nice to hear but he couldn't stop an inner voice that told him that it wasn't brave, that he should have done something more but he didn't.

It was a sin of omission. He vowed to be better.

That year he discovered he loved teaching. What better way to make money than talking about literature, writing and ideas? He got along well with his students, one of whom, Mike Janni, wrote a letter to the principal extolling his inspirational teaching which the principal included in his year-end evaluation. He was a teacher but everyday he was being taught.

He finished the year, having quit Elks Club because he found out they didn't accept Blacks, Jews or Asians. He did have some principles that were clear to him.

His wife and he headed back to Seattle for the summer where they lived rent free in her parents' basement in their house near Woodland Park Zoo. McGrath Homes hired him for the summer working construction where he made as much money pounding nails for two months as he made teaching for six months.

He kept in touch with Lyle Schwarz and Rod Molzahn, two fellow English teachers and friends, who'd become fixtures at the Washington State Drama Summer Theater Program in Pullman. They invited him to come to their final production of Edward Albee's *Who's Afraid of Virginia Woolf?* in the middle of August. He checked it with his wife and she approved.

He had a '58 Chevy four door with elongated fins that was a clunky adult car. His custom '50 Olds coupe with the louvered hood and '59 Plymouth Fury hardtop that screamed rubber and had maroon and white roll and pleat leather upholstery were distant memories.

In preparation for the trip he went to Ballard Junk Yard to buy a used carburetor because the old one choked out when you accelerated past 20 mph.

Junk yards, especially those narrow, long ones secured by ribbed metal walls with the ground turned black by oil and grease are depressing. He walked to the office and no one was there. He saw a guy under the hood of a '50 Nash Sedan, one of the truly ugly cars from that era. He said hello and the guy unspooled himself and turned to face him with a wrench in his hand.

He was a tall guy, about 6 foot 4, in stained gray coveralls with "Galt" on the front stitched in red. He knew him immediately. This was Galt Remsley, a legend when he was in his teens for his fighting abilities, his car, his popularity with girls and his general all- around hoodlumism.

He had a history with him.

When he was 15, he'd gone with Craig Munson to a Parker's Pavilion Teen Dance Night in North Seattle. They had visions of picking up girls, maybe some fast Ballard babes. Remsley was easy to spot. He held court in a corner of the dance floor, surrounded by comely wenches and three guys in leather jackets with skull and crossbones on their backs.

Galt had oilslick black hair that curled at his upturned collar and a Duck's Ass at the back of his head that looked as if it had been cut by a knife. He never saw him smile except when some guy came up to him, said something in his ear as if he was a Godfather and he and his goons left for the red-lit exit door.

He later learned the drill. Tough guys from Arlington, Anacortes or Bellingham would travel to Seattle because they'd heard that Galt was the baddest ass in Seattle and they wanted to have a go at him. They'd usually get a crony to challenge Remsley then they'd go out to the back of the parking lot and Galt would beat the crap out of them with his fists and his knees.

He was known for kneeing guys in the crotch as a final coup de grace. Once it had taken three burly cops to subdue him and put him in the patrol car.

That night he'd taken on a mission that was strangely medieval, maybe even worthy of Greek myth.

Ron Salter, the baddest guy in Edmonds, who'd been working out since he was 12 years old and was a three-year letterman at left tackle on the football team and state champ in shotput, had commanded him to arrange a fight on the Edmonds Football field the following Sunday with Remsley. He'd once helped Salter write an essay for an English class he had to pass to graduate and he evidently thought his ability to strew words made him worthy of performing the duties of diplomatic courier and proxy.

Salter's instructions were simple: arrange a fight on the Edmonds Football field at 10 in the morning on Sunday a week plus a day from this Saturday night with Galt Remsley and him.

He wasn't complimented but what could he do? When the baddest guy in school asks you to do something, refusing to do so was to invite assisted suicide.

That Saturday night at Parker's Ballroom, he approached Galt, gave his message with precise diction, making sure he said two or three times that it wasn't he that wanted to fight him it was Ron Salter, "I don't want to fight you, it's this guy named Ron Salter from Edmonds, not me." The hood leaned toward him.

He could see a dim intelligence in Remsley's eyes as he struggled to make sense of his words. His mouth cracked into a sneer. He said "I'll be there, Punk."

He was glad to escape with his life.

The fight never came off. About 30 teens waited at the football field until an hour after 10 when one of Remsley's minions showed up and told us Galt was in jail for stealing beer from a Pike Street store in Seattle the night before.

That was the end of his career as a fight promoter. He didn't know what had happened to Remsley but here he was getting a used carburetor for him, wrapping it in newspaper and charging him two dollars.

Galt didn't recognize him and he didn't remind him of what had happened 10 years ago. He didn't want to tarnish what he was, to remind him that once he was a Prince of Mayhem in the world, universally feared and admired and now he was reduced to mucking around in a junkyard.

Galt wasn't quite Odysseus in Ithaca reliving the glory days of the Trojan War, more like Diomedes imprisoned in some Land of the Dead where he endlessly did battle with cast off armor plates and greaves in the shape of bent fenders. Regardless, he was a fallen hero brought back down to earth.

But maybe that was his typically romantic, Homer-inspired self conjuring a whole story and literary metaphor around one incident and scant evidence. Maybe Remsley owned the junkyard. He probably made more money than he did teaching. Maybe he was happily married with three kids. Who knew what went on in people's lives?

He'd learned enough in the intervening years to know that appearances were deceptive and just when you thought you had the measure of someone they'd surprise you by having other qualities you'd completely missed.

After work on Friday he left for Eastern Washington about 6 o'clock. He'd called Lyle who said it took about six hours to drive to Pullman and after the show he and his housemates would party until he got there. Lyle told him he had to get to the theater so he gave him his home number and told him to call after 10 o'clock for directions.

This was the first road trip he'd taken by himself.—another marker in his path to adulthood.

Until he reached the top of Snoqualmie Pass he had KJR Rock'n'roll on the radio for company but once he entered Eastern Washington heading in the direction of Spokane all he could get was talk shows about fly fishing with blue-bass lures and bear hunting with a bow and arrow which he finally turned off.

This was in the days before freeways, when you drove through small towns with abrupt speed limit signs and speed traps to feather the municipal nest. He obeyed all the signs— he didn't have the extra money to pay traffic fines.

Driving the dark distances between towns, which increased as you got out toward the Columbia River Gorge, the darkness and lack of company or any sound except wind and the hum of the engine started to get to him.

Cars on the road became more scarce. He could see headlights from far away and it was strangely comforting to know that he wasn't alone—that he hadn't entered another world where people waited in dark places for a victim.

On one blank stretch, he was positive there was some maniac scrunching down in the back of the car, just out of his sight. He seemed to hear him breathing. He pulled over to the side got out of the car and looked behind the seat but there was no one there.

Looking toward the scrub and feathery shapes off the side of the road he heard a noise and got back in the car, perhaps escaping a psychopath's lunge toward the passenger side of the car. As he began to drive again, he looked in the rearview mirror for any maniacs and locked all four doors as his six cylinder gained speed.

He was safe but the ghosts had made their appearance.

He remembered the spring before when he was driving a lonely stretch of highway outside of Wenatchee, Washington on a long straight road in twilight. He saw something in the road ahead, maybe 30 yards, that looked like a human arm. He thought, *No, my mind's making this up* but as he got closer and passed the object he could see in a flash that it was a human arm with a gold ring on its finger and a red bolus at the stump.

He drove about two miles breathing hard then stopped at a phone booth to call the cops. He never heard what happened but it made him realize that strange things can happen in Eastern Washington on long roads.

He also knew—by now it was after 10—that he needed to call Lyle and Rod's house to get directions and let them know he'd arrived. However, every phone booth he passed— solitary booths like outposts of civilization with a single oval light fixture, usually on one side or another of a podunk town—had a cloud of moths so thick around the light that they blocked out not the night but the light. He thought of Conrad's *Heart of Darkness.*

He had a vision of using the phone then being attacked by vampire moths whose bodies contained dust and the moths would suck his blood and he would be left as a dead husk with dry powder oozing out his mouth as he tried to crawl back to his car.

He'd seen Hitchcock's *The Birds* that summer and even more than *Psycho,* that movie scared him because it made him see how something seemingly innocent could suddenly turn into a killing cloud of death.

He shrugged it off, even laughed at his fears but he still didn't stop the car until he was about 80 miles from Pullman and it was getting on past 11.

Moths couldn't turn into vampires, could they?

Ritzville at that time was what we called a one-horse town, better described as a one-street town. He drove past the obligatory gas station, general store, insurance office, post office, barber shop, church—all of them unlighted. No phone booth until he spotted one at the city limits in the back of an A&W Drive-In which was also closed and dark.

He drove to the booth, braved the blood-sucking moths, got Lyle on the phone and wrote down directions to where they lived.

Stepping out of the phone booth he saw a car with its lights on in the narrow driveway, engine running, 10 feet in back of his car blocking his way out. He froze.

Flight or Fight kicked in along with premonitory Fright. He heard a radio, the engine puffing low, and saw shadows behind the high beams of the headlights and as his eyes adjusted, he could see that the car contained four heads and shoulders. He told himself to calm down.

He heard a voice say "Hey, sonuvabitch, what color's your car?"

A strange question. He detected bravado, beer and a bear-like danger in the voice but it didn't get to him. He was smart, he'd handled young people worse than this teaching high school. He'd learned a few things.

He said, "cobalt blue", not knowing if that was actually the color but thinking he was clever and heard his voice which sounded cool, calm and detached.

His reply seemed to trigger the passenger door to open. Out of it came a tall kid, maybe 20, in a T-shirt and jeans. His shoulders seemed as wide as the door. He could see when the interior light came on there were three others in the car of like age and girth.

The moths had turned into thugs. This was a showdown, a movie Western with gunslingers facing off against each other. The kid's eyes were dark.

He glanced behind him at the wire fence, thought of making a run for it, leaping over the fence but all he could see was a stretch of flat prairie with tumbleweeds and sagebrush that went on for miles. He wasn't a long-distance runner. Besides he'd left his keys in the car.

He thought about going back to the phone booth, yanking the phone off its attachment and using it as a bolo but he knew the receivers are securely attached and didn't like the vision of him yanking impotently at the cord.

David and Goliath appeared. He looked for rocks but all there was on the ground was pea gravel.

When he was a teenager, he used to carry a tire iron underneath the driver's seat in case something happened like this but his tire iron was in his trunk and he didn't think they'd wait while he got his keys and got a weapon. He was out of options. The only thing he could do was to face them down. He knew that attitude was 80% of a fight.

All of these thoughts happened in two eye blinks or less.

He decided to tough it out. He straightened up, took a breath and began walking toward the figure behind the headlights. He did his best John Wayne intimidating walk, his lizard- badguy stare. He was a street man who welcomed a fight like a knife fighter welcomes the flick of a stiletto. Inside he was queasy. This was four against one.

He hadn't fought with a guy or guys since he was 14 and that experience had left him unsure as to his abilities. But he did have experience acting and pretending. He could do this.

When he got past the headlights and was two feet from the kid, he paused and put his hand on the fender of their car, not only to appear casual but to have a place to stop his shaking hand. He didn't realize how much his hand was sweating and as he reached the fender his hand slipped and he fell to the ground on his knees.

His cool evaporated. He'd committed a gang gaffe. He'd gone from tough guy to fool in a second and he felt his knees hard against the gravel. What to do now?

He imagined what he looked like. He saw himself from above as if detached from the scene and it struck him how ridiculous he was. He began laughing, first in short bursts, then in a flurry he couldn't stop. It was crazy, he was crazy. He was enjoying his plight.

Then he heard the kid opposite him begin to laugh, joined by the others and they all whooped and when one would stop, another would pick it up. He didn't know how long this communal laugh lasted but it went on until everyone was gasping for air. Somehow he was saved.

They offered him a Heidelberg beer in a stubby brown bottle which he took and they replayed the scene again with more laughs and chuckles. Everyone knew what was going on and it was funny to hear how each of them had the same ideas, the same sense of what was happening, how they all pretended to be something they weren't.

He asked them what they were going to do to him. The short body-builder guy said that everything closes up at 10 in this town, they were working the summer in the wheat fields, it was Friday night, nothing to do so they thought they'd have some fun with a stranger. The kid he'd faced said almost shyly, "I was just gonna beat you up a little".

He said, "I'm glad you didn't", finished his beer, got back in his car and left the A&W lot. He went one direction, they another.

Back on the road to Pullman, Camus came into his head. "What is a rebel? A rebel is someone who says yes and no." He'd said yes to laughter, no to pretense. He'd also said yes to pretense and deception and no to truth and irony.

It was complicated and he knew he was mixing up philosophy with human behavior and its absurdities but what else is philosophy good for if not to connect the two?

He kept driving through the dark and realized that what had just happened was not so much Homer's *Iliad* but more Aristophanes' comedy, *The Birds*—a play written 2400 years before Hitchcock's movie of the same name.

He'd seen a production at The Cirque Theater on the UW campus that featured the birds in human costume and the humans in bird costumes.

That was an interesting switch which made the play even funnier than it was though some of the humor in the play was so archaic you'd have to be a 5th century Greek to get it— though he was enough of a theater and history geek to laugh out loud at times.

Waves on Rolling Bay

In 1969, the first year I taught at the Island high school, my first wife, Becky, and I rented a house on Rolling Bay—one of 10 in a row of houses called Rolling Bay Walk, so named because you couldn't turn a car around in the 10 foot wide walkway that led past the houses.

Everyone parked in a gravel lot where the road ended and except for moving out, moving in and various deliveries, cars weren't allowed on the concrete sidewalk. Above the houses loomed a 60-foot cliff, parts of which would crush the house and family of a man I taught with 28 years later in a January mudslide.

Our daughter, Anna, was two. It was Becky's theory that the nuns at Deaconess Hospital in Wenatchee had given her a memory block so she wouldn't remember the pain and travail of labor—part of a conspiracy by the Catholic Church to promote childbirth. Anna had gotten through her first year of colic and once she discovered language, was bouncy, curious and happily meeting the world.

Across the walk in front of our house, four concrete steps went down to the beach from the bulkhead and when the tide was out I would often walk with Anna on the beach, turn up rocks to see the crabs, make her a peanut butter and honey sandwich—her favorite at the time—and we would sit on driftwood logs and watch the waves and the seabirds floating and flying in the sky, some diving toward the water, others in flotillas on the incoming waves.

I've always loved water moved by the moon, found in the rhythm of water on rocks a solace for the troubles of the world.

Some such feeling must have inspired Matthew Arnold to write "Dover Beach", a poem which contrasts the rattlings of war from the darkling plain with the refuge of love for another which is even more ceaseless and eternal and begins with the image of a moon over water: *"The Sea is calm tonight.*

The tide is full, the moon lies fair upon the straits."

That year I taught Debate, English and by the 2nd semester had initiated classes in Theater and Creative Writing. Perhaps this was hubris for a young teacher but I had two years of experience and the lack of those two classes in a progressive high school I saw as needful to remedy.

My new classes were met with enthusiasm by the students but not by some of what we referred to as "the old guard" who guarded the past and didn't approve of changes by fledglings who presumed to prescribe what was needed in a high school curriculum.

One such naysayer was the formidable counselor, Connie Blitzer, who my young friends on the English faculty and I called "The Red Snapper" for her dyed red hair and crustacean personality. She wrote a letter to the School Board complaining that I wasn't teaching grammar in my writing classes and that the classes I proposed didn't have anything to do with preparing the students for the "real world."

She believed in the '3 "R's"—'Reading, 'Riting and 'Rithmeitic'—in the locution of which the latter two words are misspelled and to which I would add a fourth 'R': Regimentation.

Fortunately by the time of Connie's letter I had allies in the parents of the kids I taught and a far seeing, if conservative, superintendent, Neil Nunnamaker, who approved of what I was doing. The principal who'd hired me, Fred Gunther, asked me why I didn't teach grammar in English classes as the majority of my peers did.

I told him that studies since 1956 had shown that knowing the rules of grammar had as much connection to the ability to write well as being able to name all the parts of an internal combustion engine had to do with driving a car. The time spent in teaching grammar is better spent having students write papers and showing them where and when grammatical problems occur and allowing them to rewrite the paper.

Besides, as studies show, English speakers learn practical grammar by the time they're five years old. They just don't know the technical names for gerunds, suffixes, introductory phrases, past imperfect and the like nor can they diagram a sentence, a skill as necessary to writing as intelligent dialogue is to pornographic films. Fred saw my point and supported me.

In the spring of that year I saw a film at Lynnwood Theater, the only movie house on the Island at that time, which troubled me.

It was a hunting film paired with *True Grit*, a novel I'd read. It might have been called *Safari* and it glorified the killing of exotic African animals by white hunters with high- powered rifles. It showed hippos, rhinos, lions and gazelles in full charge or flight felled by guys in safari jackets shooting from jeeps.

It showed an elephant killed by one shot through the head, a leopard felled in mid-leap from a tree. It showed the hunters afterward standing in front of the animal splayed out on a wood frame or worse, a shot of the hunter with his foot on the animal's head. For me, it was a horror film.

The last thing I killed was a robin I shot with my Red Ryder BB gun in Woodway Park when I was 11. I never shot anything else again. Taking the life of something noble that flew or ran and lived in this world seemed to me a sin.

I told my Debate class about the film the next day. They were as indignant as I was. Two of my best debaters, Ken Silver and Mark Quentin—who unbeknownst to me kept their marijuana stash in their debate boxes until a cop busted them on their way to State Debate finals and ended our hopes for a state championship—wanted to protest the movie on Friday night.

They knew I knew something about protests from my Anti-Vietnam activities.

I told them, in my teacherly and self-protective way—after all, I was a new teacher to the district and already turning some conservative heads—that I would gladly advise them and chaperone their protest but it would be best if they planned it themselves.

On Friday night I arrived at Lynnwood Theater and saw eight students with signs on sticks reading "Killing Animals? Aren't Humans animals?", "Stop the Slaughter of Endangered Species" and more simply, "This Film Sucks". They marched in a circle at the edge of the parking lot which didn't impede the customers going to the box office.

Some of them began chanting: "Kill no more"—a nicely pacifist sentiment and at only three words, easy to remember.

They seemed to enjoy the experience and after the show started we briefly talked and I went home to my family. For all of them, it was their first encounter with direct attempts to influence public opinion and make their views known and I was proud of them. They'd been peaceful, polite and non-confrontational. They were good kids.

The next week in the Letters to the Editor column, an Islander took exception to the protest. He wrote about "...this unruly mob of puppet students led by their Puppet-master teacher," who'd disturbed his Friday night at the movies with his family and how these protesters "didn't believe in the 2nd amendment to the Constitution" and aligned themselves with "hippy radicals" who were destroying America and all it stood for. Fine fuel for a rebuttal.

Thief Of Hubcaps

The day after the letter, my students were righteously indignant and with the zeal of youth, wanted to picket the man's house.

I counseled them to be secure in their convictions, to not invade private property and to take the high road, knowing that they'd expressed their dissent and that sometimes the best answer is silence. Dissent and difference is the bedrock of free speech and democracy.

The next week a letter appeared in the paper written by Dave Brown, a Seattle radio talk show host, praising both me and my students for our actions. He'd witnessed the protest and found it refreshing and "evidence of independent thought" which gave him "hope for the future in these troubled times." Rather than a puppet-master, he praised me for initiating my students into "what we need in this country—discussion, not destruction."

Welcome words and the matter soon disappeared although for weeks after I was accosted by mainly senior students in the restroom, questioning me about my 2nd amendment views and handing me NRA brochures which I politely took and said I would read but didn't. I'd read enough and heard enough in college to know what side of the argument I was on.

A month later I came home to an empty house. Becky had taken Anna to Seattle for the day to visit her folks. It was a Friday, the sun was out, the school week over. I grabbed a beer and went out on the front porch. The waves were gently rolling in a shush.

I saw a family of grebes—two adults and three greeblings (is that a word?)—floating on the waves. Occasionally one of the older grebes would duck its head and disappear under the surface of the water then return and place the catch into a young one's mouth. I watched and watched.

I heard a rifle crack. I saw one bird flip over in the water. Another shot. At first I couldn't understand what was happening, then I knew. The shots were coming from 4 houses away where the park ranger lived with his 16 year-old son.

I ran toward their house and looked up to see the 16-year-old on the 2nd story sundeck. He had a rifle with a scope aimed at the water.

I screamed "Stop, stop! What are you doing?" I must have looked and sounded like I'd just escaped from Bedlam. He answered reasonably, "I'm shooting at the birds."

I replied, "Why?" He didn't have an answer. I looked toward the water.

One grebe had been winged. With the other wing, it was attempting to fly but all it could do was turn in circles. I said, "Okay, kill that one. Put it out of its misery but don't ever shoot again." I turned my back and walked away. I heard three shots but couldn't look. I walked home, went inside.

I called up the State Fish and Game Department and told them about the shooting. They told me that grebes were a protected species, that the fine for shooting them was $1200. and possible jail time. They asked me if I wanted to file a report and prosecute.

I told them I'd get back to them which I never did. I talked to the ranger later that afternoon and he told me he'd deal with his son who'd done stupid things before. I'd seen the kid on the Walk, said hello and he seemed to be a good kid.

Thief Of Hubcaps

I didn't want revenge, I just wanted him to understand what he'd done. He'd killed half of that Grebe family for fun, because it was a nice Friday afternoon and he could do it. He could squeeze a trigger and take a life.

I made spaghetti and salad that night after Becky and Anna got home. I read Anna a story about a French girl who gets lost in the jungle and an alligator befriends her and helps her find her parents. I kissed her good night, don't let the bedbugs bite.

I told Becky what happened, that I was glad Anna wasn't there to witness the killing of the birds. I told Becky I needed to go outside for awhile. I knew I couldn't sleep until I cleared my head.

I sat on a log and looked toward the lights of Seattle. The full moon shined a path of light that stretched halfway across the Sound, ending on our beach. I looked to my right and saw something in the moonlight, turned by the incoming waves. I got up and walked closer. I saw feathers and a humped shape pulsed by the tide.

I walked into the shallow water and picked up the grebe with the shattered wing. I held it with both hands and turned it toward the light so I could see better.

The eyes were lifeless marbles but I looked into them hoping to see something but whatever had been there was gone and wouldn't return. I raised the bird above my head almost as if it was an offering to the moon or some remorseless god. I held it that way until my arms grew tired. I was doing some sort of ceremony and I wasn't sure why but it seemed important.

I felt like a priest from the Paleolithic, that every death, every leaving, affects us all, that what passes must be recognized, even honored by someone or something taking note.

I also felt a bit silly. What was I doing, a grown man with a wife and child, grieving for a bird and concocting a weird ceremony? What was a dead grebe or three killed by a gun in the scheme of things?

I placed the grebe on the log and dug a hole in the sand. I placed the bird in the hole, said some words of apology and covered it back up. I didn't mark the grave. The tide would have washed the marker away.

I looked again at the moon against the dark water, walked back to our house on Rolling Bay Walk and before sleep the final lines of "Dover Beach" came to me:

> *"And we are here as on a darkling plain*
> *Swept with confused alarms of trouble and*
flight
> *Where ignorant armies clash by night."*

Brave New World

Kenny Fukyama took a class I'd conceived in my second year of teaching I called "Literature of the Individual" which I later shortened to "Lit of I" because the counselors said the title wouldn't fit in the registration slot.

What is an individual but an I? The first line of *Hamlet* is, "Who's there?"—a question pursued until the end of the play when Hamlet goes to "the undiscovered country from whose bourn no traveler returns." even though Hamlet has been visited by his dead father in Act One.

The class included Hesse's *Siddhartha,* Rostand's *Cyrano de Bergerac*, Steinbeck's *East of Eden*, Huxley's *Brave New World*, and other works. Students referred to the course content as "Mac's favorite novels" and they were except for *Cyrano* which I included because it's romantic, I love the play and it's an evocation of living a life in brave sorrow with idealism and courage. The play also portrays the rift between appearance and reality and like *Macbeth*, illustrates the truth of, "There's no art to find the mind's construction in the face."

Sometimes there's a well of sorrow impossible to draw.

Kenny was a star in the class. His essays were incisive and intelligent. He understood my forays into metaphor and meaning. Unlike others in the class, he seemed to enjoy the complications and conundrums of becoming an individual, of finding one's self. He listened to me and other students with respect and intensity. He was innately kind.

He was and still is, one of my favorite students, with a gentle nature and a whip-smart mind. He seemed happy in the world and I encouraged him to major in English in college.

What did Kenny look like? He was neat; he had intense, serious eyes that sometimes lifted into a smile which turned inward and closed. He had dark, short hair. He was respectful of authority. He never said much in class but you could tell he was churning and turning ideas in his head.

Sometimes his glance went through you to some place you could not tell. I don't remember ever hearing him laugh out loud or get angry. He seemed to have a tight leash on his emotions but perhaps that's wisdom in retrospect.

The summer after he graduated high school he committed suicide. It seemed as they say "out of the blue" which indicates that it happened without warning, without clouds or signs of cataclysm—the way a cyclone can suddenly appear on a clear day, the way you can be walking in mild weather and be immolated by lightning, how you can be driving on a pleasant evening and be struck by a careening car or even a falling meteor from the sky and everything changes and we look for reasons and can't discover them.

A clear sky doesn't guarantee safety.

We searched our memories for signs of depression or despair to no avail. Kenny was always so even, so content, so warm and caring of others. The suicide gave us pause— when such a successful and seemingly happy kid could die at his own hand, how could we prevent such things in the future? What had caused him to despair?

We never found out and sometimes, as we learn when we grow older, we have to reconcile with that frustration and realize that sometimes there's nothing we could have done, that what goes on inside others is sometimes locked away like a safe with 10,000 tumblers and an unbreakable combination. It's a secret sorrow that never speaks until it's mute and we read the news and scour our thinking with regret at what we might have done to prevent such a loss.

And the sorrow passes on to the living from the dead and diffuses until something comes back to remind us of what happened.

One spring night in 1976 the three-story brick building built in the 30s that faced High School Road burned down. Suddenly the high school lost half its classrooms, the school office, cafeteria, library, and a building that had served a generation or more of students and teachers.

Today you can see the six-foot-long stone pediment that used to cap the top of that building in front of the existing campus in the back of benches that face High School Road. It serves as a reminder of what was and what remains. Not many people realize where this stone has been or what it once represented.

The day after the fire—which was started by three students as a lark fueled by beer on an otherwise boring night when they didn't have anything to do and decided to break into the high school, take some duplicating fluid from the copy room, douse it on costumes taken from my 3rd floor Theater storage area and light them on fire—we English teachers were summoned to the school to go through the books in the 3rd story storage room to see what we could save and what to throw away.

We needed the books for the rest of the year when we would be teaching in portable classrooms— elongated trailers that resembled squat dirigibles.

Today this task wouldn't be permitted. The building would have been sealed off, secured by No Trespassing signs and patrolled by guards but this was a different time.

We walked through the charcoaled timbers and wet mess of lathe and plaster up the staircase to the bookroom, avoiding the 1st floor which still steamed and dripped from the fire hoses of the night before. We set to our work which consisted of fanning the pages of the books to see what was within and tossing the rejects into large garbage cans.

I was thumbing through a copy of *Brave New World* when I noticed something strange.

Above each page on the right hand side was a stick figure composed of a head with no eyes, two arms without hands and two legs without feet.

Thief Of Hubcaps

As I fanned the pages from the back of the novel, the figures grew smaller and smaller until they disappeared at the end which was the beginning of the book. The figures were so calibrated that you couldn't tell the difference between the size on facing pages— you could only see the difference by comparing the figures 10 pages apart or so.

It was a work of art, motion by design, created by someone who was both artistic and obsessive. I looked at the facing page.

The reverse was the pattern. If you thumbed backwards, the figures started small, then grew larger at the end. It was a mirror, with two events replicating each other in the middle then pursuing different ends and depending on which side of the book you started from, you met with disappearance to appearance or appearance to disappearance.

Fascinating.

The figures were drawn in pencil, exact replicas except in size, almost as if they'd been stamped out in a mold, memorized by a machine that reduced the image by 2% with each replication which of course wasn't possible in those days when home computers didn't exist.

This was welcome relief from time spent in the tedium of glancing at pages of text to determine whether the book should be tossed or saved. This was worthy of saving.

I looked at the student names in the glued-in label in the front of the book on the inside cover and at the end of the list, the last person who'd checked out *Brave New World* was Kenny's name. He'd written

Kenneth Alan Fukyama in a cursive that was delicate and clear.

It was out of the blue. I leaned back in my chair and every noise vanished as if I was in a dun cloud of cotton bats.

I thought of how much time and pain Kenny had taken in his solitary toil. I thought about what message he was sending eightyears before. I wondered whether the suicide of John Savage in Huxley's novel had anything to do with Kenny's suicide. I wished I'd seen his message when he turned in his book.

What was he trying to say?

No matter how you looked at the pictures they went from more to less, less to more, beginning to end, end to beginning. It was a puzzle that depended on perspective. And what was the end and what the beginning?

The drawings worked the way old cartoons worked kinetically in the era of silent films—a series that slightly changes from frame to frame and allows the viewer to perceive motion, action and story without human beings being filmed.

The title of Huxley's novel comes from Miranda's speech in Shakespeare's *The Tempest.* She's been raised on an island by her father and other than her father and his servants—Ariel the spirit and the enslaved Savage—she hasn't seen humanity.

When Miranda finally sees the sailors of the world she says: "O wonder! How many goodly creatures are there here! How beauteous mankind is! O brave new world that has such creatures in it!" and when we realize that the sailors are drunk and Miranda's lines are at the least ironic and at the best naive, we understand the irony of Shakespeare's play and the irony in Huxley's novel.

John Savage lives in a society of shallow escapism and superficial values. It's a society he can't abide and he ultimately hangs himself in despair.

I wish I had known more.

I say without irony that Kenny was brave and wondrous and beauteous and then he was silent.

I write this in shadow as an attempt to give him a voice and save his message to those who might understand and for a moment, remember a goodly creature who once lived on an island.

Sniper

You know this is what happened.

In 1975, the Biology teacher calling roll pronounces Michael Wellesley's first name as Michelle. It was Michael's first day at a new school. Some dirtbags in the class immediately laugh when Michael answers in his high voice: "My name isn't Michelle, its Michael, Michael."

Exactly the wrong thing to do and the boys have a target.

At 16, Michael's a kid who hasn't matured physically or emotionally. He hasn't learned the tough law about showing your hurt: if you let on you're upset and god forbid, start to cry, the wolves of school will tear you apart and they'll keep tearing as long as you twitch. A boy must suppress his vulnerability, his sensitivity, his emotions.

That same semester you have Michael as a student in Speech class. The first assignment is to tell a story. He tells the class that he was adopted, that he was Jewish, that his parents had died in the Holocaust. His voice breaks as he describes how they'd gone to the gas chambers.

He tells us how a German soldier had taken him out of the line of prisoners at the age of two and given him to a peasant couple who lived outside the horror of Auschwitz. He ends the speech by saying, "I can't go on" and hangs his head.

After he sits down, you ask him if what he said was true. He says it was. You try to give him an out, to find a "teachable moment" and he turned it down.

This is the moment in class when a teacher is flummoxed. The speech was obviously fictional, gleaned from reading and imagination and perhaps a misguided attempt to impress his peers. If he was 2 in 1944, he'd be 35 years old in 1975.

Though you grant much leeway in the realms of fancy and imaginative storytelling, the assignment was to tell a true story about something that had happened to you in the past and Michael's story is obviously untrue. The class is quiet when he finishes, not out of respect for his suffering but out of disbelief at his blatant lie.

You speak to him after class and cautiously make him aware of the problem with his speech. One gives allowances for the craziness of teenagers but also, you're never quite sure if you're dealing with mental illness, drug-induced fantasy or schizophrenia. You've run into trouble with that distinction over the past years.

He tells you most of the speech was true. He was Jewish. He was adopted. When you ask him about the Auschwitz aspect, he says it could have happened and since most of the speech was true, couldn't some of it be false?

That's a good question, one that straddles the line between biography and fiction.

Memory's a magician you can't trust to be true and even now you question your memory of what Michael said. How could he not have known his speech would be doubted? Was he purposefully inviting ridicule for some mystifying reason?

Perhaps he learned from that experience since the rest of the quarter goes more smoothly for him. He throttles back on his speeches, one can detect a quiet intelligence though he always sits alone in class and when you see him in the halls he's never with anyone else.

That spring you hold auditions for *Winnie the Pooh and the Blustery Day*, a play that will travel to the elementary schools in the area. You think it might be good for Michael so you encourage him to audition, to be part of the theater program because high school theater is a place where everyone finds a place.

You get the tech geeks, the smart kids looking to bolster their resume for college, kids who love to play make-believe, kids who want to be actors and most, if not all, learn to work together for a common goal.

There's jealousy of course and mean-spiritedness but there's also a wonderful kind of community and a shared sense when the play is over that they've accomplished something important and even today, you get notes from ex-students talking about how theater was the best part of their high school life.

Thief Of Hubcaps

You cast Michael as one of four rabbits who operate as a kind of Greek chorus to the loveable Winnie the Pooh. During the 10-week rehearsal period you sometimes give Michael and Fritz Wolf, a young proto-hippy who's wise beyond his years and looks like John Lennon complete with peeper glasses, a ride home from rehearsal when they need one.

On one such ride, you stop at the Chevron Gas Station just down the road from the high school.

You're all outside your beat up station wagon. Fritz pumps gas, Michael washes the windows—which is a nice thing for him to do—when the activity bus rumbles by. You hear voices yelling: "Hey, Michelle," "Hey Fag," and other insults. Michael doesn't respond—he's learned that much in the past year.

Fritz, who plays the lead role of Winnie the Pooh, looks after the bus and says,"They yell like that because they're afraid."

He speaks it as if he's just realized it, almost as if he isn't talking to you. You say, "You got that right, Fritz."

At the first performance at the elementary school on the Island, Michael goes missing 5 minutes before curtain. You ask Bobbi Jo Madison, the stage manager, what happened. She says someone said something to Michael that he took the wrong way and he took off in the direction of the woods to the north.

You ask her what was said. She says that it was something about Michael's makeup, that his lips were too red.

You know why he's left. After a year or more of being savaged about his manhood, being called 'Pansy' and 'Queer,' he's touchy, paranoid. He reads insult in what's meant to be helpful advice.

The boy who tried to help, standing next to the stage manager, says he didn't mean to be mean. You believe him. He's a good kid. You tell Bobbi Jo to hold the curtain until you get back.

In the woods, you have a flash of disbelief. Here you are looking for a 5 foot9 inch rabbit in the woods. You spot the white faux fur of his costume before you see Michael. He sits with his back against a large maple tree. He ignores you. You kneel down.

There's a moment of despair. What can you say? How can you fix the world? You say the usual clichés about struggle and survival, fighting against the idiots, about finding something to keep going for and he finally gets up and you walk with a fully costumed rabbit back to the grade-school auditorium and a nice performance of *Winnie The Pooh and the Blustery Day*.

By the time Michael's a senior he's developed a turtle shell and his fellow classmates have put aside, more or less, taunting him—at least that's your take.

In the spring of that year he stops by your class after school and tells you he's enlisting in the army after graduation. You listen, nod, affirm his decision to what degree you can, feeling all the while that this is exactly the wrong thing to do. You fear the military will tear him apart with its manly code but you hold your tongue. When a kid wants to do something you support him. You lose track of him for three years.

On a summer's day doing your usual summer carpentry work as CEO of The Sensitive Carpenters—a fringe construction company with one employee, you— you drive to the lumber yard to pick up material.

Thief Of Hubcaps

Walking toward the truck is a young man you recognize as Michael.

He's filled out. In place of slunched shoulders he walks squared and confident. He holds his head high and muscles have replaced baby fat. He wears jeans, a flannel shirt and carries a leather tool holder on his broad belt. He leans into your open window.

Mac, great to see you.

Michael, wow. You're out of the army.

Call me Mike. Yeah....I'm home.

He helps you load plywood and 2x6s, smiles and waves when you leave. You've been wrong about what the army would do to him as you've been wrong before about what might happen to other vulnerable kids.

You're glad you were wrong and though you have trouble at first remembering to call him Mike, over the course of the summer you get used to it.

You stop by one afternoon at the lumber yard and Mike tells you he's getting married and asks if you'll be an usher. He says his older brother, whom you've never met, is going to be the best man. Of course you say yes but you also wonder why he's asked you to be part of the wedding party.

Young people choose their close friends, not a former teacher decades older than they are but this is a request you can't turn down. You ask him how many other ushers there'll be and he says, "You're it." He tells you there'll be about 50 guests at the wedding in North Seattle.

You arrive in your best suit, wearing a pale blue shirt with a Modigliani tie. When the ceremony begins there's maybe 10 people in the pews. Mike's bride, whose name you can't remember, doesn't seem nervous or giggly or hyper as most brides do in your experience. You begin to have a feeling that things aren't quite right.

You go to the reception at the bride's house and it's a sad affair—not much jubilation, toasting or wedding cake fru-fra, let alone the click and flash of cameras. You attempt conversations, have some snacks, chips and dip, a couple of glasses of Gallo wine, wish the couple well and drive home.

On the ferry, you go to the top deck and look over the rail into the water which whitens and courses away into the twilight. Something buzzes in your head but you've done your duty, what you could, for a kid you've always liked.

Two years later you hear the news about a sniper on the Island, who'd stationed himself on Sunrise Hill adjacent to the highway and shot at passing cars on the road with a 30.06 rifle. One of his bullets had gone through a car's windows between the front and back seats. Another had winged a trunk.

The police caught him after he'd fired about 10 shots and took him to the Kitsap County Jail in Port Orchard.

It was Michael.

Some things are fitting and some don't fit, for all we try to force them into comprehension. What didn't fit was that Michael always seemed a gentle person. He was mainly kind to unkindness. Why would he want to shoot and perhaps kill people he couldn't see? What had happened in the two years you hadn't seen him?

Thief Of Hubcaps

You speculate about a failed marriage, a loss of a job, the kind of snap that occurs when people veer into violence but you don't know and still don't know.

What does fit as you hear about the trial and sentencing for attempted homicide is that nothing comes from nothing and a part of you wishes you could find each boy who had abused Michael and speak to them, even drag them into a court of law where they would know that what they said to Michael was as surely a trigger as the one that Michael squeezed to shoot at faceless people who traveled on a road he could only see through his sniper's scope.

He'd come to a place where he couldn't go on. We shoot when we've been shot.

Looking back after 30 years, you can't clearly remember Michael's face, perhaps because you've seen so many others like it in the course of teaching these many years.

What you do remember is a boy who had a chance but for lack of kindness, lost it—another kind of manslaughter.

The Chicken Lady, Heidi, Fishy, Amadeus & Molly

Between marriages, after your 2nd attempt has flared out into a whimper, you rent a house on Seaborn Road on Port Blakely Bay in 1982. For two years and beyond, with your two youngest daughters, you're a solo dad—without a woman for the first time in 20 years.

It's a Camelot without Guinevere and the attendant travail. It's a time you and your daughters remember with affection.

Down the road in the woods there's a waterfall of sorts that courses down a steep bank. The kids call it Paradise Falls and in the summer they ride the three-foot falls on plastic garbage bags with Cat Downs, the neighbor girl who lives across the street.

Across the street you and the kids can walk down the neighbor's driveway to their dock and jump into the waters of Puget Sound in the summer or fish for perch in all seasons. Molly's eight, Heidi 10.

One summer Saturday you head off to Seattle to visit Seattle Center, go on rides and to satisfy mainly Molly, play a game for a quarter in one of the sideshow booths that involves pulling levers to manipulate a lead ball through a maze to try to end up at the bottom of the glass device.

If you earn enough points you're rewarded with garish prizes of puffy animals, fluorescent sunglasses or Chinese pillows with Seattle Center stitched in bright red thread on its blue silk surface.

Molly's maniacal at this game. She always pleads for just one more chance and you usually cave in. What's a day at Seattle Center for if not for indulgence and spending money you don't really have on your kids?

You pull onto the ferry in your beat-up mustard yellow '56 Ford pickup with a screwdriver that serves as a transmission stick. The girls want to go on the upper deck to take in the sun and wind so the three of you creak out of the truck doors and walk through the parked cars to the stairs that lead above.

You spot an aging DeSoto two-door which has been converted to a truck by removing the trunk lid and half the top. It's gloriously rusty and ramshackle.

You hear a voice like a chicken coming from a driver crouched behind the wheel whose head barely pokes above the steering wheel. She stares straight ahead. You hold both girls' hands and feel their grips tighten as you approach the car.

The woman's bent over the steering wheel with two claw-like hands gripping the sides. She wears a motley shawl of multicolor—green, red, pink. Her face puckers into a mouth that's toothless and sucked in and she opens it off and on making a great imitation of a brooding chicken,

Paaawwwk.   Paaawwwk.   Paaawwwk.

The girls hands tighten even more but they don't say anything. They don't stare at the strange woman whose face looks like a dried potato, who wears on her head a checkered babushka with what looks like chicken fluff on top of it in the weird car. You've told them that it isn't polite to stare at people who we might think are strange or to make a stranger feel uncomfortable by saying something that might offend them.

There are many strange things in the world and your kids are good kids—polite and sensitive as their father, or at least learning to be so and succeeding as often as young kids do with occasional and understandable lapses. You're proud of them and still are to this day as you are of all your children and grandchildren.

You reach the top deck and sit down on a metal bench. The girls look at you with wide eyes and whisper—because this is a secret, something to speak of in hushed tones,

Dad, who was that?

Following your lead, the girls look around to see if the Chicken Lady has flown and squawked up to the upper deck. You lower your voice to mirror theirs:

That was the Chicken Lady.

Who's the Chicken Lady?

The Chicken Lady helps out parents when their children don't mind. When kids misbehave, their mom

or dad can call her and she'll immediately come over and make them mind.

Molly and Heidi accept this definition by nodding their blonde-haired heads. They're respectful, serious in their silence as if they've just found out another secret of the adult world. You smile and say:

First thing we'll do when we get to Seattle Center is have a Slush Puppie.

And that's what you do. You ride favorite rides—the Roller Coaster, the Spinning Teacups—eat hot dogs by the spouting fountain on the grass and of course, play the Ching-a-Ching Drop-ball game and Molly wins a panda bear. Heidi throws softballs into a basket and winds a purple-beaded necklace which she wears to bed that night after you play Stravinski's *Firebird* and tell them again the story of Fire Bird and Water Bird—our improvised and dramatic tale set to Stravinski of two young girls walking in the woods who see a magical bird of light so beautiful it outshines the sun until one misty morning when it meets Water Bird, the villain of the piece.

The story has a happy ending. That's essential for going to sleep and you kiss both of them good night as you always do.

This is also the summer when Sasha, a friend of Molly's, tells her that if you turn off all the lights, look into a mirror and say "Bloody Mary, Bloody Mary, Bloody Mary," Bloody Mary will appear with her back to you then slowly turn around so you see not only her bloody baby but blood on Bloody Mary's face.

You tell Molly it's not a true story—there's no such monster—but you see in her eyes she's not convinced. You say, let's test it out.

You go into the bathroom and turn off the lights. You look into the mirror and chant the invocation. You wait and nothing happens. You tell Molly to repeat the ritual. She stands on the bathroom stool so she can see herself in the mirror, hesitates then whispers: "Bloody Mary, Bloody Mary, Bloody Mary."

She looks around. You open up the shower curtain. You whisper "Bloody Mary, are you there?" The only sound is the furnace starting up, sending warm air into the dark bathroom.

You say, "So much for Bloody Mary," and go into the kitchen to make Pork Butt, potatoes and peas for dinner.

Pork butt is a family favorite, a chunk of meat like a roast which you'd chosen one day shopping at the local grocery store because you admired the name and had never seen it before. The first night you cooked it with garlic and a glaze of parmesan, counted one, two, three and everyone took a tentative bite. It was sumptuous—moist and tasty.

You leaned back in your chair and said: "Girls, that's mighty good butt." and it became a running joke. The girls would ask, "Dad, can we have Butt tonight?" or "How about a Butt sandwich for lunch?"

Molly, at eight, wants to be a veterinarian. At various times you had cats with names like Nymphy—a young mother who screeched when she received the barbed penis of her cat consort—Park and Bench, (deliciously named by a kid in preschool), Mrs. Dalloway (after the Virginia Woolf novel), Horace and Hoover—Hoover named after a vacuum cleaner which your Poetry prof, Nelson Bentley, suggested, who had cats named Electrolux, Dustbuster, Eureka and Kirby.

Thief Of Hubcaps

Molly harassed you to buy her a goldfish in a plastic sack when you went to the Kitsap County Fair that summer though you told her these goldfish were famously short-lived. You relented by the end of the day and she named it "Fishy"—not quite up to the level of the previous names but it had a nice cachet.

You bought a fishbowl, feed and some figurines of castles and mermaids to entertain Fishy but that first night Molly played with the fish by inserting her finger into the bowl. You told her fish didn't like to be petted but when you went off to do laundry in the basement, you returned and found her with her finger in the bowl.

In the morning Fishy was fins up and you buried her at the foot of the outside stairs in a patch of dirt that held the Pet Graveyard along with some anemic daffodils.

Each of you said nice things about the fish named Fishy, planted a stick cross to mark the grave and holding hands, sang "Battle Hymn of the Republic" together which you always did at the conclusion of services for pets. You're not sure how or why you chose that song but it seemed appropriately uplifting for the internment.

Molly also had a guinea pig she'd named Amadeus after you'd taken the girls to see the movie of that name and to hear the soaring music of Mozart. Though you admired his namesake you weren't fond of Amadeus.

You've had a fear of rats since you and Dave Richards chased one when you were 16 at his Dad's waterproofing warehouse and trapped in a corner, this foot-long rat turned, seemed to grow another eight inches, contorted his face, hissed and you both ran out the door. Amadeus wasn't a rat but he belonged to the same family.

You tell her she can keep him if she takes complete care of him and she does, feeding and grooming this furry creature of brown and white who looks like a pygmy cow without horns dressed in Naugahyde.

You say hello to Amadeus in the morning as you prepare "Dad's waffles" for the kids—actually Eggo store-bought but the girls enjoy the myth of you making them—but other than moving the cage to get him some sunlight, you avoid intimacy.

Flea season for the cats arrives in August. You buy flea collars but when the girls wake up with red bites on their legs and arms you know it's time for drastic action. The next weekend the girls are scheduled to visit their grandparents, Grampa Dick and Gramma Marge in Longbranch, about an hour's ride from your house.

You take them there on a Friday night and on the way home stop at a store in Silverdale for munitions. After perusing the instructions which state that one bomb will kill every flea and mite in a 600 square-foot enclosed space, you decide to get two bombs—the upstairs is close to 700 square-feet and has a corner room. You want complete annihilation and you figure that more is more.

Saturday morning you close all the windows, take Amadeus down to the basement and hang him and his cage on a nail underneath the open floor joists. You place a sheet over the cage in case any vapors from above seep through the floorboards.

You return upstairs, set off the bombs and still holding your breath, shut the door tight. You work all day framing a hip roof for John Cross, an ex-student.

When you return nine hours later, you open the front and side doors, the windows and go to the basement to retrieve Amadeus.

He's mort, as the French say, looking very peaceful, lying on his back as if he's sunbathing. But he's absolutely dead and your heart falls, not so much for Amadeus as for Molly. You immediately call her— bad news delayed is bad news mislaid.

Honey...Amadeus died today...

Before you can add details, she starts wailing, sobbing. You listen to her, bite your lip. She suddenly stops crying as if shutting off a faucet.

Can we have a funeral?

You say of course, you'll get everything ready for when they get back home. You like the way Molly sees the funeral as an antidote to grief, a way to get something good out of something bad.

You've read enough Poe to know about bodies decomposing but because you'd taken Geology instead of Biology as an undergraduate, you thought that decomposition of organic material was caused by air— after all, when you wrap food in plastic, it prevents mold and breakdown.

Thus, you carefully wrap Amadeus in a Hefty Bag out of which you squeeze all the air, and place him in his basement cage in this hot August heat to await the funeral.

The girls are supposed to return Monday but call to ask if they can stay another day for one of Gramma Marge's rummage sales.

The girls arrive on Tuesday afternoon and Heidi skedaddles over to Cat's house to show her the loot from the rummage sale which includes several scarves and frilly dresses. You ask her if she wants to attend the funeral and she tells you to go ahead without her. You respect that.

Heidi's tolerance of Amadeus matches yours and perhaps she knows Molly wants some privacy for her mourning. Besides, she and Cat love to play Dress Up. an early indication of Heidi's acting career which will take shape 10 years later and continue on to New York and the stage.

After you help unpack Molly, she asks if she can see Amadeus.

You walk outside and show her the burial site you've dug in the garden plot at the foot of the stairs, halfway between Fishy and Mrs. Dalloway, the cat you found frozen on a winter morning in the back of the house, back arched and teeth bared as if she was fending off an attacker. You go to the basement to get Amadeus from his cage.

When you lay him on the concrete floor and remove the plastic shroud his skin pulses with maggots. You see them underneath his belly, his throat, his chest. Some of the maggots have broken loose and lie like plump macaroni around his hindquarters. You hear Molly say, "Dad, can I see Amadeus now?" You say, "Just a minute, Honey."

You know you must act quickly. You take Amadeus to the other side of the basement where you keep a giant can of Raid to extinguish wasps and bees. You know Molly would be horrified if she saw the maggots.

Thief Of Hubcaps

You spray the body—perhaps the wrong thing to do. The maggots become agitated and the Raid foams up on Amadeus's skin creating chemical splotches of bubbling foam.

Molly seems to sense something's wrong. You hear her voice quaver as she again says, "Dad, can I see him now?"

As you move toward the sink with its attached water hose you say "Give me one more minute." The maggots are bad enough, the foam's even worse. You place Amadeus on the concrete floor and turn on the hose.

As you spray the foam, patches of his skin tear off, one of his eyeballs and all of his right cheek come off, exposing the bone underneath. The foam's gone but now he looks as if he's died of leprosy and been bathed in sulfuric acid.

By now, Molly's crying. "Dad, can I see him now?"

You change your plan. "Honey, I think we'll have a closed casket funeral."

You cut a piece from one of the girls' baby blankets—a pink and blue affair with white ribbons—swaddle up Amadeus and hold him in your arms like a baby. You go outside. You give the deceased to Molly and she places him in his grave, stands up and looks at you. She knows what's next. You take her hand and begin.

'Amadeus was a good gerbil. Whenever I said good morning to him, his eyes answered back good morning." Now Molly's turn and her voice doesn't break or falter. It's brave.

"I love you Amadeus and now you're gone. But I won't forget you and wherever you're going I hope you get enough to eat. Bye, bye, Amadeus."

Silence for awhile. You hear Cat's door from across the street open and Heidi's quick steps. She slows down when she arrives and from the other side, takes Molly's hand and tilting her head, looks at her.

You see in her chocolate-drop eyes a sister's compassion, a smile that suffers and sustains. You begin the funeral song and soon your voices join,

Mine eyes have seen the glory of the coming of the Lord,
He is trampling out the vintage where the grapes of wrath are stored;
He hath loosed the fateful lightning of His terrible swift sword;
His truth is marching on.
Glory! Glory! Hallelujah! Glory! Glory! Hallelujah!
Glory! Glory! Hallelujah! His truth is marching on...

Several truths rise in that summer air, the three of you together, singing that Civil war hymn in which mourning is accompanied by bravery, in which the songwriter writes of seeing something of the way things are, even in the midst of death and loss, even when a pet gerbil goes untimely into the dark beyond darkness.

And as you always did when you finished that song, you look up at the sky, seeing there a seagull floating out towards Port Blakely Bay, a miracle of white wings against a blue background that seems as insubstantial as air, as fragile and lovely as the time when you mourned with your children and sang by the graveyard that contained Fishy, Mrs. Dalloway, Amadeus and patches of daffodils.

Ripples in the Time of Oz

Some stories we hear are fiction yet when we hear them we believe they actually happened. Other stories actually happened but seem so fabulous in the telling that even the person who lived the story doubts its truth. This story is of the latter stripe.

He was the director.

He'd directed over 100 plays at Bainbridge High School from 1968 to 2004. The current theater space was completed in 1977 after the old high school building on High School Road was razed and a larger building took its place.

After a decade of moiling on the medieval Commodore Middle School stage, he wanted to do something amazing for the new stage's first season so he chose *The Wizard of Oz*—a favorite of his since he'd read L. Frank Baum's Oz books after seeing the MGM movie in the '50s as a 10-year-old. George Harvey, a veteran 4th grade teacher at Wilkes, was in charge of set building and his 4th grade students auditioned for the 16 Munchkins.

He cast the play and rehearsals began. He'd never directed an epic musical theater production before but he had the brazen confidence of a novice.

The technical challenge in mounting a production of *The Wizard of Oz* is the change between the opening scene in Kansas and the following scene in *Oz*. Set changes longer than a minute invite charges of incompetence by the audience, if not mass retreat to the exits.

George's idea was brilliant: four different backdrops to fly down from the loft along with two wing flats at the sides that would turn to portray Munchkin Land, the Yellow Brick Road, the Emerald City and the Wicked Witch of the West's castle. His final inspiration was to have a two-foot wide rainbow arcing over the 50-foot-wide stage that would reach 15 feet into the air at center stage to welcome Dorothy and the audience to Munchkin Land and Oz.

As the captain of the Titanic must have felt before he hit the iceberg—the director was unaware of impending disaster.

Final dress rehearsal was done without set changes. Kansas was complete but Oz was a distant vision. George and the stage crew were madly painting scenery flats in the hallways next to the theater and once the rehearsal was over at nine o'clock, 12 students, including George and the Director, painted until 1 o'clock in the morning on a school night.

Even today, if you look closely at the concrete floors outside of the theater, you can see traces of emerald green paint embedded in the concrete aggregate for which he was excoriated by the head custodian.

Opening night with its electric air: a full house, actors in makeup and costume, Munchkins safely stowed in the choir room. Nelda Christianson, a senior piano whiz, plays the overture.

Curtain's up and we're in Kansas where Dorothy sings "Somewhere Over the Rainbow" most beautifully and after meeting Professor Marvel, the cyclone begins with a whoosh of wind that quickly becomes a roar. Dorothy runs to the makeshift house at stage center, goes inside and as the lights dim, the wind rises and the curtain falls to applause. All is well. On to Oz!

Nelda begins reprising "Somewhere Over the Rainbow". After three minutes he hears the sound of hammers and voices behind the curtain. At 10 minutes, the director takes the stage to announce that it's opening night and, "We're having technical problems".

He tells Nelda to keep vamping "Over the Rainbow." and goes backstage to the Land of Pandemonium: George at center stage yelling at the fly loft: "Drop the Munchkin Drop, No...not that one, that's the Witch's castle" He sees 12 different stage crew members running around like headless chickens. He realizes he'd only be in the way so he returns to the audience.

Twenty minutes and counting.

He tells Nelda to keep playing "Somewhere Over the Rainbow". She gives him a worried look and continues plunking the keys.

At 40 minutes he goes backstage to see George—a short man with a prominent belly wearing a

15-pound nail belt—12 feet up on a tripod ladder at center stage with a hammer flailing away at the final two ¼ -inch-thick strips that complete the rainbow.

This is before the age of cordless screw guns and to nail two pieces of plywood together 15 feet in the air without backing is both foolhardy and heroic.

He watches as the stage manager underneath the ladder pleads, "Mr. Harvey, Mr. Harvey, when can we open the curtain?" George doesn't skip a beat, keeps banging away and says, "As soon as I get this goddamned rainbow nailed together."

He smashes a final blow and the rainbow's complete. Nelda finishes her endless loop of "Over the Rainbow" with a triumphant flourish and the house lights go down after the longest set change in history at 52 minutes but the production gets better.

Now we jump to 1985, eight years later. Many of the kids who were Munchkins in the original *Wizard* are seniors in high school and want to do the show again. He's ready to return to Oz.

The show's superb: 30 seconds to transform Kansas to Munchkin Land among other artistic touches but it's the final performance that carries the most weight.

It's SRO—standing room only. Afterwards, he walks out to the football field to cool down after the show.

He sees a lime-green Dodge Barracuda race through an opening in the cyclone fence, spin a swerve that harrows the grass, speed to the east goal post, plough a dirt-flying circle and speed back toward the 50 yard line. He steps out of the dark onto the field and raises his arms to the oncoming car.

Thief Of Hubcaps

Fortunately, it stops. He sees 3 kids inside the car he doesn't recognize on some sort of teenage payback mission. He tells them, "Okay, the fun's over, you've got one minute to get out of here before I call the cops." They get out of the car—big kids in muscle T-shirts.

The biggest kid says, "You think you can stop us, old man?"

He doesn't know the answer to that question. He's getting older, not ready to take on three teenagers but behind him, he senses three figures.

They step forward and it's Tin Man, Scarecrow and The Cowardly Lion in full costume and makeup. The boys in front of the car blink as if they've entered an alternate universe. The Cowardly Lion, who played the Mayor of Munchkin Land 8 years before, growls in character: "You'll have to go through us first."

The boys meekly drive away from that football field of Bainbridge, Kansas and looking up, the director could clearly see a shimmer of emerald green in the night sky—light from a land that shimmers more true than truth.

English 156: Crossing the Lines at Puget Sound Naval Shipyard

After being kicked out of Boy Scouts along with
two other 12 year olds for smoking toilet paper in our
tent on my first campout, reading in my teens *Johnny
Got His Gun* by Dalton Trumbo, *Catch 22*, *Company K*,
Wilfred Owen's "Dulce et Decorum Est" and other
novels and poems decrying the savagery and
senselessness of war, having by disposition

a resentment of rules, regimentation, group
thinking and proper paragraph breaks,

being forced to take ROTC in college, barely
escaping being drafted into the Vietnam fiasco, being a
part of war protests and agitating against military
excursions into Iraq, Afghanistan and other locales, I
hesitated to take on a class for Olympic College

teaching Business English at Puget Sound Naval Shipyard in Bremerton.

However, this was my first year as an instructor at OC in 2006 and I didn't have much choice in choosing what I wanted to teach. I accepted the offer.

It wasn't quite like inviting Gandhi to teach Martial Arts to Bengali assassins or Picasso to teach sexual abstinence to Castrati but it was close.

I understood that my responsibility was to guide these young men and women in the basics of writing, reading and understanding the English language in the context of an organization devoted to the military and its requirements. The textbook was decent if uninspired and covered necessary situations, reports and nomenclature inimical to clear communication and exact information.

I read the syllabi of previous instructors which supplied a mountain of spelling tests, vocabulary tests and prosaic assignments. My mission was clear, my duties specified even unto the weekly tests.

I could do this and in my hubris I determined that I would not simply be a Gradgrind, a widget stamper, but an instructor of Business English the likes of which had not been seen. I would take what I was given to teach and give it an Emily Dickinson slant.

I would do what Mozart did with "Twinkle, Twinkle, Little Star"—I would add arpeggios, departures, glissandos and transform a potential Zone of Dead and Boring into an Archipelago of Adventure and Inspiration. I would combine the Seven Labors of Hercules with the Canticles of Leibowitz and prove that any subject explored with deep-browed eyes and brain will yield its own beauty.

Students in the class ranged in age from 20 to 35. The class was part of their apprenticeship at the shipyard for which they were paid. Most of their time was spent learning construction, scaffolding, insulation, welding, plumbing or other trades necessary to the workforce of PSNS. At the end of three years they would have an Associate of Arts Degree, training in their particular trade and a long term job that promised financial security and a government pension. Many were Navy vets.

I received a security clearance for areas on the base I would be frequenting. I had a photo ID and bar code that allowed me access through the security gates.

I would meet them in the afternoon twice a week for a three hour class when they were fresh from lunch and their labors in the field. It was a good group, a typical mix one would find in any college classroom—the solitary kid who's a bit of a nerd, the comics, the crusty veterans of the military, the shy ones, the anxious ones who pursue grades for the sake of grades. I liked the heft of their surnames: Rocky, Lester, Sophia, Juanita, Nate, Red, Paliki, Joshua, Sonia.

The second week I was walking out of Building C4 after class when a fellow instructor came along beside me. He asked me how the class was going. I said "Fine" and wasn't it a nice day?

He concurred. I said, "See you soon," and started toward the exit gate patrolled by men and women in Navy uniforms wearing standard-issue holsters with imposing pistols. I took the shortest route toward the gates.

Thief Of Hubcaps

Three foot wide walkways in the yard are denoted by white paint and marked "Pedestrians Only" but they're sometimes not the quickest and most reasonable way to get from one place to another.

He caught up to me again and said, "You know, at PSNS we don't walk outside the lines." I said, "Oh, thanks, I'll remember that." I don't think he detected any irony in my response. It was a nice metaphor to walk with to the parking garage two blocks away.

I dressed as I always dress—multi-colored Converse sneakers, ties that featured Van Gogh, Cirque de Soleil, James Dean and polychromatic patterns, purples, pinks and never camo as some of my students wore. They paid attention in class and greeted my odd ways and dress with acceptance if not appreciation.

They laughed at my jokes and seemed to enjoy the way the class was unlike any they'd ever taken. They did their assignments with precision and dedication, sometimes turning in 10 pages of homework from three different assignments on a single day as well as daily spelling and vocabulary tests.

I used the spelling and vocab tests I'd been given but modified them. I added words like *harlequin*, *tumescent* and *ineluctable* to the vocab tests. I had them write a detective story using the spelling words. It wasn't that I was being subversive. I did everything I could to make each class an event, something to remember.

I imparted my philosophy: find a way to have fun with whatever you have to do, use your imagination, think of other ways to accomplish the same tasks, refuse to be bored and savor the opportunity to do what you must do. I was having fun, the students were learning and I kept pushing myself to give them what they were giving me: challenge and good work.

Of course, the class wasn't all Mr. Chips and lightning.

Sometimes, as Twain said, it was lightning bugs, even a hard grind and after about a month the honeymoon phase that every teacher enjoys with a new class had settled into a routine of mutual expectations: turn the new assignments in, pass the homework back with comments as to how to improve, take spelling and vocab tests, read and discuss the assigned chapter, learn to outline a paper, write the five-paragraph essay and other rudiments of Business English.

My class was becoming mundane, a word I'd given them for Vocab #3.

I needed to find a way to shake up the class and give them something out of the ordinary. Chapter 5 focused on workplace protocols and spent several pages on writing an incident report. I had an idea.

All learning from textbooks is abstract. It must be applied, made real by direct experience. I knew that discussing how to write an incident report and giving a quiz on the reading would be a typical approach unworthy of me and produce not only lethargy in my students but narcolepsy in myself. I would approach the material in the most visceral way possible.

I would have them witness an incident and then write about it. I would engineer a scene that would convince them what they'd witnessed was real and dangerous.

I would create the experience of being in a place where their emotions and adrenaline would be so charged that, as the text stated, they would have to put aside their emotions and attempt to recreate what had happened in words and write a clear, objective account of the event.

I'd had a like experience before when I was teaching high school at in the early '70s. Everett Thompson, a close friend and I heard about a university class that witnessed a staged shooting and then were asked to write about it.

The description of the event by the students was as varied as the writers themselves. Details were left out, chronologies inverted, facts invented. Clearly, emotional states alter objective truth. We decided to stage a shooting in Everett's senior- level high school English class.

I also teach and direct theater so I have numerous blank pistols—starter's pistols which serve as safe props to use when a gunshot is required onstage. The scenario was that I would walk into Everett's classroom, start yelling about a romantic tryst with my wife, shoot him in the chest and walk out of the room.

Everett would be dead on the podium. We cleared the plan with the principal and adjoining classrooms and awaited the day of the shooting.

I walked in shouting, the class quieted and watched as we yelled at each other and I pulled out my gun and shot my friend with a .32 blank and he collapsed. I heard later that the room went quiet for about 10 seconds then someone said: "Okay, no more English for today."

Everett came back to life, I walked back in and while the experience was fun and exciting for the students, it didn't work as a learning device.

This time it would be different. My students didn't know my background as an actor and theater guy, they were older and less sarcastic and the Island resembles Bremerton the way Disneyland resembles downtown Detroit.

This time it was 2006 on a Naval base, post 9/11 with a nation attuned to school, college and post office shootings with strict injunctions against firearms carried by anyone except military guards. I needed to choose another tack.

The class already thought I was strange. Why not pretend I'd gone wacko, over the edge, around the bend?

I met with the director of the apprenticeship program and told him what I had in mind. I asked him if he'd take me out of the classroom when I slammed the door to the hallway and then direct the class to write up the incident. He approved my plan and liked my innovative approach.

He said he'd get the security guard to take me away so he'd be free to instruct the class as to their duty.

Before the bell rang to start class, I sat in front on a high stool. Unlike every day since the start of the quarter, I didn't greet the students as they came in. Every once in a while, I'd softly moan, run my hand through my hair, shake my head. The bell rang.

I looked up and said, "Where are we?" I twitched my lips. I touched my nose. Some of them laughed but most of them looked at me intently. I got up and started weaving around the room. I stuttered. I took the one-foot pile of homework papers and said, "I could stand on these, jump off and commit suicide. I...can't....do this...anymore."

I stood on a chair and climbed on one of the tables that served as desks for the students. I took out my Zippo and said, "What would happen..." (by now I'd adopted a low chuckle following words and phrases and pretended a demonic glee) "...if I lit this lighter on this ice cream cone?" I held the lighter up to one of the fire sprinklers.

Justin Delgado took me seriously. He said we'd be drenched in water and have to evacuate the building. I said then we could go home but what was the use of that? I started shouting numbers, doubling them into millions. I slammed against the whiteboard saying, o god, o god, o god. I reeled to the hallway doorway and hit it with my fist.

I knew I'd convinced them. They were frozen, wide-eyed, stunned by my berserk behavior, my voice that creaked, broke and rose from a guttural wheeze to a manic screech. The security guard took me into the hallway.

Through the open door I could hear the director say, "We've been worried about your instructor. We've had reports that he needed help. Stay seated. I'll be back."

In the hallway the security guard said that he was listening and "God, you convinced me. Are you an actor?" I said, "Yeah, a bit, I had some training." He said, "Wow."

The director walked back into the room, assured the class that I would be cared for and told them that they'd obviously witnessed an incident and as with every incident, he needed a report from eyewitnesses.

He told everyone to write what they'd seen, heard and experienced.

We went to his office to decompress. I began thinking that my performance had gone too far. Maybe I'd traumatized some of the students. I'd initially said that they should be given 15 minutes to write their account but I came back in 10 minutes.

I walked through the door and told them I was acting, pretending. I reminded them about the reading for today and explained why I had done what I'd done. We discussed what they'd seen. Two women asked to be excused and I gave them permission.

Red said that he wasn't completely convinced. He was one of the sharpest kids in the class and I liked him. I asked for their incident reports. About half were blank. They said they were so upset they couldn't write. Others had the sequence wrong, imagined details that hadn't occurred, and misquoted me.

For the next hour we went over the difficulty of writing accurate reports and the effect of emotion on judgment and perception. The two young women never returned and they weighed on my mind but I pushed the niggling thought away. Sometimes students had to leave during class for other reasons—appointments with supervisors or family duties.

I hoped this was true but something was in the air.

At the end of class I received a note asking me to stop in at the director's office after class. He told me he'd had the two women in his office for an hour.

One had a father who had chased her around the house with an axe when she was 15 until the police finally arrived and took him away. The other woman had a husband who'd snapped one night, beaten her up and dragged her into an alley and tried to stuff her in a dumpster.

The director told me he'd calmed them down and explained to them why I'd acted the way I did. He said I was a talented instructor trying to teach his students. He said he finally told them to go home for the rest of the day, that they would talk more if they needed to.

I got their phone numbers and called them that afternoon. I apologized; I was abject, sorry, remorseful. I knew I'd done damage. I knew I'd crossed a line. I told them I owed them. One woman said, "How about an 'A' for the class?" We both laughed.

The quarter ended on a nice note.

They presented me with a Naval Base hardhat they'd requisitioned from Supplies with "English 156" on the side, "Avuncular Pedagogue" on the front and written in permanent marker, their names and messages using words like "Indubitably", "Decadent," "Oxymoron," "Synesthesia," "Hiatus," even "Friend" and "Awesome Teacher." They'd learned some vocabulary.

I learned again there are some lines you shouldn't cross. Betraying a trust when that betrayal might cause a person to relive a terrible memory is one such line. You don't throw cherry bombs at a VFW picnic.

I've kept the hard hat on a shelf in my workshop since that time but as a way to invoke the past in the present, it's sitting here now on the dining room table as I type. When I brought it inside this morning from my workshop it was so dusty I had to wash it in the sink and now it looks brand new, white and shining.

The gift and the lesson is finally a good memory, one that I will not lose but like most memories it's a troubled mix of fondness and regret written indelibly with permanent markers of red, purple, black and green that age and dust have not diminished.

Violated

It was misconceived.

The last speaker to speak in my Public Speaking class on this particular night, a young man who'd taken my Beginning Acting class the quarter before and was now taking this class, stood at the podium ready to begin. He reminded me of my son in law, Earl—the same calm, short hair, intelligence and forthright manner.

He'd taken a liking to me the previous quarter which was a compliment I honored and which I attributed to his need for affection coming from a place I did not know but could dimly sense. The first assignment was to tell a true story.

He began with, "I was violated last quarter on this campus," and the audience and I immediately went into that electric shock/absorption/silence that attends danger and confession.

My first thought was, *Good for him. He's going to get something off his chest. I hope he's reported it.*

Many of the speeches already given had been powerful and wrenching—deaths of fathers, mothers, disappointment in love, loss of a child, stories of being beaten by a parent but this was different.

This was about a person on our campus, a sexual violation, and we were rapt.

Barry said that his abuser was a professor on this campus, that during last quarter when he'd arrived "bright and bushy-tailed," looking forward to his first college experience, he's signed up for this instructor's class. He'd seen him in the Student Commons and the instructor had put his hand on his shoulder.

Barry described it as a sexual come-on and when he responded in a startled way, the man had excused himself by saying "Oh, sorry, I thought you were someone else." Barry told us he knew that this was an excuse, that he meant the gesture as an invitation to sex. He said, "That Sonuvabitch" with clench-teethed venom.

I began thinking that he might be speaking about a man close to my age whom I'd seen at the start of the fall quarter who'd disappeared about halfway through the quarter without any explanation.

We all try to find reasons for a mystery and Barry kept us in suspense, wondering who he was talking about and what further had happened. He was doing what I asked the students to do for their first assignment: speak the truth, get the audience's attention and don't be afraid to be dangerous, to take a chance.

For the most part they'd done this and I felt again what I'd felt before in classes I taught: a gratitude for young people—in truth, several people were in their

50s but at my age anyone under 50 is young—who actually listen and act upon what I ask them to do.

Clues to the abuser's identity were woven into the speech in brief descriptions. The abuser had white hair, somewhat stringy, he sometimes said weird things that were hard to follow, he forgot what he was saying at times and he dressed well, if a little outrageously.

These clues gave me pause.

I do have white hair though I'd never thought of my hair as stringy, I do say things designed to be out of the ordinary to keep my students' attention, I sometimes, in the flurry of trying to reach and teach ideas, get lost because so many thoughts congregate.

And the clincher: I like clothes. I like to wear scarves and bright colors—yellow, purple, pink. I have 60 pairs of Converse tennis shoes, some in patterns that Miro and Salvador Dali would find interesting, another pair that resembles Dorothy's ruby slippers for men.

He couldn't be talking about me, could he?

When I had Barry as a student the quarter before he'd been a model of devotion to the class. The first assignment in Beginning Acting was to write a silent scene for one person to be performed by another member of the class. I did this purposefully because most students taking beginning acting think that acting is about being clever, using words to one-up their partner.

The trick to acting is what's happening inside— words mean nothing without internal belief. His scene had been good and I'd given him a high 'B' and told him, along with the rest of the class, that all papers submitted could be rewritten, that if the rewrite was a good one, the old grade would disappear and the new grade would take its place.

It's what I do in every class I teach: a good writer is a rewriter. Grades are superfluous. What matters is what we learn.

After I passed back the papers he rewrote the scene and turned it in the next day. The following day he asked me if I'd read his rewrite. I told him I hadn't had time but detecting his intensity and fearing he might be a grade-grubber, I asked him why it was so important to him.

He said that no teacher had ever taken his ideas seriously before or made so many comments and he wanted to improve the piece. This was welcome news to an idealistic instructor so I spent time helping him improve his writing on this and other assignments.

He was a disciplined director in the scene work, perhaps a bit compulsive but I admire someone who wants everything just so. And he was a good kid. He meant well though at times he was socially awkward but that's part of being young for most people, especially guys.

He received a 3.8 in Beginning Acting, a high grade for me, and signed up for Intermediate Acting in winter quarter. After the first acting class he asked me if I would accept him on the wait list for my speech class. He needed to take another class and seeing the class was taught by me he'd chosen Public Speaking.

I told him I'd sign his permission form to take the class. I told him that we had a history, he was a good student and I'd be happy to take an overload. Besides, it was a compliment to me that he'd sampled what I was and had to say and wanted more.

Thief Of Hubcaps

Repeat students are like repeat customers in construction work which I've done to make extra money for 40 years—they've seen good work and believe in you enough to have faith that you'll treat them right and do quality work. It's an ego stroke and compliment which I humbly appreciate and do not crow about as I know it's often not the result of superior teaching but of happening to meet the student when the student's ready to learn.

Time and chance happens to us all—sometimes with good, sometimes bad, results.

I'm doing now what Barry did in his speech. I'm not letting my audience in on what happened. I'm using suspense but also giving information that helps to understand why what happened happens.

He was accusing me of being his abuser, of being a pervert, a homosexual predator of the worst stripe. This began to sink in through my disbelief, my—what more fitting term than naïveté—a belief that when one acts out of a firm commitment to the best in a student, good things result.

I searched my memory for anything Barry might have misunderstood or any particle where I might have exceeded a boundary. Nothing came to mind. I've been accused of many things but never of coming on to a male student.

What did come to mind was an incident some 15 years before when a student wanted to kill me and I was completely unaware of what was going on inside of him and until the police got involved I never suspected the kid was anything but normal and a student I liked and nurtured.

Was Barry a victim of some mental disorder, a schizophrenic who'd snapped? Had I dropped into a parallel universe? Was I living in a Kafka short story?

I thought of stopping the speech, confronting Barry with, "Wait a minute. Are you accusing me of being a predator, that I abused you?" I thought of calling Security.

I knew this was a dangerous time and then, because I have faith in people and I knew Barry, I figured that he must have a reason to say what he was saying. I hoped I would find it out and everything would be okay. I waited to see what would happen.

He seemed to arrive at a conclusion. He said, "And this man is sitting in this room tonight." He looked directly at me and I could feel everyone's eyes turn in my direction.

He paused and began talking again while he walked toward where I was sitting at the end of the third row of tables. I didn't hear what he was saying. My heart was in my throat.

I looked at his hands to see if he was carrying a gun or a knife. I looked at his pockets to see if he was concealing a weapon.

He walked to my chair and said, "Stand up."

I stood up.

He reached out toward my shoulder. Involuntarily I jerked backwards. I had no control over this reaction. It was pure instinct originating in survival and fear. He put his arm around me and began talking again.

I couldn't hear what he was saying, there was a roar in my ears and I could feel my heart thumping. I felt him squeezing my shoulder once, twice, three times in—what was this? Affection? A come-on? I didn't know and asI began to gather my wits I realized he was praising me.

He was saying "...here's a man I admire, a man who gave me a place at this college, who speaks wisdom, who's a wonderful teacher and human being." He was smiling.

I was paralyzed.

The whole class breathed again, they started talking to each other. The tension was broken. They were relieved. They realized that this was all a joke, a ruse designed to fool them into thinking something was the truth and then magically let them discover what was actually the truth.

After I got my breath back and somewhat dizzyingly walked to the front of the room we talked a bit about what had happened and I scanned the faces to see if anyone had believed the story, if anyone was visibly upset.

I couldn't detect anything, though one student who was 35 and a Navy vet serving at Bangor Naval Base said he had his cell phone in hand ready to call 911.

I asked for volunteers to begin the next round of speeches—the informative speech. Nine people quickly raised their hands and we mapped out what would happen the next week and the class went well. Several people, after the class ended, stayed to talk about their topic and get advice and ideas.

It was a good class. Everyone seemed to have put aside any aspersions on my character and the disturbing nature of Barry's speech.

I also liked the kid and believed in his goodness. As Yakov Bok said in Malamud's *The Fixer,* "I live like an optimist because I cannot live at all as a pessimist."

Besides, at my advanced age, I'd made the same mistake of unintended damage when I crossed the line at Puget Sound Naval Shipyard some four years before. If I could forgive and understand myself, how could I not forgive and understand Barry?

We easily find fault in others. What's harder is to accept responsibility for our own actions, to know that the events that happen to us are often caused by our own designs. And regardless of the rue and pain they cause, we have a story to tell, something to learn from.

But there's always more, isn't there?

Stories don't stop. They attach to the future and derive from the past. Just as there were things about the women at PSNS I didn't know or foresee there were things about me that Barry didn't know.

Memory's like a thread of string that attaches to a minotaur's cave inside our heads and sometimes when we see the string again we're not sure if it leads into a cave where we'll forever be lost or if it leads to a place we can escape from and be found. How can we tell when we've crossed this path before which way is out, which way in?

All we can do is choose a direction and follow it hoping that the string won't disappear if we take the wrong way.

Sometimes we must go back to go forward.

Thread

One of the essential oddities of high school life is that though every student professes a reverence for the individual this reverence is defined by a narrow corridor.

The idea is to be outré without being strange, to be a rebel not a reclusive twit, to be stylishly weird not clumpingly frumpy.

You've come to believe that the true individuals of a school are the outcasts who are maligned for their difference and then, over the course of time, become invisible because they don't matter—in many ways they have no matter and become invisible.

Sometimes these alien beings find each other and survive, other times they're imprisoned in a cell of their own devising, unable to understand why they're so separate. Without perspective they reach a vanishing point and disappear even to themselves.

You do not pretend you were aware of this oddity when you attended high school. Like so many other teenagers you were intensely self-centered, aware of little else other than your own hormonal directives, scrabbling to find a way within the gilded way. You always thought others blessed with confidence and abilities beyond your ken. You envied them.

When you became a high school teacher you could see into the social matrix and begin to understand its vanity and cruelties without being repulsed. Though this life was curious it wasn't without a certain charm and you knew that the experiences of that transient time teetered on a thin balance—that a slight shove or snap of the thread could send a good person into the abyss.

You'd seen it happen.

A teacher is absolutely a part of this web but he's also able to see the filaments upon which it hangs and know that those whose world consists of living on the web, no matter how precocious or perceptive they are, can't see how the web secures itself to invisible stanchions that appear only when seen in a certain light. One must be outside of something to be able to see inside that something.

When all we know is an ocean that swims with fish how can we imagine a land to walk?

Devin Merkle seemed perpetually wide eyed, like a puffer fish brought to the surface. Not that he was blown up—he lived within his own world. He seldom spoke and then only with a barely audible voice that apologized itself for speaking. He dressed in disguise— earth tones, flesh tones, colors or the lack of them that melded into the walls, the institutional rugs.

Thief Of Hubcaps

He had black hair and black-rimmed, thick glasses. He was a solid B student who was exceptional only in his isolation. You met him in 10th English and from that semester on, he was in every class he could take from you—World Lit, Expository Writing, Lit of I, Senior Lit and a friendship possible between a teacher and a student took shape.

You said hello to him in the halls, you smiled when he came into your room, you encouraged him to speak in class though this seldom worked. You liked him for his difference. You looked out for him in his seclusion as you attempted to do for other students you saw as solitary.

In the early 90s, students could choose their teachers at registration for the next semester. Teachers had 30 tickets for their classes and would station themselves in various parts of the gym and hand those tickets on registration days to students after writing their names on a roll sheet.

Devin, you remember, was always in the front line for a ticket to your class and this devotion flattered you. It's nice to be appreciated.

By the time of Devin's last semester of his senior year, he'd taken every class you taught except Theater. And there he was on a January day first in line, asking for a ticket for Theater.

A surprising turn of events for one of the most introverted students you'd known. But you thought, good, he's taking a chance, he's branching out—maybe he sees a way out of his confinement through acting, through discovering the larger world that drama and plays explore. Maybe he realizes that high school isn't the world or even the end of the world.

You were pleased. You'd seen other students in the past suddenly open up, "bloom" as they say, given water and air.

Mary Harmon was such a student, so painfully shy in the 9th grade that she couldn't look you in the eyes, a girl who turned red whenever she had to answer a question, even answer the roll call. And then, by her sophomore year, she was the pianist for the spring musical beginning to call other musicians to account for missed notes and weak rhythm.

By her senior year she was a student director giving advice and issuing directives with all the aplomb and self-confidence of a Makarova. Sometimes, as Old Lodgeskins, the Cheyenne chief in *Little Big Man* says, the magic works. Sometimes it doesn't.

That semester after the initial acting exercises designed to allow the student a safe place to explore different roles and ways of acting, to become different people, to throw off pretense and act honestly, to be part of a group united by a common purpose, you decided to do a 45-minute piece about date rape with the class called *Shadows in Our Lives*.

It would be performed for English and Health classes in the school and spoke frankly about the scourge of date rape using vignettes, monologues and snippets of scenes involving thresholds of sex and intimacy. The counselors approved. The play went well.

You remember Devin did a monologue about a kid with a crush who can't express his feelings to the object of his affections that ends with confusion and questions about sex. He did well. He was honest and convincing. His voice had grown—he could be heard in the back rows.

Thief Of Hubcaps

At the end he was pleased by the applause and you were pleased that he'd come so far. Another victory for self-expression and the healing nature of the arts.

Sometime at the end of January you received a phone call about 9 o'clock in the evening. After you said hello, the voice, which was obviously disguised, said "Sic, Sic, Sic." You thought he was saying "Sick, Sick, Sick"—that you were a sick person. You said, "Thank you," and hung up.

Some kids in your classes thought some of your ideas and poetry you taught was sick, as in having a perverted mind. They were often kids who were sheltered by their parents or prevented by their religion from considering other points of view.

You believed that one of the teacher's duties is to acquaint his students with a wider world with varying perspectives and attitudes and some of it should be disturbing, some of it should be challenging. You meant thank you in irony but also in earnest—you saw it as a compliment of sorts.

You'd received harassing phone calls before. It's part of the job description of being a teacher. You're bound to make enemies—if you're popular with everyone something's wrong.

You soon learned to have fun with the calls, to meet insult with humor, to realize that you've become part of someone's education which means for some, trying out an anonymous phone call. You'd done the same when you were 13 or 14. It was a creative adventure.

The next time he called he said the same thing over and over like a mantra, "Sic, Sic, Sic... Sic, Sic, Sic... and you realized he wasn't saying "Sick, Sick,

Sick" he was saying "6, 6, 6"—the name of the Anti-Christ in the Book of Revelations. You'd been elevated to an eminence worthy of the Devil in the Apocalypse.

You said in a matching sepulchral tone: "Welcome, that's my name and number. Come inside... it's the end of the world. 6...6....6." You could hear the caller breathing on the other end. He hung up. You smiled.

On Valentine's Day he called again.

You remember it was Valentine's Day and you'd given your wife a weird 1924 Duart Hairdresser's Appliance with hanging electrical cords that ended in hair clips which resembled an early 20th century torture device. It still works and sits on your entryway deck in case any visitors need a quick curl-job.

You once used it as a stage prop for a re-enactment of the birth of Frankenstein's Bride. You've since added a stuffed armadillo on top of the device. You admire the strange.

This time was different though equally strange.

Is Satan there?

No...he's attending a Wild Pig Barbeque but if you call back in an hour he should be home.

You were beginning to enjoy these calls. It was an invitation to improvisation, an entertainment which happened every two weeks, always on a Sunday night at 9.

Next time, same question:

Is Satan there?

No...there is no Satan here nor do we believe in Satan. We believe in satin...the silk of it, the sensuousness. We wear it always. Even our underthings are satin.

Thief Of Hubcaps

After two or three requests for Satan you grew tired of the monotony. Your caller hadn't learned the concept of variety and surprise.

This time when you heard the same question you answered by screaming into the phone as loud and as long as your breath held. When you paused to breathe he'd hung up and the calls stopped. Screaming, like magic, sometimes works.

You think sometimes that telephone calls are like bird calls. The ring of a phone resembles the call of some birds we hear in early spring. It's a way of saying hello. It's a way of saying "We're here." With birds, as with people, we sometimes don't understand what's being said or why it's being said.

All we hear is the call and as much as we try to answer, we're never sure if our answer is enough or even approaches what's behind the call. We're often blind as moles.

In the 90s and perhaps even now, the high school had a final awards assembly for seniors the week of Graduation. Like all assemblies these gatherings are a chance for some students to get attention and best of all, notoriety.

Cheerleaders prance and dance, speakers and performers in skits vie for who can be most entertaining, most outrageous. The band plays, coaches speak inspirationally and most people come away in high spirits. It's a way to unite the student body, to have 1200 people in the same room cheering for each other, laughing with each other, bonding in a village ritual that's predictable and sometimes worthy of intense gossip and talk afterwards.

For some it's a way to make your mark and test the line of what you can get away with. Some things you can, some things you can't.

Cross dressing is permitted and always a sure-fire audience pleaser. To see a jock flouncing in a frilly dress inspires roars of approval. The football tackle with an early beard and booming biceps who stuffs his chest to look like a bosomy chorus girl and moves his hips like a strumpet becomes a demigod.

At one such assembly a young man who would later become a regular on "Saturday Night Live" stuffed his crotch and lip-synched and gyrated to Michael Jackson's "Thriller". The performance was amazing. The audience hooted and hollered. The principal and vice principal frowned.

The principal hauled him into his office after the assembly and threatened 3 days of suspension for "inappropriate behavior" during an assembly. The young man's defense for stuffing his crotch with a foot-long bratwurst so he looked like a tumescent matador on penal steroids was that if guys could stuff their chest to look like they had enormous boobs why couldn't he stuff his pants to look like he had an enormous penis?

He was an advocate for sexual equality. Aren't dicks as important as boobs? The defense didn't fly but the kid had a point and as it turned out, a career in comedy.

You were scheduled to hand out the Drama Awards at the end of the hour-long assembly which usually ran at least 10 minutes over. Drama awards were scheduled last as an antidote to the endless awards for sports, academics and clubs which tended to drone on and on.

Thief Of Hubcaps

Your actors always did a mock Academy Award Ceremony for best actor, best techie of the year which featured clips from the musical, the one-acts and the straight play. They did weird, actorly things which they cleared with me beforehand. They dressed up in costumes that ranged from television sets to arthropods on stilts. It was dramatic.

It was a chance for Drama to be placed on equal footing with Athletics, good for the program, good for the kids and you welcomed the chance for them to be recognized.

What you hadn't recognized was that Devin had, what's the word—acquired? caught? been afflicted with?—paranoid schizophrenia that year. He heard voices that told him he was the Son of Moses and his mission was to kill the Anti-Christ.

He'd chosen you as the Anti-Christ.

You've always enjoyed playing different roles—Henry Higgins in *My Fair Lady,* Judd, the necrophiliac-pyromaniac in *Oklahoma*, Jonathon in *Arsenic and Old Lace* who's murdered 12 people, Grandpa Joe In *Wonka* at the Pioneer Square Theater for 160 performances—but these were parts for which you'd auditioned and got paid for. You hadn't auditioned for Devin's play but you were cast as the main character.

Which, in a way, was a compliment.

His plan was to cut your throat with a butcher knife in front of the student body at the awards assembly. It was ingenious.

You would be introducing the Drama Awards with some sort of shtick whether it be a disappearing arm, a magic trick involving smoke and a fake bird or pretending to swallow your tongue or eat one of your eyeballs and Devin would approach you from the side with a butcher knife.

He'd take you by surprise, cut your carotid and you'd bleed to death within seconds. The audience would cheer and laugh. They would be amazed at how real the blood looked, how it spurted from your throat, how you convulsed and spasmed on the ground and finally died with a shudder and then you were still. How dead you looked. How dead you would be.

At the time of course, you didn't know that anything was "afoot," as you love to say in theater lingo.

You also didn't know that the night before he'd taken his family's butcher knife from the kitchen and stowed it under his bed to take in the morning. He'd also—this kid who'd never tasted alcohol or taken drugs—procured an upper, a pep pill, because he'd started to worry about whether he could handle you if you struggled.

You were in good shape and outweighed him by 30 pounds. He was a spindly 5 foot 8 inches and abjured athletics. The pill would give him the energy and resolve he needed.

He took the pill first thing in the morning and was so wacked out by the rush he forgot to take the butcher knife. This omission was solved in 1st period Calculus when he borrowed a Swiss Army knife from a classmate with the excuse that he needed it to open a package before the assembly. Everything was in place.

Your place at the assembly was always by the Senior section of the gym bleachers where you would stand with other English faculty and friends and watch the madness.

You weren't fond of the Orwellian chanting and the competition among the classes as to who could yell the loudest. It seemed Fascist and Groupthink but to be charitable, it was also, for many, a necessary exercise in group flagellation.

Toward the end of the assembly, Barton Steen, the vice principal, came up to you and said the assembly was running longer than expected and asked if you could cut Drama's time from eight minutes to three.

This was fuel for instant dudgeon. You'd long resented the emphasis and pre-eminence of athletics to the near exclusion of the arts not only at your school but at other high schools. You told him if you could only have three minutes you'd as soon cancel. He blithely said, "Okay," and walked away.

A junior girl you knew asked if you'd pass out flowers to the seniors as they exited the gym at the end of the assembly on the east side. You said 'sure' and as you were on the west side of the gym, ducked underneath the bleachers to get to the assigned exit.

Which was the moment when Devin looked for you where you usually stood.

When you emerged from under the bleachers and could see the gym floor, the student body was in an uproar—laughing, screaming, shouting.

You saw Devin with a microphone in back of a new teacher, Clara Thomas, who taught Humanities. His arm was around her throat and he was shouting into the Mic which had chosen at that moment to go mute. The kid on sound was madly plugging in connectors to get the sound back. All the assembly could hear was unintelligible rant.

You thought to yourself, "Wow, look at Devin...three months ago he was so introverted he could barely look you in the eyes and now he's entertaining the whole student body. That's what drama can do for a kid."

You saw Ben Madison, a student body officer, go toward Devin and Devin slash at him with his Swiss Army knife. From the other side, Dave Ellick, the principal, grabbed at his shoulder and Devin cut him against his ribs. You could see a red line on Ellick's white shirt. The audience was quieting down, realizing this wasn't a skit.

Two teachers, Bim Prince and Jim Dow, grabbed Devin and lifted him over their heads and took off for the outside exit. By now the audience was mute in collective gasp. It's the reaction when your eyes can't understand what your brain knows to believe and you freeze.

In the tomb of the gym, as he was carried out the doors, Devin yelled, "You'll remember me for this!"

The vice principal dismissed us to our rooms. An instant buzz of talk, wide eyes and some girls crying. Outside we heard the sirens calling "oh no, oh no, oh no" in rise and fall. We went back to our rooms and discussed what had happened though none of us knew why it had happened.

We attempted to get back to normal. You were disturbed of course, You had a history with Devin and knew what he'd done was irrevocable and self-destructive. Was any of it your fault?

5th period a counselor came to your room and said you were wanted in the office. She would take over your class. You were interviewed by two detectives from the Kitsap County Sheriff's office.

They told you about Devin's plot, that you were his target. They asked you what you knew of him. You realized you didn't know enough but did your best to explain the relationship.

Devin was headed for Port Orchard and the county jail. The principal had escaped with superficial cuts—his shirt and T-shirt had protected his ribs. The new teacher was upset and as it turned out, wasn't in school for the next week—in fact, she resigned her position and moved back East.

Devin was arraigned but before his trial, was remanded to Bellingham and the state mental hospital for evaluation and ultimately, treatment for mental illness.

You were placed under protective custody, a court order that provided you be notified if Devin came within 100 miles of where you were and if so, you could ask for police protection. You believe the order ran out about 10 years ago but you weren't worried when it was rescinded.

You found out through a lawyer friend that in the month after the incident his family had moved to Montana, that after Devin had been in the mental facility for four years he was released and in the late 90s was married with two kids, had a job as a truck driver in Montana and seemed to be doing fine.

This was good news to you. You harbored no grudge against Devin and wished him a happier life.

What you did harbor was paranoia of sorts. You seemed to have caught it from Devin and it manifests itself at odd times—some predictable, some not.

You never attend large assemblies of any sort, especially at school. You do go to plays but sit at the very back of the theater in the last row. When you go out for breakfast or lunch, even in a bar with friends, you sit facing the door so you can see who comes in.

When you do construction work you tell your fellow workers that if they've returned from somewhere, if they haven't been inside the building where you are working, they need to start talking, singing or whistling once they're 30 feet away.

You've scared some of them by your reaction when they've silently approached you from behind. You freak out as the saying goes. You're scared and scare them—usually by turning toward them, putting up your hands and shouting "Ha!" as if you are some sort of Kung Fu madman and it takes awhile for your heart to stop beating hard.

You usually laugh in relief, your friends apologize and you sit down to gather your wits and realize there's no danger, it's all in the past.

Then there's the odd event and the past comes up like swamp gas bubbling up from something buried underneath. Walking through the woods at night you hear a noise as if someone walks behind you. You see in the dark vague shapes that resemble a human form.

One night years after the incident, you had a dream where you were shot by two police officers in the street. They took you to an office where they told you to wash the floor and they pushed you inside a standup coffin. You wanted to tell them you had two bullets in you that you were worried about but you couldn't speak.

A young man you'd known before, one of many wonderful students who've been in your classes whose names sometimes escape you but who you recognize from their face, told the cops that it wasn't right the way they were treating you. He took you by your hand and led you into another room with candles and two overstuffed chairs. You sat across from each other, your knees touched.

He took out a straight razor and began stropping it. He lathered your hands and arms. He began shaving the backs of your hands with the pearl handled razor, cutting into them so quickly you thought you would bleed but you could see no blood in the white lather. The light from the candles yellowed the room of shadows, lightened the dark.

Kindness and warmth shone in the young man's eyes as he inspected his work.

You woke in a panic. You searched for an answer as to why this dream was so unsettling. You knew beyond knowing that the dream contained a message, a meaning, if you could only tease it out, if you could follow the thread of where your unrest came from. The dream ended well, why did it still have you in a shudder?

It wasn't in the straight razor or the two bullets—you'd been dealt much worse in other dreams—and then you got it. The rub was in the kindness of the shaving of your skin which had seemed a welcome relief in your dream. It was the opposite of what you'd first thought.

You realized that what he was doing was preparing you for some sort of slaughter, some ritual you didn't know about or imagine was possible.

It came from a darkness you couldn't penetrate—like Devin's voice shouting, "You'll remember me for this." though now it's not a strangled shout in a silent gym you hear—it's more a whisper that joins a clamor of similar voices in a hushed jumble you hear in your head singing and mourning what's passed and perhaps still to come.

Frog in the Crawlspace

After my father lost the bulk of his money through the deception of a business partner in a fishing resort he planned to build in La Push, Washington, we moved to our house in Mountain Lane at the foot of Hummingbird Hill.

For the first 2 months, we boys slept in sleeping bags on army cots outside the living room in a covered open area. We'd wake up with our bags covered in frost.

Inside, stairs led to an unfinished basement—what was called a daylight basement. My dad hired a Norwegian carpenter named Sven Nygaard, a taciturn, hard worker who always had a chaw of snoose (the Norwegian term for chewing tobacco) in his cheek and who told me, in a rare burst of volubility, that chewing snoose had saved the four teeth he had left in his head and he opened his mouth wide to show me the ones that remained.

Sven finished the basement in knotty pine paneling, built two bedrooms on each side of a hallway and a bathroom with a shower, toilet and sink along with a laundry room abutting the stairs that led from the top floor.

Each bedroom had two bunk beds and the two younger boys, Lee and Timmy, slept on the daylight side. My brother Gary and I slept on the side closest to the bath/utility room with me on the top bunk and Gary on the lower bunk.

I liked to be on the top bunk—like a cat loves a perch— and I could easily jump the 5 feet it took to get into bed. After sleeping outside, it was good to be snug in a three-sided space.

Tim and Lee were 13 and 11, Gary and I, 17 and 15. The walls of our bedrooms reflected this difference. Tim and Lee's side displayed pictures of Stan Musial, Jackie Robinson, Don Heinrich, Bob Houbregs, the A.P. All American Football team for 1955 and other athletic ephemera.

Our side was a synthesis. Pictures of comely females in inviting poses, their lips parted as if to initiate a liquescent French kiss, congregated with our Babe Ruth League Baseball group photos and pictures of athletes like Bob Feller and Willie Mays in action shots—Feller just as a fireball left his arm, Mays rounding 3rd heading like a torpedo for home plate, seeming to target Jayne Mansfield's cantilevered boobs in the adjoining thumb-tacked glossy.

Looking from our bunk beds you could see the exposed structure at the foot of the concrete slab of a four-foot-high crawl space with floor joists and post-and-beam construction on hard clay. Soon after we started sleeping downstairs, my dad and Uncle Carl built a concrete block wall to close off the crawl space.

We were being sealed in or something was being sealed out.

All of us boys loved Cowboy and Indian movies, what one of our neighbors in Ballard, Joe Schwab, called, "Goddamn-giddyap-shoot-em-all-to-hell Westerns."

When I was in 2nd grade I had a Roy Rogers lunchbox with a Trigger thermos. My heroes on screen were Hopalong Cassidy, Randolph Scott, Gary Cooper, Lash Larue and John Wayne. My heroes in books were Crazy Horse, Cochise, Geronimo and Sitting Bull, and as far as heroism and loyalties went, I saw no difference between them.

My brother Tim and I especially admired the stealth and secret language of Indian scouts. We saw them in movies sneaking up on a wagon train or cavalry campout at night and to communicate their location or warn of danger, they'd imitate bird sounds and each one meant something different depending on what the scouts had agreed to.

A night owl's hoot might mean all is well, the caw of a crow caution, the whistle of a whippoorwill to keep moving. The possibilities were endless.

After our bedroom lights were turned out and we'd said our good nights—in that interim between wake and sleep, in that secure silence—Tim and I would send bird calls to each other through the hallway between our open rooms and depending on the emotion and inflection of the bird sound and the bird chosen we would send each other different messages before we slept.

I would caw like a crow, there would be a waiting silence, then Tim would whistle back a whippoorwill. Another pause and I would send another message, a different bird, another whistle into the dark and so it would continue for 10 or more minutes until one of us would whistle and there would be no answer and we'd know our brother was asleep.

I can't remember Gary or Lee joining in though they might have.

Perhaps they were sounder sleepers or thought we were silly or perhaps they were silent listeners to our nightly drama. I'd like to think the latter. It's always good to have an audience and every night the script was different.

Sometimes we'd start with danger, then go to attack (usually the scrawk of a raven). Other nights we'd play two different owls, sometimes in mating season and the possibilities of calling "whooo" with different shadings and questions intrigued us. Sometimes the owl sounds broke into stifled hoots of laughter as we imagined what each of us was asking.

That was part of the fun—to have the other brother break bird-character with laughter or suddenly to introduce a woodpecker by tapping our fingernail against the pine, to know that we both understood what we did was our way to entertain our brother and speak in a language other than words.

It was always birds, never crickets or wolves or other creatures that call in the night. In my metaphysical age after reading volumes of books on natural history, the messaging of whales, the way all species communicate with each other with sounds that originate within themselves, I believe there's a link between the undiscovered countries of sleep and death and the presence of birds.

Before entering a place where strange visions and fear might abruptly materialize it's wise to be cautious, to have another beside you when you to visit a place in your head where you're so entirely alone.

In the crease between conscious and unconscious—that entry into nightmare or things not of this world—to apprise a bird is to travel with a companion to navigate the night and return to the day.

Larks herald the dawn, nightingales announce the night and in our long genetic past, we've always paid attention to the circling of kites, the chorus of a squall of gulls, the badinage between crows and hawks or the zing of a high pitched yellow-rumped warbler. Birds send messages beyond our ken.

Sometimes I see birds against a vaulted sky as in a dream. Eagles, sparrows, gulls, cormorants, ospreys, blue heron and crows whirl and glide like notes from a terpsichorean fantasy, float on spread wings or beat to rise and call to each other and to me. I call back.

I've done so with wolf calls and some few friends know this and answer back in a way beyond words. What do we say to each other? What is a call but a way to say "I'm here"?

That Sunday, after Uncle Carl and Dad had placed the last 8x8x16 Greystone block and mortared it in, we had dinner and an hour of Ed Sullivan's Variety show after which we trundled off to bed.

Just before sleep, we heard the bass thrump of a frog from behind the wall—a strong double syllable like the click of a cylinder into a latch. We laughed—it was so unexpected, so surprising, to have a frog so close, so loud. The frog went silent.

Minutes, then again he resumed his rhythm and we boys laughed and so it continued with first the frog then our laughter which lapsed into silence, then again the frog and at some point all of us, including the frog, became quiet or at least couldn't hear each other.

Monday and Tuesday we awaited the frog like an invited guest after lights out. On Wednesday we heard another note. The rheee-eep became weaker, less strident.

I thought of Edgar Allen Poe's "The Cask of Amontillado" where Fortunato is trapped behind the masonry wall in Montresor's wine cellar. The frog was captured but how? It must have been the space between the wall and the crawl space—he must have fallen the five feet into the narrow gulf and even frogs can't vertically leap that distance.

The next morning at breakfast we told our dad about the frog, how we had to do something to save it, that he was getting weaker.

My dad was a kind man, used to the strange behavior of young boys but even he could resort to sarcasm: "Yeah, I'm going to tear down the wall to free an imprisoned frog." The discussion ended, we finished breakfast and went to school.

The decline became more pronounced as we traveled the weeknights and into the weekend. Not only had the croaks became less abrupt but the pauses between them grew longer. No longer did the croaks produce laughter—now we were tuned to the silence between them, waiting to hear if the frog still lived.

We had become witnesses to a solitary death.

Thief Of Hubcaps

It's strange now to remember. How each of us boys in the dark traveled behind that wall, somehow extended ourselves into another darkness and though we could not see the frog, how the frog was more real than ourselves. It was a kind of preparation for the future which I didn't realize at the time but understand now.

On Sunday night, one week after we first heard the frog call, none of us spoke of what we knew must happen. Another part of us wished for silence at night which we could have taken for escape and freedom—whether of death or liberation—and perhaps these two are the same at some point.

My sense is that none of us, after we were quiet from the punching of pillows and rustle of blankets, slept.

We waited as if deathbed witnesses, hoping for the best, awaiting the worst. The first croak that night was so low we could barely hear it. A long stretch of silence that grew, then finally another dispirited rheee-eep.

Finally, a bolt of sound, almost a paroxysm. It was a towering rheee-eep before the fall. It was higher in pitch and at the end trailed off into another kind of silence that expanded.

No one moved or laughed, each of us alone in our beds, in our heads. In my upper bunk, I remember waiting as something came into me that I hadn't known before and can't define even now.

Later I would hear someone say "He croaked." in place of "He died." and later still, I would hear a singer's last concert referred to as a swan song and I would read that swans are said to sing a final note before they die which Dr. Johnson referred to when he wrote "Swans sing before they die/Some people should die before they sing."

My purpose here is to sing the song of the frog and tell a story which has remained with me for six decades.

Perhaps, knowing the end and having breathed the bracing air of the past and how we lived through so much, we can't stand it that all of this has been for nothing, that it will disappear with us, that our existence ends when we do.

In the ensuing years I would be attendant to dogs and cats as they breathed their last and sometimes they would bite before they died or worry their heads as if they were trying to shake off death. I've heard that sometimes people do knitting motions with their hands before they die.

All of this, along with the throes of frogs and swans, a final protest against death, a claim upon the world of our place in it, our struggle to keep living, a vainglorious attempt coupling courage and despair before vanishing into oblivion.

That night almost 60 years ago, we heard the youngest brother Lee, who was least likely to do so and in my memory never made bird calls or whistled before we went to sleep, sound a low call close to breathing to break the silence. I hear it still:

"Toowhoo, Toowhoo."

Whistle Back, Wave Goodbye

When you were a kid, you could whistle loud enough to be heard across a football field on a moon-filled night with no one in the stands and a friend hiding somewhere in the dark who heard you and whistled back.

At 70, you don't think that's possible. Your whistler won't whistle much these days. Your friend, Charlie, who works with you on construction projects, sometimes whistles when he's in a good mood, you're doing exquisite work and the day has some sun in it. You like to listen to him whistle though you've never told him so but he'll read this book someday and know you do.

Something you do religiously is wave to people who are going away.

You wave after they've visited your home— Tell, Rick or Roger for a Seahawks game, Richard when he magics your computer, a student you're currently tutoring or some ex-student who's dropped by. When you leave one of your kid's houses or drop them off at the ferry, you wave until they're out of sight. If you're in a car, you honk at someone you know which is another kind of waving.

You'll stand on your porch and wait until they back their car onto Windsong Loop road and you'll wave at each other until they turn at the stop sign. When your wife Merry leaves in the morning to teach middle school Science or when you leave to teach college classes, you always wave to each other.

And every time you lift your arm, something cinches in you like a harness attached to a tree so you won't fall.

You wave because someday you may not be there to wave or they may have gone elsewhere and you don't want the last time you see them to be without a wave which seems to you to be not only goodbye but "Stay well," as the tribal people in South Africa say, until we meet again.

Maybe a story is a way of waving.

When you were 12 you were called a momma's boy by your friends on Hummingbird Hill who you used to walk to school with. Most mornings there would be four of you—Bob Bean, Lea MacQuarrie, Danny Irwin and you.

You'd see them through the family room window coming down the alley and head out to walk with them down the dirt path that traversed a 30 foot high gully above the bulldozed road that led to school.

When you got to the dirt road at the bottom of the hill you could look up toward your house and see your mom silhouetted in the living room window which looked west toward Puget Sound. You would know she was there and it felt good to know.

You would keep walking for another 30 feet and before you entered a grove of tall fir trees, where you'd stop and wave to your mom and she'd wave back. You'd even say "Bye, Mom!" out loud though it would have been impossible for her to hear you even if you shouted. She was behind thick glass.

This gave your friends ammunition to call you "Momma's Boy" and you'd hear it sometimes on the playground at recess. "You're a momma's boy.' This gave you pause. You didn't want to be either a boy or accused of needing a momma though you were both.

When you turned 13 in March, you decided you were done with being a momma's boy but you had a problem. You still loved your mom and liked to wave at her. You tried to satisfy both urges—a remedy you found out later was a Hegelian synthesis which worked so well for M.L. King and non-violent protest in the '60s.

You'd walk with the guys and just before you were out of sight under the looming fir branches, you'd slow your pace, turn back toward the window and quickly wave. It seemed a good solution at the time and your mom must have noticed what you were doing, but she never said anything about it. She'd already raised 3 kids who'd gone through the crazy of apprentice teenager.

You practiced this deception the rest of the year and into the next and sometimes, you're sure, you forgot to wave but if you were without witnesses on that dirt road to school, you always remembered.

When you turned 15, some of your friends had their driver's license so you'd sometimes get rides to school or ride in your brother's car, though those trips were scarce and only happened when he owed you a favor. At some point, you probably stopped waving.

When you were 15 in 1956 you went to your first Bona Fide Teenage Drinking Party. You got a call Sunday afternoon from Danny Irwin and he asked you if you wanted to go to a beer party that night at Mary Jane Hannah's house just below Hubbard's Folly about a mile away.

You said yes of course. You agreed on a virtuous excuse: a study session for Biology at George Lemier's house.

You met Danny at 7 at the corner of Daley Street and 10th Avenue under a lone streetlight. You wore the Tweed wool overcoat you'd gotten for Christmas that year which you thought you looked cool in. It had a collar you could turn up.

It was long enough to go past your knees to mid-calf and you believed the coat was a synthesis of film-noir private detective and 19th century brooding mystery—a cloak that Heathcliff from *Wuthering Heights* might wear as he wandered the moors inviting the gaze of young women in need of ravishment to ponder his rakish profile. You wore it every day to school and every weekend to dances.

When you walked in the side door from the carport you entered another universe.

"Be-Bop-a-Lula" by Gene Vincent and the Blue Cops blasted from the record player. Guys in white T-shirts and low-slung jeans with girls draped on their hips lounged in the front room, against the walls, like modern gargoyles with gargolettes. Smoke from Lucky Strikes and Camels filled the rooms. You saw two open cases of Olympia beer on the kitchen counter along with some dead soldiers—a term you learned from your brother for empty bottles.

Olympia beer was the beer of choice for teenagers in the Pacific Northwest. If you tore off the paper label on the glass bottle, the reverse side had between one to four dots.

The belief was that one dot meant you got a kiss from a girl, two and you got a touch of breast over bra—what was called a "dry feel", three was passage under panties and four was the Armageddon of intercourse.

Guys would save the four-dot labels in their wallets like they'd save a winning lottery ticket today. You imagined they thought there was some sort of distribution center they could go to filled with nympho teenage girls with whom they could redeem their labels for a roll in the hay.

One guy you knew, Royal Roles, had so many four-dotters his wallet bulged his back pocket like a piggy-back buttock.

You later found out the dots were from different bottling factories and designated where the bottle came from, whether it be Olympia, Tumwater, Vancouver or Seattle, Washington. A prosaic end to a promising myth.

You and Danny took it all in. This was far better than learning about zygotes, gametes, mitosis and meiosis—which you could never figure out the difference between. The phone rang and Mary Jane yelled, "Turn down the music."

People listened when Mary Jane spoke. She was 5 foot 9 with linebacker shoulders and a head of hair like a hurricane.

Once she'd broken a Ballard guy's arm in a rumble with Edmonds hoods at the Alderwood Manor playfield. He'd stuck his arm, hand up, into the open window of her car. She rolled up the window and pulled down hard, breaking his arm at the elbow.

Mary Jane Jankowski could have whipped half the hoodlums at Edmonds High in a junkyard fight.

A guy on his way to the party was on the phone. He'd spotted three cop cars above the house. The sharks had circled. You and Danny bolted for the door but not before you each grabbed a beer from the open case.

You ran outside into the adjoining woods and took the back way toward Hummingbird Hill. Whenever you saw headlights both of you jumped in the roadside ditch.

It was an epic night—two stolen beers, narrow escape from the cops and your first Teenage Party without parents. You hid the beer in the pocket of your overcoat before you got home past your curfew and sneaked in the basement door.

Monday morning. The bane of all teenage boys and most adults.

You heard your mom's voice calling down the stairs, "Wake up Bobby. It's a new day." You groaned and went back to sleep. You heard her again, this time louder. "If you don't get going, you'll be late for school. Breakfast's on the table." She didn't say it like a warning, more like an invitation to breakfast.

You clutched the covers more tightly and rolled over.

Thief Of Hubcaps

After five or more minutes she reverted to the ultimate threat, "If you don't get up real snappy, I'm going to come down there and get you." You rolled out of bed, took a fast shower, combed your hair, pulled on your jeans, T-shirt and headed upstairs.

Your mom made breakfast for your dad and four brothers every morning and had devised a schedule that was both inspired and efficient for her shopping and peace of mind.

You can't remember what you ate on all the mornings but you remember Saturday was blueberry pancakes with two strips of bacon, Sunday, waffles and grapefruit, Monday, fried eggs sunny side up served on wheat toast with link sausage and always, a small glass of squeezed orange juice and all the milk you could drink.

Every morning she set the table with a clean tablecloth, blue plates with scenes of rural England you can still see in your head, silverware at the side on top of a folded linen napkin. Other than taking your dishes to the sink after you'd finished breakfast, your only responsibility was to eat what your mom made.

When you got to the table, breakfast was still hot. Your mom had warmed it in the oven and you sat down without a word and began eating. Your mom looked at the wall clock and said you'd have to be quick or you might be tardy.

In the back of your head you remembered you had two tardies—three was the magic number that got you an hour of detention after school. You kept eating. Maybe you nodded— probably not, you were in a foul mood.

Next thing you knew your mom was standing by the table with your overcoat in one hand and a bottle of Olympia beer in the other. She'd gone downstairs to get your coat, to help you not be late. She said, "Bobby, what's this?" To gain time, you said "Oh...wow..." and then you had it.

Oh...Gerry Morse must have put it there. He was at the study session last night and he's never liked me. Of course.... that's it. He was trying to get me into trouble...

She waited until you were out of words and then some. She looked you straight in the eyes.

Bobby, you know in your heart what's right.

You shoved your unfinished plate back, got up, grabbed your coat and book bag and headed for the door. You were furious. You threw open the door, then slammed it shut as you yelled "Go to Hell!" You don't know if she heard you or not. Maybe your words were covered by the door slam. You hope so.

You went down the angled path, your book bag banging on your shoulder. You could barely breathe. You walked as if possessed, each leg a piston.

You clenched your teeth, ground them against each other. At the bottom of the hill you kept going. You said "goddamit, goddamit, goddamit" over and over until you got past the overhanging trees and stopped.

It was as if you'd run for two miles through a storm. You took deep breaths. Finally you got it. You realized you'd taken out your shame at being caught with a beer by getting angry at your mom who had gotten you out of bed and made you breakfast.

Thief Of Hubcaps

How could you have done that? Not only had you lied to her, you hadn't even taken your dish to the sink. Something caught in your throat. You knew in your heart what was right.

You walked back toward the house and looked up at the front room window.

Your mom was still there. You looked at the shape of her far away, framed in the morning light.

You held up your hand and waved. She waved back. You waved again. You could feel a smile breaking your face. You waved again and waved until your arm got tired. It was call and response beyond words but you knew what was being said.

You also knew you'd get a detention but it didn't matter and something moved behind your eyes that mixed sorrow and happiness. You waved a final goodbye over your shoulder as you began running toward your school and left your mother alone in her watch at the window that looked over the cliff.

Thirty years later you're teaching at the high school. Abe, your mom's second lover, had died 10 years before. He had a heart attack while your mom and he were talking on the phone in the morning and something went out of her when he died.

She was still sweet and gracious but age was starting to take its toll. A car slammed into her from behind when she was stopped at a red light on the bottom of a hill fronting Highway 99 and she was put in the hospital for a week.

After her first stroke, you and your brothers put her in Krista Rest Home near Richmond Beach where she had a second stroke after a couple of months of living in her small room. You signed a paper requesting

"No Extraordinary Measures" which meant that if she had another stroke they'd let her go.

You visited when you could but probably not enough. You were raising two kids, doing drama productions with rehearsals every school night except Fridays. Every Friday you could manage, you'd take a ferry, drive to Krista in time for your mom's dinner. You never called to say you were coming, you knew she'd be there. Her days of going out were over. You'd walk into her room and look into her eyes. She couldn't speak by this time, only a low garble, but you could tell by the look in her eyes and her mouth that contorted into a remnant of smile that she recognized you.

You'd feed her applesauce, pureed meat and small bits of vegetables. You'd take the glass with the flex straw and put it to her mouth.

You'd tell her stories about the last week, how the girls were doing, what play you were directing. It seemed to calm her and when you left you'd lean down, kiss her forehead and say goodbye, then say it again before you went out her door toward the parking lot.

On one of those last visits you brought school pictures of the girls for her to look at and put next to her bed where she kept framed photographs of her six children and 12 grandchildren, along with Dad and Abe. One of your brothers was gone by then but you hadn't told her. Maybe part of her knew.

By now you know that older people know more than we think and moms certainly know more than we realize they do. When a child leaves this world, the parent feels it in her blood. It's a kind of osmosis, one term you did learn in Biology.

Thief Of Hubcaps

You fed her, talked your monologue and held her hand.

After a couple of hours you look at your watch and know you have to get going. You have a ferry to catch, a rehearsal early the next morning and some prep to do before you can sleep plus there's a babysitter to drive home. You kiss your mom on the cheek, give her hand a squeeze and go out the door.

You always look back to where you've been especially if it's a place where someone you love is in a hospital or nursing home. You remember doing this when you saw your dad for the last time at Beck's funeral home. When you left your brother's hospital you looked up toward the 6th floor where you knew he was and hoped he was recovering from his trouble.

You look back because you believe, in a strange way, that you can somehow send your spirit to your loved ones even if they're not there to see you.

Krista Rest Home had two two-story buildings connected by a ground level glass enclosure so the folks could get from their apartments to the dining room and common rooms without being in the weather.

Standing by your car in the parking lot, you look toward the buildings and see your mom in the middle of the glass passageway in her wheelchair, belted in so she can't fall out.

The night nurse stands by her side. Your mom has a blanket on her lap and a shawl wrapped around her shoulders.

You stare. She's never done this before. Somehow she must have gotten through to the nurse that she wanted to see you one more time and as you watch you see the nurse take your mother's hand and lift it in a wave. You raise your hand and wave back. You wave again, and again.

That night you missed your ferry and to this day you miss your mom. But every time you wave when you leave someone or someone leaves you, you wave— not to bring them back or say goodbye but for a moment, to remember the time you had together.

As if a raised hand could travel the distance and reach the other.

Acknowledgements

With appreciation to my friend, editor and techno-guru, Richard Davis, friends who've read initial drafts—Dave Richards, Brother Tim, Mark Nichols, and Nancy Rekow—my wife, Merry, who patiently listens to my ravings and my children and grandchildren as well as the characters who've taken part in this adventure.